A MOST C
MA

The breathtakingly handsome Earl of Huntingdon is determined to take a bride, and equally determined that his marriage to Miss Georgina Pierce will be a business arrangement only—after all, he has been wounded in love before. But there is unexpected passion in his innocent wife, and he soon begins to look forward to many days—and nights—with her . . . until he shockingly discovers that her promised fortune has been squandered. Though Georgina rightly protests that she knew nothing of it, Huntingdon is wounded to the core.

Spirited Georgina surprised herself by agreeing to marry the earl—a man she's just met. The handsome nobleman proposes that she exchange her fortune for his title, but from the moment Georgina first waltzes across the ballroom floor in his arms, she realizes she can easily give this handsome, haunted lord her heart. . . . But first she must teach him that there is one thing far more important than money and position—and that is love.

LORRAINE HEATH

To Marry an Heiress

An Avon Romantic Treasure

AVON BOOKS
An Imprint of HarperCollins*Publishers*

This is a work of fiction. Names, characters, places, and incidents are products of the author's imagination or are used fictitiously and are not to be construed as real. Any resemblance to actual events, locales, organizations, or persons, living or dead, is entirely coincidental.

HarperCollins*Publishers*
77-85 Fulham Palace Road
Hammersmith
London W6 8JB

ISBN: 0 00 775080 3
www.avonromance.com

This edition published 2005
First Avon Books paperback printing: September 2002

Printed and bound in Great Britain by Clays Ltd, St Ives plc

For Ann N.,
who knows how to keep
Christmas well,
with love

Sandra Avila

a small fortune during America's civil war. That he had done so by defying the blockades didn't matter. Following the war, he'd sold much-sought-after items at what some people considered exorbitant prices. He'd also dabbled in land speculation, and it was rumored he'd recently taken an interest in railroads. Apparently he was a jack of all trades with a golden touch.

"But American women, especially those from Texas, particularly those from Fortune, are not always . . . malleable," Ravenleigh stated.

Devon quirked a dark brow. "Had a bit of trouble taming the little wife, did you?"

His cousin narrowed his pale blue eyes in warning. Devon knew it was a foolish man who taunted his benefactor. As a rule he tended not to be foolish. Proud, yes. Beyond measure. But foolish, no.

Pride was a dominant family trait, and true to form, Ravenleigh would not add sparks to to the dying embers of gossip. Although Devon readily admitted Ravenleigh seemed more than content now, he had heard the rumors bandied about that his cousin's Texas bride had not initially adjusted well to life in her new country.

"These women were forged in the fires of a difficult life. They are accustomed to independence," Ravenleigh informed him in a tightly controlled voice.

"My next wife shall have all the independence she craves. All I desire is her wealth, in exchange for which she will become my countess. I understand these Americans long for the respectability our titles afford them."

Although he'd yet to be introduced to Miss Pierce, he could not help but wonder if she was aware that her father had let it be known that he was eager to purchase a titled husband for her.

"Although our society is fraught with marriages of convenience and political alliances, I can imagine nothing lonelier than being married to someone you do not love," Ravenleigh said.

Not wishing to crush his glass as the dark emotions roiling through him took a firmer hold, Devon carefully placed it on the polished marble table beside the chair and stood. "Then you possess a deplorable lack of imagination, Cousin."

He strode to the window and gazed out on the well-manicured garden.

Loneliness was watching respectability stripped away bit by agonizing bit. Isolating himself so others would not witness his fall from grace. Projecting a false image to the world so no one would know his true sorrow, his immense fears, his incredible woes. To face everything alone. To desperately want to weep only to discover he no longer possessed the comfort of tears.

Now he was precariously balanced on the precipice of losing all he loved. His family's estate. The dwindling respect of his peers. His own self-respect and his damnable pride. Seeking Ravenleigh's help in his quest for deliverance had gouged his vanity, and the wound continued to fester.

"Huntingdon, I could see my way clear to loan—"

"Don't!" Devon clenched his hands until his forearms ached with the effort to restrain himself. He wanted neither pity nor magnanimity from the man. "I refuse to become a charity case as long as I possess the means by which to avoid it. I have but one thing left to barter: my title, in exchange for an heiress. It will have to suffice."

Closing his eyes, he imagined Huntingdon as it should have been: grand, bold, majestic. Not as his father had left it: strongly resembling an aging dowager who spent far too much time drinking.

Shaking off the well-worn cloak of resentment, he forced his thoughts to return to Miss Georgina Pierce. Georgina. He didn't fancy the name, but in truth he wasn't overly concerned with compatibility. He had married once for love and had no intention of repeating that ghastly mistake.

"Are the ladies about?" Devon asked.

"No, Elizabeth took the girls shopping."

"Good. We shan't have to worry about being disturbed once Pierce arrives. What is your impression of his daughter?"

"That she is not overly fond of England."

Devon glanced over his shoulder. "How can she not be?"

"Our world is extremely different from theirs. While I was in Texas visiting Kit, I could not help but be grateful that *he* was the one Father had sent away and not me."

"You weren't the one creating scandals," Devon reminded him.

"If only the reasons behind his going had been that simple." Ravenleigh shook his head. "But that discussion is best left for another time. Regarding

Georgina . . . I suspect it will not be enough to gain her father's favor. You will be forced to gain hers."

Devon grinned cockily. "Don't underestimate the family charm. I can exude it in abundance when necessary."

"You would do well not to begin in a manner you do not intend to maintain."

"I shall do whatever I must, Cousin, and the lady will be grateful for it. I assure you that I can play the part of attentive husband." He turned his face back to the window. "Do you ever think of Clarisse?"

"Every day."

"How do you suppose your current countess would feel to know how often you think of your first wife?"

"I suspect she knows. As I'm well aware, she often reminisces about her first husband."

Devon swallowed hard before confessing, "Margaret hated me before she died. Pierce's money will ensure his daughter does not harbor the same sentiment toward me."

"I must admit to not knowing Georgina well, but she hardly strikes me as a woman who would *hate* under any circumstances."

"We can only hope." Because hate had the ability to slice a man to ribbons. To make him feel less of a man. Perhaps the worst of all, to cause him to despise himself. He'd loathed looking at his reflection in the mirror. And unfortunately, his home possessed a beastly number of mirrors.

A subtle knock on the library door broke into his morose thoughts. How quickly introspection could sneak up on him, haunting, stirring up a past he hoped to put to rest expeditiously with the attainment of an heiress.

"Milord, Mr. Pierce has returned," the butler announced. "As you requested, I informed him you required his presence in the library."

Devon stiffened. The hour of his deliverance had arrived, and none too soon. Left to his memories much longer, he'd no doubt resemble a thunderous black cloud when he greeted the man whom he hoped would serve as his new benefactor.

"Give us another moment," Ravenleigh said authoritatively. The door clicked shut.

How easy it was to command when a man stood on top of the mountain, how difficult to regain his footing as he was toppling off.

"Would you like me to stay?" Ravenleigh asked quietly.

Devon shook his head. "You've done quite enough by making Mr. Pierce aware of my needs and arranging our meeting. I prefer you not witness my supplication."

He winced as Ravenleigh scraped back his chair. He doubted the drop on the gallows echoed as loudly. In the sparkling-clear window, he saw his cousin's hazy reflection. In his own windows at home, he saw nothing but smudge and dirt.

"I'll inform Mr. Pierce you're ready for him." Ravenleigh placed his hand on Devon's shoulder. "For what it's worth, Kit found himself in a marriage of convenience, and it's worked out splendidly."

Devon was truly glad Ravenleigh's twin brother

had found contentment in his new home, but the past few years had taught him that dreams existed only in the dominion of children and fools.

"Don't hold your breath waiting for my happiness, Cousin. I've never possessed the reach with which to grasp it, and that aspect of my life is unlikely to change."

Ravenleigh's hand fell away as his cousin's footsteps echoed through the grand library. Devon bowed his head and prepared himself for the selling of his soul, pride, and self-respect.

His face rigid, unemotional, Devon turned.

A gray-haired, slightly balding, pot-bellied man in ill-fitting clothes shambled into the room.

"Mr. Pierce, may I present Devon Sheridan, Lord Huntingdon," Ravenleigh said.

"Huntingdon, huh? What goes with it?" Pierce asked.

Devon cocked his head slightly, as though the action would help him decipher the strange question. "I beg your pardon?"

"You're *what* of Huntingdon?"

"He's the Earl of Huntingdon," Ravenleigh supplied.

Pierce smiled, displaying crooked teeth. "I knew that. I know a lot about you, young fella. I've been checking you out ever since Chris here told me of your interest in my daughter."

Chris? Never in Ravenleigh's life had he been addressed as Chris. Devon suppressed a shudder at the inappropriate informality, appalled by the man's lack of respect for his cousin's title.

Ravenleigh cleared his throat. "If you gentlemen will excuse me, I'll leave you to discuss your business."

"'Preciate the howdy-do, Chris," Pierce said.

Good God. Devon could only pray the man's daughter didn't speak as though she'd recently fallen off a turnip wagon. While his cousin closed the door quietly behind him, Devon gave Pierce his undivided attention.

Pierce narrowed his eyes into darkened slits, studying him as though he were some prize stallion on the bidding block. Devon endured the scrutiny because he recognized he had little choice in the matter. He was willing to do whatever necessary to achieve his goal. As a result of primogeniture—his blessing and his curse—English heiresses were few and far between.

Lord Randolph Churchill had recently wed an American. American ladies had so charmed the Prince of Wales when he visited their country that he was now inviting them to England and into his social circle—much to the chagrin of his mother, Her Majesty Queen Victoria.

Devon had little doubt that in a few years Americans would be taking London by storm and a desperate man would be able to select from a veritable feast instead of settling for the crumbs. But he did not have the luxury of waiting until the fare improved.

Whatever Pierce was looking for, Devon wished he'd find it soon so they could get on with this meeting.

"So you're wanting to form a partnership, are you?" Pierce asked at long last.

Devon nodded curtly. "Indeed I am."

With a lumbering gait, Pierce continued across the room. Devon had intended to place himself behind the desk to gain an advantage, to be perceived as the one offering instead of the one reduced to asking.

But with typical American brashness, Pierce dropped into the large leather chair behind the desk, rested his sturdy elbows on the polished mahogany top, and eased forward.

Devon held his position by the window as though he were guarding the Crown Jewels instead of his pride.

"Did your cousin explain the conditions under which I might be agreeable?" Pierce asked.

Might be? Devon had expected all the bargaining to occur on his side and be to his advantage. After all, he was offering to marry the man's daughter. Still, he replied succinctly, "He did."

Pierce leaned back in the chair and repeatedly tapped the tip of one finger upon the desk. A most irritating sound.

"Nothing in the world is more precious to me than my daughter, Mr. Sheridan."

"Huntingdon," Devon stated firmly.

Pierce's bushy eyebrows nearly reached the top of his balding pate. "What?"

"When in England, you should address a peer by his title. Mine is Huntingdon. My cousin's is Ravenleigh."

"And if my daughter should cotton to marryin' ya, how would she be addressed?"

Cotton to marrying him? Was there any reason why she wouldn't?

"As my countess, she would be addressed as Lady Huntingdon."

"Countess. I like the sound of that. Just kinda rolls off the tongue like hot honey. Lady Huntingdon." He grinned broadly. "I like it just fine."

He patted both palms on the desk, a little rat-a-tat-tat, as though he was a drummer in Her Majesty's army. "Let's get down to business, then. I've been making inquiries about you since your cousin told me you were interested in marrying my daughter."

"Indeed?"

"They say you treated your first wife well."

His chest tightened as the memory of his Margaret coursed through him, seeking purchase he couldn't allow—not now—not when he was on the verge of arranging a marriage that more closely resembled a business venture. He had spent hours dazzled by her beauty and done everything in his power to give her all her heart desired. But in the end, nothing had been enough to keep her. "And that fact interests you because . . ."

"I'm only interested in dealing with a man who will treat my daughter kindly." He leaned forward again, his gaze hardening. "Do you know what it is, Sheridan, to love a gal so much you'd gladly give your soul to the devil simply to see her smile?"

"Huntingdon. And yes"—he swallowed hard—"I know the boundaries that surround a love of such magnitude."

Pierce scoffed. "Maybe the rumors I've heard about you aren't true, since it's obvious you know nothing about it at all."

"I beg to differ. I am well acquainted with a love of great magnitude."

"If you were, you'd know it has no boundaries. None whatsoever. That's the kind of love my daughter has in her heart."

The man was breathing heavily, his eyes bulging, his cheeks flushed. This meeting wasn't progressing as Devon had envisioned. "May I offer you a bit of my cousin's port, Mr. Pierce?"

Nodding, Pierce settled back in the chair and rubbed his fist over his chest. He gave Devon a weak smile. "That kidney pie I ate for lunch doesn't seem to have agreed with me."

Devon strode across the room to the liquor cabinet. The decanter clinked against the glass as he began to pour the wine. "I've made inquiries regarding you as well, Mr. Pierce."

He set the decanter aside, walked to the desk, and extended the glass to the man he was beginning to view as his adversary. "I know you're a shrewd businessman."

"My daughter is not a piece of property." Pierce snatched the drink from his hand. He downed the liquid in one long gulp before slamming the glass on the desk and skewering Devon with his glare. "I've no interest in dealing with a man who views women as such."

His mind swirling with the implications, Devon returned to his place by the window. "I assure you that I meant no offense, nor would I deem her an object. As my countess, she'll want for nothing."

A gleam entered Pierce's eyes. "That's what I'm counting on. But I have three conditions you must agree to before I'll give my blessing to this venture."

"What would those be, Mr. Pierce?"

"First, my daughter is never to know about this arrangement. You are to make her believe you find her beautiful, you're in love with her, and that's the reason you asked for her hand in marriage."

Make her believe she was beautiful? Dear God. What sort of woman would need convincing? An unattractive one obviously. Love her? Devon wasn't even certain he knew what the word meant anymore. Still, he gave a brusque nod.

"Second, my daughter loves children. You are to give her as many as she wants.

"Finally, you're to remain faithful to her. If I discover otherwise, I'll have you gelded. Even from the grave."

Devon spun around and faced the window. He felt as though he were a whore, selling himself to this old man so he could rebuild his estate.

"What exactly will my agreement to your conditions purchase me?"

"Unlimited access to everything I have—after the marriage, after I see she's happy."

Devon had not expected such prodigious generosity. He could quickly restore Huntingdon to its former grandeur. He looked at the gray skies and inhaled deeply.

"I accept all your conditions. We shall need to

meet with our solicitors to negotiate the marriage settlement."

"I've got no problem with that, *once* I see she's happy."

Turning away from the window, Devon gave him a long, hard perusal. "You'll have to sign the settlement papers before I'll apply my signature to the marriage license."

"I'll sign on the day you tie the knot," Pierce stated. "Once you're married, I'll transfer money over to you. The happier she is, the more generous I'll be."

"We shall have to arrange an introduction."

"She's attending some fancy ball with Lauren tomorrow night. You can start wooing her there."

Devon bowed slightly. "Very well. I shall count the moments until tomorrow evening."

"I doubt that. I've never known a man to welcome Cupid's cramp, but I'll promise you this, Huntingdon. She'll make you a far wealthier man than you can imagine."

Devon hoped the old chap spoke true, because he could imagine quite a bit.

Chapter 2

"At tonight's ball, if you wish to speak to a gentleman, you simply catch his eye and snap your fan closed." Lauren Fairfield demonstrated the proper protocol with a coy batting of her eyelashes that reminded Georgina Pierce of the rapid beating of a hummingbird's wings.

Curled up in a plush chair beside the window, Georgina slowly sipped the flowery pekoe tea. The serving girl who'd brought her the steaming brew had explained it was suitable for morning but not afternoon or evening—as though Georgina truly cared if the proper tea was poured from the teapot at the appropriate time of day.

The things these Brits fussed over and were concerned with baffled Georgina no end.

"If I've a mind to speak to someone tonight, why can't I just walk across the ballroom and talk to him?" Georgina asked.

Not that she would consider talking to one of these Englishmen, much less approaching him. Or any other man for that matter. She couldn't determine a topic that they might find fascinating. During the few conversations to which she'd been privy, the men had spoken to the women as though their heads served no other purpose than to provide a place for their hair to take root.

Rolling her blue eyes for the hundredth time since Georgina's arrival, Lauren plopped onto the bed. "Because that's not the way it's done, silly goose. I'm certain if you could simply master the proper etiquette, a gentleman would favor you with a dance."

Georgina had always thought her friend beautiful, but the years away from Texas had added a grace and confidence that came from knowing how she fitted in the world. Georgina had yet to figure out that aspect of her life.

Shortly after the war her father had uprooted her and her mother so he could deliver goods throughout Texas. Since she'd finished her schooling by then, her education hadn't suffered. And in some ways she'd learned more than she'd ever wanted to know—about people and what they considered important.

"Ah, Lauren, it ain't my etiquette that's got the men shying away from me." They'd attended two balls since her arrival, and she'd yet to attract anyone's attention. Although in truth she hadn't come here with flirtation in mind. Her features were as plain as the day was long. She was as steady as a rock—which more often than not made her as dull as muddy water.

"'Ain't' is not a word. Please desist from using it in my presence."

Unable to believe how easily she could rile Lauren these days, Georgina grinned. "I simply do it to irritate you."

Lauren stuck her nose in the air and looked down at her. "I'm well aware of that. I don't remember you being quite so annoying."

"I don't recall you bein' such a prude." Georgina followed her comment with a small chuckle to mask her quandary. While she cherished her friendship with Lauren, she also found herself discomfited by Lauren's love of societal rules, rules that in New York had served to humiliate her.

Three years ago, her father had decided they should stop their wanderings, establish roots, and set up residence in New York. But they found none of the warmth and acceptance they'd left behind in Texas. Georgina was certain the "old money"—those who comprised the socially elite—were responsible for her mother's death. They had snubbed her and her mother in public, had pointedly never issued them an invitation to their balls. Her father's hard-earned money made no difference to their social standing. They were never accepted, and acceptance had meant everything to her mother, who had grown up in poverty.

Georgina had been taken aback when she'd first seen Lauren after so many years of separation. She fought not to equate Lauren with the Knickerbockers of New York, the people she'd come to loathe for their pretentious displays of snobbery.

Lauren touched the closed fan to her right ear.

"I know I've changed," Georgina said solemnly. But her friend was a far cry from being the same as well.

Georgina continually searched for the girl who had run through the flower-laden fields with her, climbed trees, and sneaked out the window at night to meet her by the creek. Beneath the vast, star-filled sky, they'd woven their dreams of marriage, husbands, love, and children. They'd promised to remain friends until they died.

She'd felt bereft and alone when Lauren had left Texas eight years ago after her mother had married Christopher Montgomery. She'd hardly cared when a few months later her father had decided to sell their house in Fortune and take her and her mother with him on his travels.

Lauren placed the fan in her lap. "So you *do* know the language of the fan."

The language of the fan, the glove, the handkerchief, the parasol . . . Why couldn't these people be content to simply talk to each other? Why did they have to play these irritating games? It didn't seem quite honest to have all those objects do the communicating.

"I took a gander at those books you loaned me. The rules over here seem foolish. If a man is walking down the boardwalk in Texas, he tips his hat to me and says, 'Howdy, miss.' Here a man can't tip his hat unless I give him some kind of bow, and until I speak to him, he can stand in front of me until the cows come home, but he can't speak to me."

"Because this is civilization. In England the men are gentlemen."

"You don't consider Tom to be a gentleman?"

Lauren bolted off the bed and stomped to the window that overlooked the most beautiful garden Georgina had ever seen. Elizabeth Montgomery's adoration of roses was evident everywhere she looked. Cuttings in crystal vases adorned each room.

"Why did you have to mention him?" Lauren asked.

Georgina shifted in the chair, tucking her legs up beneath her, not caring one whit that she was wrinkling her skirt. Perhaps the Knickerbockers had been right in excluding her from their society. "I thought you loved him."

Lauren stroked the burgundy velvet drape a servant had pulled aside first thing that morning. "As a child loves another child, perhaps. I was only fourteen when we left Fortune. I barely remember what he looks like."

"Is that the reason you haven't bothered to ask about him since I've been here?"

"Why should I think of him when he's forgotten me? He promised to write, and I've never received a single letter from him."

"Maybe because he's been too busy making a living."

"Do you ever see him?" Lauren cast her a sideways glance reflecting such longing Georgina knew her friend did indeed think of Tom—and often.

"From time to time when Papa's business takes us

back through Texas. He's a very respected trail boss. He gets top dollar, because he's hard-working—"

"The gentlemen here don't have to work. Therefore they have plenty of time to devote to the women they love."

"If they don't work, where do they get their money?"

"They inherit it."

Georgina set the delicate china teacup on a little table with spindly legs that didn't look strong enough to support it. "They have to do something to generate income."

"Maybe they invest it. I don't know. I just know they don't have to *work*. They don't sweat. I remember when Tom would come over at the end of the day, he smelled no better than a cow, his clothes were dusty, and his fingernails had dirt wedged beneath them. English gentlemen are always clean and they smell nice."

"There's nothing wrong with honest sweat and dirt."

"Except that it's reserved for the lower classes," Lauren said softly. "We're above all that here."

Georgina noticed that Lauren was drawing the fan absently across her cheek. "I love you" according to the language of the fan. Was she thinking of Tom? Was Tom the reason she'd declined the numerous marriage proposals that had come her way?

"You're a full-grown woman, Lauren. You could go back to Texas any time you wanted."

Lauren scoffed lightly. "I daresay I'd fit in as well there as you seem to think you do here."

A fit Georgina knew was as easy as trying to snap into place a wooden puzzle piece that had somehow managed to get associated with the wrong puzzle. Hadn't their years in New York taught her that? She'd been incredibly relieved when her father had told her they'd leave the mansion they were leasing in New York. But instead of going back to her beloved Texas, they'd sailed to England. Georgina had been heartbroken. She wanted a home, but more she wanted to feel as though she belonged somewhere.

With a sigh, Lauren turned away from the window and strolled gracefully to the canopied bed. "I wish you'd select a fan. I spent most of yesterday afternoon on Regent Street, searching for one I thought you'd like."

Georgina eased out of the chair and walked to the bed. A dozen fans were spread over the burgundy comforter. "I suppose I think of a fan as something to cool you off in July, not something that tells a man what you're thinking."

"People here are much more sophisticated than they are in Fortune. I felt as though I was a country bumpkin for the longest time. I thought I'd never be accepted." Lauren's eyes filled with understanding. "Is that the reason you don't think the gentlemen have asked you to dance? Because you lack the sophistication to which they're accustomed?"

"That and other things." Georgina picked up an enormous fan and opened it, spreading wide the ostrich plumes. The wounds delivered in New York were still too fresh. She couldn't explain to Lauren how she'd tried to fit in once and had failed miserably. "I could hide my face with this one."

"There's nothing wrong with your face."

"Except that it's not elegant or dainty. And I have a tendency to speak my mind, a habit some men find unappealing." She tossed down the fan. "I'm not comfortable in the parlor, Lauren. I'd rather be outdoors."

"Then you shouldn't have come to England during the Season. You should have waited until August, when we'll be in residence at the country estate."

"I didn't know about the Season when Papa told me he wanted to come over here. I just wanted to visit with *you*—not with all these prim and prissy people who set my teeth on edge with their high and mighty ways."

"You're my guest, Gina. People will think I'm rude if I don't take you to the dinner parties and balls with me."

"Well, we certainly can't have people thinking *that.*" Georgina reached for a fan with intricate flowers carved into the ivory leaves. "I'll carry this one to the dance tonight."

Lauren flung her arms around Georgina and hugged her tightly. "You *haven't* changed. You still care more about others than you do yourself. Maybe some lucky gentleman will notice you tonight. Wouldn't it be splendid if you married a man with a title? You could stay in England, and we could visit all the time."

Merciful heavens. Marrying a stuffy old English dandy was the last thing Georgina wanted.

* * *

"You have to tell her, Nathaniel."

Nathaniel Pierce wasn't certain if he was sitting in the day room, the morning room, or the afternoon room. He simply knew he was in a room, but he also understood that those with money preferred to give their rooms a name, as though in doing so they not only added to the importance of the room, but increased their own significance as well.

Elizabeth Fairfield Montgomery was an exception. She stood near the window, giving him a pointed look that indicated she'd accept no argument on this matter. She and Edna, his wife, had been the best of friends. They'd written often until Edna's death.

He wiped his roughened hand over his mouth. "I don't want Gina to know that I had anything to do with Huntingdon's interest in her."

"Nathaniel, you can't *give* her a fairy-tale romance and a storybook marriage," Elizabeth insisted.

"Why not? I'm an old man who made mistakes."

"Only when you gambled."

Only Elizabeth would remind him of his greatest failing. He'd amassed fortunes only to lose them when Lady Luck turned against him. Many a night Edna had cried while he'd been rubbing elbows with the demon of gambling. He'd stop gambling to halt her tears.

And when he'd climbed back onto the mountain of gold, he'd taken her to New York . . . and her tears had returned.

"It was more than gambling, Elizabeth. I never

should have taken Gina and Edna with me. Traveling from town to town. Sleeping in the wagon when we couldn't find an inn. Never staying in one place long enough for either of them to make any new friends. I didn't realize women needed to have friends nearby. Now I can give Gina back some of what I took from her."

"She doesn't feel as though you took anything."

"I feel it!" He lunged out of the chair. How could he explain the loneliness his daughter had experienced? She'd had no friends other than those she'd left behind. Although they'd always rolled from one town to another, she'd never complained. That wasn't her way. She simply accepted what life dished out and made the best of it.

Too late he'd realized the unfair cost of his ambitions. She'd never been courted. Or wooed. Or made to feel special. She'd never had beaux lined up at her door, seeking her favors.

He'd thought New York would provide her with the opportunity to obtain a husband. Instead the experience had only worsened her isolation, had made her feel more apart. She'd been the country girl striving to fit into the city life.

He'd brought her to England, hoping to find her a husband, someone among the aristocracy who would appreciate her. Someone to show those New York Knickerbockers that his daughter was good enough.

"Huntingdon's right for her, Elizabeth. I went to the village on his estate. I talked to those who know him—"

"You made inquiries about him?" she asked, clearly horrified.

He'd made inquiries about all of them—every aristocratic man who'd approached him in the gentlemen's clubs or the gaming hells. Huntingdon alone had chosen a clandestine meeting. Huntingdon alone wasn't lounging in clubs and running up debts.

By God, he wasn't lazy. Nathaniel would give him that. The man had tried his damnedest to better his situation. Familiar with the instability of wealth, Nathaniel felt comfortable giving the man a leg up. Every aspect of life was a gamble. He was gambling now that his instincts were honed, that he'd measured the man accurately.

Huntingdon wouldn't squander the money he acquired when he married Gina. Nor would he squander the happiness she could bring him.

"I wanted an unbiased impression of the man. He's loyal to his tenants and his land. He'll be loyal to Gina."

"At least let her know that he has an interest in her."

He supposed there would be no harm in that approach. If he handled it properly, Gina would be none the wiser regarding the exact conditions of the marriage. Huntingdon would no doubt court in haste. He supposed it was to his advantage to prepare his daughter for the man's suit.

As soon as the marriage took place, he'd make arrangements to have it announced in *The New York Times*. Yes, sir, his little gal marrying an English aristocrat would curl the hair on a few of the matrons' heads.

Georgina stared at the ball gown draped over the edge of the bed. The yellow shade reminded her of a healing bruise. She'd stopped counting the bows when she reached twenty-five. As for the feathers that lined the back collar and would press against her head . . . what in God's name had the seamstress been thinking when she'd agreed to make this abominable creation?

Georgina knew what her father had been thinking. A man of excesses, the beauty of simplicity completed eluded him. How could she possibly wear this atrocious garment to tonight's event?

With a sinking heart she set a large box on the bed. Inside was the gown that had only just arrived from the dressmaker. Incredibly elegant, it consisted of nothing more than simple lines. She'd fallen in love with the deep blue satin the moment she saw it. The hero of her dreams always possessed eyes of that color. Eyes that hid a tortured soul. A soul calling to her to lend strength and wisdom—

A knock on the door brought her abruptly back to the present and the hideous gown. "Come in."

Her father shuffled into the room, sweat beading his brow, his nose and cheeks ruddy. In spite of the cool climate, he always looked as though he were on fire.

"What do you think of the gown, darlin'?" he asked, as though he'd discovered buried treasure that had been lost for centuries.

She certainly wished it hadn't been dug up, but she wouldn't hurt his feelings for the world. "Oh, Papa, it's"—she glanced at the dress; how to disguise the truth without lying was a game she'd played with him since she was a child—"it's like nothing I've ever seen."

"I knew you'd love it! You're just like your mother used to be. Too easy to please. Lord, I miss her more each day."

Her heart went out to him. Pneumonia had taken her mother last year. Pneumonia and a broken heart brought on by society's cruelties.

Her father's face suddenly brightened. "I talked with a fella yesterday. Devon Sheridan."

She didn't particularly like the manner in which her father had said that—as though he'd recently acquired some new property. "Devon Sheridan?"

His smile grew. "He's titled, gal, and he's asked for permission to call on you. I've granted it."

She dropped onto the fainting couch situated at the foot of the bed. She tried to steady the thunderous beating of her heart. Lifting her gaze, she felt the dull ache in her chest grow as she contemplated the pleased expression on her father's beloved face. "Why would he want to call on me?"

"Because the man knows true beauty when he sees it. He confided to me he's been watching you from afar for some time now." He stepped closer, grabbed her hand, and squeezed hard. "I'm sure he's contemplating marriage, and I'm sure he won't be long in asking."

With trepidation slicing through her, she felt her

skin prickle as though a thousand ants crawled over her flesh. She'd never met the man, and she seriously doubted anyone was watching her from afar. "But Papa, I only came here to visit, not to live."

"No reason you can't stay here. Besides, you and Lauren were always like two peas in a pod. As you grow older, it's a good thing to stay close to those who knew you when you were little. Helps you to remember your roots, feel secure in their hold."

"But my roots are in Texas." She didn't want to hurt him by pointing out that if he thought roots were so important, he shouldn't have pulled her out of Texas to begin with.

"And a harsher land there will never be."

"But I love Texas."

His face crumpled as though she'd plunged the recently sharpened blade of a knife through his heart. "Lord, Gina, I thought you'd be gladdened. You're always talking about how much you want children, and you can't have them if you ain't got a husband."

She wanted children more than she'd ever desired anything in her life, but it took more than simply acquiring a husband. It took getting intimate with him, an act that required fondness, caring, trust . . . certainly too many things to name. "But Papa—"

"Shh, now." Awkwardly he knelt in front of her and skimmed his knuckles over her cheek, the love reflected in his eyes bringing tears to hers. "I know what it is to want a child, Gina. Your mother and me were married twenty some odd years before you blessed our lives. I want to leave this world knowing

I've done my best by you and you have someone to share your life with. Someone who can appreciate all you have to offer."

Alarm skittered through her at his somber mention of leaving this world. "Papa, are you keeping something from me? Are you ill?"

"Of course not, but I'm an old man growing older, and I'm getting tired. I want you to be happy. I want you to have that young 'un you've always wanted so desperately."

"But an English lord, Papa? I think I'll get bored out of my ever-lovin' mind married to a man who does nothing but play. I'd rather marry a costermonger. At least he works up a sweat."

"A man with a title will give you respectability, a place in society that I couldn't give you in New York."

Her heart tightened as the truth dawned on her. "This trip was a husband-hunting expedition, wasn't it?"

Her father ducked his head as though embarrassed that his grand scheme had been discovered.

"Don't you see, Gina? He's got to be an Englishman, an aristocrat. A man with a title. To show those New York bitches who shunned your mother that she was good enough."

"Oh, Papa. Mama was so much better than them—"

He jerked up his head to reveal tears welling in his eyes. "You know that, I know that. By God, I want those Knickerbockers to know it. To know we were all good enough."

"Revenge is not a reason to get married," she said softly, her heart aching for his agony.

"It's not revenge. It's practicality. You're long past a marrying age. We're here in England. Why not marry an aristocrat? Be a countess. Have your children. Do this for your mother. She'd want to see you happy."

"I didn't come here looking to get married."

"I know you didn't, gal, but give this young fella a chance. If you don't like him, I'll find someone else for you."

He spoke as though he was deciding on a new piece of furniture or a bauble. Something insignificant, not a person who could forever alter her life. She'd always followed his advice, acknowledged his greater wisdom, and sought his counsel. How could she now turn aside his plans?

"Why did you choose this particular man?"

"Because he loved his first wife something fierce and spoiled her rotten."

"He was married?" The tapestry of his grand scheme was revealing its unbecoming threads as she unraveled it. Why would she want a man who had already been married and acquired certain expectations regarding a wife's behavior? If she was to marry at all, she wanted a man who understood her need not to be tethered.

Her father nodded sagely. "She died three years ago. He's been mourning ever since. Only came to London a few days ago to visit with his solicitor. Doesn't usually go to the parties around here, but then he heard about you."

She could well imagine what he might have heard about her. She simply didn't fit in this society.

"Then I'll be competing with his memories of his wife."

"Nah, not once he gets to know you well. He'll love you as much as I do. Maybe more. Besides, he needs you, gal. You could make him grateful for his days."

She averted her gaze, because it hurt to see the hope reflected in her father's eyes.

"Why do you think he'd make a good husband?"

"He was never unfaithful to his wife—a rare thing among these gents. Most treat their mistress better than they do their wife. But not this fella. He doesn't drink to excess. He doesn't gamble."

Unlike her father. A man of excesses indeed. When he drank, he drank until he lost all reason. When he gambled, he lost fortunes. Fortunately, he seldom engaged in either activity. Shortly after they'd arrived, he'd begun disappearing for a few days here and there. She'd assumed then that he'd gone in search of places to gamble. Instead it sounded as though he'd been hunting down a husband for her.

"You like him," she responded gravely, as though gloomily accepting her fate. But he wasn't presenting her with a ball gown she could remove at the end of a long evening. He was offering her a husband, a mate for the remainder of her life. Years and years and years. Marry in haste, repent at leisure. Wasn't that how the old saying went?

"I like what I've seen of him. I went to his estate,

without him knowing, of course. Talked to his tenants, the villagers. I know the sort of man he is. I understand the sacrifices he's willing to make for his land—sacrifices most of these men wouldn't be caught dead making. He'll do well by you. If not for me, then at least for the memory of your mother, give him a chance."

She didn't want to remember all the days her mother had waited for the arrival of an invitation that would never come, waited for someone to call on her. No one ever did.

Georgina gave him a tremulous smile. "I'll give him a chance."

Her father's grin shifted the wrinkles in his face and made him appear much younger. "You won't regret it. Now get ready for this ball. I have a feeling he'll introduce himself tonight."

She cast a speculative glance at the gown her father had purchased for her. If Devon Sheridan approached her while she wore it, she'd know he was a desperate man. A desperate man indeed.

Chapter 3

As Georgina stood beside Lauren in a corner of the ballroom, she couldn't help but be overwhelmed by the extravagance—the glittering world of crystal chandeliers, marble floors, and mirrored walls. Dozens of large flower arrangements made the air nauseatingly sweet. Although the area reserved for dancing was open, the perimeter was crowded with small tables, chairs, plants, and statuettes.

Georgina always felt as though the walls were closing in on her. At times she found it increasingly difficult to breathe. Even when she walked through the city, she was bothered by the hordes of people. Her only respite came in the wee hours of the morning, when she went riding.

She couldn't possibly contemplate marrying and remaining here. If only something grander than loneliness awaited her in Texas.

"Stop twirling your fan," Lauren whispered harshly.

Georgina stilled, grateful for the distraction. "You told me to hold it in my left hand to signify I was interested in making someone's acquaintance. That's what I'm doing."

"No, you're *twirling* it in your left hand, which is a signal you love someone."

And she certainly didn't love anyone. Had never loved anyone beyond her family and Lauren. She'd longed for a gentleman to love her. To look upon her as so many of these young men did Lauren.

Would Devon Sheridan gaze upon her with appreciation? She contemplated what she might have done to garner his attention. Nothing of significance came to mind. In truth she could not help but feel that her father had taken some action.

And yet would a match based on mutual needs be such a terrible thing?

She was twenty-six years old, and love continued to elude her. And although she had not come to London searching for a husband, she couldn't help but speculate on what it might be like to be truly accepted into this circle. To have a husband and in time children.

She desperately wanted to give her children roots deeply embedded in familial history. What better place for that than England?

But her heart belonged to Texas. Her father wasn't only asking her to consider marrying a man she didn't know, but he was asking her to give up her dream of returning home to live.

Georgina glanced around, wondering if Devon Sheridan had arrived. She hoped her father was wrong, that the man wouldn't approach her here. She didn't know all the rules and subtle nuances. Memorizing them wasn't the same as applying them.

"You're twirling the fan again," Lauren said in a whisper.

"I can't help it. I hate just standing here, waiting. Maybe I should go home."

"Don't be silly. I'm trying to decide who would find you the most interesting, so I can introduce him to you."

She hadn't shared with Lauren her father's amazing afternoon revelation. Lauren would only encourage her to accept the man's suit. It didn't matter that they had not one thing in common—not their heritage, not their language, not their values. It was an odd notion: that a country born of another could have rebelled to such a degree it hardly resembled its mother any longer. But Georgina assumed that result was the natural evolution of a child. To seek its own path, its own destiny. To be forever different.

Besides, Sheridan might not show, and she didn't want to appear the fool for halfway wishing he would.

"Of course, we'd have more success at finding you a suitor if you'd worn something"—Lauren's gaze roamed Georgina's length—"other than that ghastly gown your father purchased."

"It pleased Papa for me to wear it."

"Don't you ever take into consideration what would please you?"

"It pleases me to please Papa."

Suddenly Lauren dug her fingers into Georgina's arm and whispered in a low, conspiratorial voice, "My God, I don't believe it. Huntingdon is here."

"Huntingdon?"

"Papa's cousin." She surreptitiously wiggled one of her fingers in the direction of her gaze. "Over there. The wickedly handsome gentleman talking to Papa."

Georgina had always thought it was a wondrous expression of Lauren's closeness to her stepfather that she called him Papa.

Squinting, she gazed across the ballroom. The man talking to Christopher Montgomery was dark, not only in coloring but in demeanor. She couldn't explain the reason he seemed mysterious. And it seemed as though, like her, he didn't quite belong. Even from this distance, she could determine that his black double-breasted jacket was well tailored, yet it appeared that he'd outgrown it slightly.

Did men outgrow their clothing? She supposed so, if they put on weight, but Huntingdon didn't appear to have an ounce of fat on him. And he looked to be well past his growing years.

Maybe it was the breadth of his shoulders, completely unlike those of the men surrounding him. She imagined him working the land in Texas, a vision he would no doubt have taken exception to. When a few gentlemen had visited Lauren, Georgina had discovered lifting a teacup was work to an English peer.

She suspected Huntingdon engaged passionately

in sports of some kind. Far be it from the nobility to get their hands dirty in honest labor.

How could she ever consider marrying a man like this—one she'd never be able to respect? Even if she liked him, how could she admire him, when their values were completely different? And without veneration, she knew it was doubtful love would ever exist between them.

"How can they be cousins when they look nothing alike?" Georgina mused. An inane question, but at least it served to bring a halt to the arguments rushing through her mind with the force of stampeding cattle.

"They say there is gypsy blood on his father's side—it's quite scandalous. His mother was Papa's aunt. That's how they come to be cousins."

Gypsy blood. Yes, she could see that now. His skin possessed a swarthiness, unlike the deathly pale coloring of the other gentlemen in the room. Maybe his complexion was part of the reason he looked out of place—physically he simply didn't look dandified or spoiled.

"Why are you surprised to see him here?" she asked Lauren.

"He seldom attends balls or social events. I've never even been to Huntingdon, because he's never invited us, and it's simply not done to go uninvited. He and his wife called on us shortly after we arrived, but recently he has become a bit of a recluse."

Georgina watched as Huntingdon wended his way through the crowded ballroom with poise and confidence, almost prowling. His movements reminded her of the panther—black, sleek, and restless—she'd observed at the London zoological gardens.

She didn't know why she sensed he had a strong urge to roll his shoulders as she'd seen so many cowboys do before they hoisted their saddles onto their horse's back. A roll starting at the hip and working its way upward almost poetically.

She enjoyed the natural grace of a man when he was working hard. It was appreciation, not lust, that she felt when she watched a cowboy exerting himself. The rhythm of muscles bunching, coiling, flexing, tightening. Muscles that looked firm even when they were relaxed.

Sheridan, wherever he was, probably had limp limbs and weak hands.

Lauren's fingers threatened to cut off Georgina's circulation.

"Oh, my God, he's coming toward us," Lauren whispered frantically.

And Georgina realized that somehow, some way, she'd managed to lock her gaze with Huntingdon's—or at least it might have appeared that way to him. When in truth, she'd only been admiring his form, a shape that seemed out of place in this ballroom. During her observation, without thinking, she'd pressed the handle of the fan to her lips: "Kiss me."

She could only hope he hadn't thought she was flirting with him. She'd never purposely attract the attention of a married man, and Lauren had just told her that he had a wife. She wondered where the woman was.

Georgina would certainly want to share the evening with her husband if she had one. She didn't understand the thinking over here. Marriage was a partnership, two people working together to secure happiness.

She couldn't do this. She absolutely couldn't marry one of these men. Having nothing in common with any of them, she didn't feel comfortable around them. Besides, she'd always hoped to marry for love not convenience.

But the undeniable truth hit her: if she didn't latch onto this opportunity now, when would she marry, when would she have children? In reality marrying an Englishman could prove to be an ideal situation. She'd noticed it was impossible at these functions to know who went with whom. Husbands and wives, with a few exceptions, seldom interacted much.

She could marry the man, have his child, and hardly ever see him again. Her life wouldn't be much different from what it was now—except that she'd have a son or daughter to love. A son or daughter. Could she marry a man and use him to gain what she dearly wanted?

She had no business being here, waiting nervously for some desperate man to approach her. Maybe Sheridan had caught sight of her in this awful gown and changed his mind.

"I'm going to get us some punch," she said. And while she was at it, she'd locate the carriage and simply sit in it until it was time to go home.

"You're not leaving me. I'll introduce him to you.

It's only proper. Besides, he might ask you to dance, and other gentlemen will surely follow suit."

But he made her nervous, the way he strode toward them with apparent single-minded purpose. Someone snagged his attention, and he stopped. A reprieve.

"Maybe we should take a walk in the garden," Georgina suggested.

"You won't find a beau in the garden."

"Lauren, I'm not really looking for a beau."

"Why not? You could stay in England, and we could grow old together, remain best friends forever."

Hadn't her father suggested practically the same thing? Were they conspiring? "Have you talked with my father about me getting married?"

"Of course not. Your father and I seldom speak, but now that I've said it, it sounds like a splendid idea. Maybe we could even marry brothers, so we'd attend all the same family functions. Now, that's a thought."

Huntingdon was on the prowl again, acknowledging people with a mere nod as he made his way across the room.

"You know, the more I ponder your introduction, the more I realize Huntingdon might not be a bad match for you," Lauren murmured.

"I thought you said he was married."

"No, I said I'd met his wife."

Georgina wanted to screech. Honestly, sometimes she felt as though she was communicating with someone who spoke in a language alien to her. Marriage, wife. She couldn't figure out how any difference existed between the two.

"It stands to reason if you met his wife, then he's married," Georgina pointed out.

"No longer married. Widower."

Everything within Georgina stilled as a horrid thought hit her. "What's his name?"

"I told you. Huntingdon."

Damn this English tradition that gave people in the aristocracy so many names. "No, I mean—"

But it was too late. Huntingdon came to an abrupt halt before them. Georgina was grateful to see his intense gaze had shifted and locked onto Lauren. It had probably been on Lauren all along. Georgina had simply been unable to tell because of the distance separating them.

The gaslights flickering in the chandeliers glistened on his black hair. Threads of silver graced his temples, adding to his distinguished demeanor. His eyes matched the blue of the gown she'd planned to wear this evening.

"Lord Huntingdon, it's such a pleasure to see you this evening," Lauren said softly, elegantly.

She spoke with a confidence Georgina continually admired. She was again reminded how her friend had grown into an elegant lady, and the differences between them seemed to be as vast as the ocean that had separated them for eight years.

"Miss Fairfield, I assure you the pleasure is undoubtedly all mine."

His voice was a low, rich rumble, and Georgina could well imagine him whispering seductively in a woman's ear. What she couldn't imagine was the reason Lauren thought he'd be a good match for her. She really should have told her friend about Sheridan. It could make for a most embarrassing moment if Lauren decided to try to play matchmaker without knowing her father had already taken on the role.

"May I say you look extremely lovely this evening," he continued. "As always."

A soft blush lit Lauren's cheeks. "You are too kind, my lord."

"Hardly, Miss Fairfield, but I do appreciate beauty when I happen upon it."

He shifted his attention to Georgina, and she felt the full impact of his intense blue gaze. But within his eyes she noticed something now she hadn't before—a profound sadness, a haunted mien characteristic of the men she had known who returned from war. Had this man fought a battle and known defeat?

He slid his gaze back to Lauren and arched a brow as well as a corner of his mouth. A wry smile that did nothing to detract from the fine shape of his lips.

"Oh!" Lauren almost hopped. "My lord, forgive my rudeness." She turned to Georgina. "Miss Pierce, may I present Devon Sheridan, the Earl of Huntingdon. Lord Huntingdon . . ."

Georgina's fingers turned icy cold as her worst fears were realized. Never in a hundred years could she marry a man whose features were chiseled to perfection. A man such as he far exceeded her reach. What had her father been contemplating?

Lauren's voice became little more than a buzz as

she prattled on about something, something to do with Huntingdon. Georgina saw him make a movement, and she feared he might be on the verge of grabbing her hand and kissing it. Even though they wore gloves, she didn't want the intimate contact.

Tucking her hands in close to her waist, she knew her withdrawal must have been evident, because he seemed to draw back as well, his gaze speculative. She clutched her fan with both hands. What were the signals for "Go away," "I don't like you," "You're as handsome as sin and we'd make an odd pair"?

She couldn't think, couldn't speak, could barely breathe.

Unlikely scenarios scrambled through her mind. Maybe two Devon Sheridans existed. Surely this man wasn't the one who had spoken to her father, the one he expected her to marry.

He tilted his head slightly in a semblance of a bow. "Having recently met your father, I can honestly say it is an honor to make your acquaintance at last, Miss Pierce."

He *was* the one! And with that certainty, his interest in her became painfully obvious.

She studied him more carefully. His white silk waistcoat was straining against its buttons. The cuffed sleeves of his jacket were frayed around the edges and sadly out of date. Men weren't wearing cuffed sleeves this season. His tight trousers had also seen better days. His shoes, though polished to a shine, revealed worn leather.

Unlike the other men in the room, he hadn't bothered to keep up with the trendier fashions. Some might attribute his slightly unstylish attire to the fact that he'd been in seclusion after the loss of his wife, but Georgina felt certain that she knew the truth of his situation.

As she'd suspected, the man who had expressed an interest in her was an impoverished nobleman. She could decipher his reasons as though he'd engraved them across his forehead. These men who lived off the hard work of their ancestors were spoiled, and when the coffers were empty, they found it much easier to marry money than to earn it.

Then he smiled fully, exhibiting a charm with which he'd no doubt been born. And she realized that if she bore his son, he would resemble his father. He would know what it was to be adored. And he himself would be titled.

Wasn't that the way English law worked? The entire estate and its title passed down from father to eldest son. She'd seen the deference given to the first-born sons among the aristocracy. She hated to admit that she'd be pleased to give her son an advantage in life. But was it advantageous to have everything handed to you?

Was she really any different from the man standing before her? She wasn't foolish enough to think she'd earned his love or his interest. He needed an association with her father, and marriage to her was the most expedient route.

"Miss Fairfield won't chastise you for speaking to me now that we've been formally introduced," he said.

But she could think of nothing intelligent to utter.

I know who you are. I know why you're here. We will not make a good match.

And yet she really didn't know if the last was true. He looked as though like her, he, too, wished he was anywhere else.

"The cat seems to have gotten hold of her tongue," Lauren said with a soft chuckle.

"So it would appear," he said solemnly. "Might I inquire as to whether you're enjoying your holiday in London?"

"Uh, yes, Mr. Huntingdon, I am." She didn't know why neither her brain nor her tongue seemed to want to function.

"What do you fancy most?" he asked.

Strangely she thought he sounded as though he truly cared. What if he really did have an interest in her beyond her father's money?

"I enjoy riding Lord Ravenleigh's horses through Hyde Park in the morning."

"My cousin does have a fine stable of animals." He bowed slightly. "If you ladies will excuse me, I shall take my leave before I arouse jealousy among my peers for dominating your time."

Georgina watched him walk away. She didn't want to be fascinated by his supple movements, didn't want to wonder what it might be like to dance with him, to have his undivided attention.

"We've been spending all day, every day together. When in the world did you go riding?" Lauren asked, breaking into her thoughts.

"In the morning long before you're awake."

"Who is chaperoning you?"

"No one. I'm an adult. I ride alone at home. Why not here?"

"Because the rules are different here. And for goodness sake, if he speaks to you again, remember to address him as my lord, not Mr. Huntingdon. The proper form of address is extremely important if you want to make a good impression."

Georgina had little doubt she'd made an impression. Perhaps having met her, he would report to her father that he no longer had any interest in her.

How odd that she suddenly found she had an interest in him.

Chapter 4

Devon had feared gaining his introduction to Miss Pierce would arouse the curiosity of the other gentlemen in attendance and they might seek her out as well. He'd worried that he'd forfeit his advantage if she were smitten by someone who possessed the ability to offer her more than he could. But if anyone had noticed, he was apparently not intrigued.

Devon had yet to see Miss Pierce dance.

After several attempts, one insistent fellow had lured Miss Fairfield away from her friend. Left on her own, Miss Pierce neither conversed nor flirted but seemed to prefer the company of potted palms.

He spotted her hidden behind the graceful fronds, peering out as though she wasn't quite certain what activities one engaged in while in attendance at such an affair. Twice his gaze had clashed with hers when she'd discovered him watching her.

She did not play coy, as most women did. She appeared to be a solitary soul, and that notion appealed to him immensely.

She was unfashionably tall and slender. Her skin was dark, almost weathered, as though she'd spent a good deal of time in the sun without benefit of a parasol. Her reddish-brown hair was beginning to droop, as though a lover had repeatedly tunneled his fingers through it. But he hadn't seen her saunter away for a secret assignation.

Her clothing was garish beyond measure. He did not as a rule take notice of women's fashions, but he was fairly certain hers was *not* in vogue. However, a reputable seamstress could change that.

Convincing her that he found her beautiful and had fallen in love with her would be no easy task. It would take precious time he did not have the luxury of wasting.

He doubted he would ever consider her beautiful, and he knew beyond any doubt that he would never fall in love with her. Yet he was pleasantly surprised to discover that she did indeed intrigue him.

He caught sight of her slipping through the glass doors leading into the garden. He supposed if he was going to make his intent to court her known, she'd provided him with the perfect opportunity. As unobtrusively as possible, he followed her outside.

He found her standing at the edge of the porch, gripping the wrought-iron railing. He wondered if she was as disappointed in the evening as Margaret would have been had she garnered so little attention.

Men had fluttered around Margaret as though

they were bees hoping for a sip of nectar, even after he and she were married. Their constant attention had led him to the discovery of a jealous streak that caused him to see red. He doubted it would ever surface with Miss Pierce as his wife, and that notion caused him a great deal of relief.

He did not consider her hideous. Only unattractive. Yet as he neared her, he realized she wasn't truly plain. She simply possessed no feature that stood out and grabbed one's attention. Limned by moonlight with the forgiving night shadows cast around her, she appeared almost . . . lovely. In a lonely sort of way.

Like any woman, she deserved a man who appreciated what she had to offer, not a man whose claim of interest was sparked by the coins jingling in her father's pockets.

For the length of a heartbeat, he debated the cruelty she might one day accuse him of if she ever learned the truth. He would simply have to bury it deeply and cover the lies with false glitter.

"The beauty of the moon pales when compared with your loveliness." He cringed. Devil be damned. That was the most awful thing he'd ever murmured to a woman.

It had been years since he'd played the courtship game, and he'd grown unaccountably sloppy. All he'd needed was one little lie, one tiny flirtatious comment, and he'd have had her nestled within his palm. The problem was that he didn't truly want her in his palm. He only wanted his fist around her father's money.

He was fairly certain she'd never had a compliment thrown her way. Otherwise, why would her father be willing to purchase what she had yet to obtain? Why had he insisted that he convince her that she was beautiful? Why pretend to love her unless she had no experience with being loved?

He had expected her to turn to him with adoring eyes. Instead she continued to look at the lawn shadowed by the moon.

"Consider me plain, my lord. Consider me dull. But never, never consider me stupid."

She faced him then, one eyebrow arched, daring him to deny her accusation, daring him to give her another compliment. He could do no more than wish a great gaping hole would suddenly appear and the earth would swallow him up. She gave a small nod, as though his silence confirmed her suspicions, and turned her gaze back to the lawn.

"You must be a desperate man," she said quietly. "What did my father offer you?"

So much for keeping his promise to her father that she would never know of the arrangement. But if he did not uphold his end of the bargain, would her father honor his? Or would he locate a man more adept at deception?

He debated the wisdom of denying her father had offered him anything, but how long would it take a relationship built on the foundation of a lie to crumble? To woo her with false flattery was one thing. To boldly lie . . .

As though sensing his dilemma, she said, "I won't tell him you confessed."

"Unlimited access to his wealth."

He clenched his jaws and balled his fists at his sides, hating the need he heard shimmering in his voice. The desperation she must have also heard.

Her silence spoke loudly. She'd wished to humiliate him, and now she was relishing her accomplishment. He didn't need this degradation, nor did he want it. He'd find another way to handle his ghastly situation. He turned on his heel and began to walk away.

"I'm not opposed to your suit, my lord."

He stopped but refused to look at her. This experience was more humiliating than meeting with her father.

"I've been standing here silently playing devil's advocate with myself. What if I married you? What if I didn't? What would the future hold if I returned to Texas? What would it bring if I remained here? I'm twenty-six years old." She released a small, self-deprecating laugh. "And I've never been kissed."

He turned then, slowly, realizing that perhaps this moment was as difficult for her as it was for him. She was still watching the lawn as though she hoped to catch a glimpse of the grass growing.

"My father thinks you would make me happy."

"I would do all in my power to see that you don't regret having me as a husband."

She looked at him, her worries written in deep lines on her face. "What about you? Will you resent having me for your wife?"

"Resent salvation, Miss Pierce? I think it highly unlikely."

"What sort of marriage do you see us having?" she asked.

Although he was familiar with the pleasures and perils of marriage, he could not easily sum up the complicated answer to so simple a question. "Would you care to take a stroll through the garden with me?"

"Isn't it scandalous for a woman to be alone with a man?"

He cocked his head. "Miss Pierce, you have already invited scandal by venturing outside without a chaperone."

"A body can't even step out without someone tagging along?"

A body? *Her* body. If he brought her back flush against his chest, he thought he might possibly be able to rest his chin on the top of her head.

He dropped his gaze to her tapping foot. Her irritation was incredibly easy to read. His society provided rules for every occasion, rules a person was expected to follow. He wondered how long it would take her to adapt to the code.

"Once tarnished, a woman's reputation can never again shine," he told her.

"You care about things like reputation?"

"Indeed I do. Shall we take that stroll?"

"Without a chaperone?"

"I won't tell if you won't."

She released a small laugh that took him off guard. A soft lilt that floated on the evening breeze, an inviting warmth that caused him to think that perhaps marriage to her would not be as awful as he'd imagined.

"Seems you only worry about the rules if you think you'll get caught breaking them," she said.

"Quite so." He extended his crooked elbow toward her. "Shall we?"

She reached out as though she would place her hand on his arm, and then, as though thinking better of it, she simply said, "Just lead the way."

He dropped his arm to his side and began walking along the cobblestone path. She fell into step beside him, her skirts swishing around her. It had been an incredibly long time since he'd strolled with a lady.

Beneath the perfume of roses wafting around them, he caught the whiff of another scent, subtle but alluring. He didn't recognize the sweet fragrance, but he knew it belonged to the woman beside him. He wondered what other surprises he might discover about her.

"You were going to explain what I could expect if we got married," she said.

If? Did these Americans never commit to anything?

"Right," he answered succinctly. "Our marriage would be typical of the English aristocracy. We would spend the summer in the London house and the rest of the time at my country estate."

"*Your* country estate?"

Wealth gave her an advantage over him he didn't much fancy but knew he would have to accept. He fought to keep the irritation from seeping into his voice. It would not do at this early stage of the courtship to give her cause to doubt his sincerity. "*Our* country estate."

"How would you treat me?"

"With the utmost respect, naturally." He glanced over at her, lost in the shadows. He'd suggested the walk because he found it easier to speak when he could not look directly into the eyes of another—when pity was absorbed by the darkness. "And with gratitude. My estate, the life I have always known, is crumbling around me."

"You could get a job," she suggested.

Or slit his throat, his preferred choice if only allowed the two. "People of my station do not *get jobs.*"

"I have to confess I don't understand your aversion to working."

"A gentleman does not work. It is the one remaining aspect of our lives that separates us from the masses." Those of the middle class who were becoming landowners, those who were acquiring wealth and imitating the aristocracy. Those who could never buy their way into the position in which Devon had been born.

Men such as her father. Yet it seemed what he couldn't acquire for himself, he could boldly purchase for his daughter.

"But if it's a matter of going hungry—"

"I am not yet at the point of hunger. Marriage is an acceptable solution. Besides, your father informs me you wish to have a child. That I can give you."

"That?"

She sounded truly horrified. An Englishwoman

would be tripping over herself to gain his favor, and this woman was waging war against the subtle nuances of their conversation.

"We're talking about a child—" she began.

"I realize that," he interrupted. "I chose my words poorly. I simply meant that I have the ability to give you a son or daughter."

"And you'll be willing to give me a child?"

"Absolutely."

"Will you love this baby or resent him?"

"Why would I resent it?"

They had circled back to the spot where they'd begun their journey. She stopped walking and stared at him, giving him the distinct impression she could see through the night into his soul.

"You strike me as being a proud man," she said softly. "I suppose I worry you'll come to resent what marriage to me gained you."

"As I stated earlier, you may rest assured that particular circumstance will not happen. I grew up knowing my place in society and understanding well its cost."

Distant lights made it easier to see her silhouette. She nodded slightly, and he wondered if she'd been contemplating his words. They seemed wholly inadequate to express what he felt and what he was willing to sacrifice in order to ensure the well-being of Huntingdon. It was not so much the present that concerned him, but the future . . . and the past.

He felt as though he was disappointing those who had come before and failing those who would come after.

"Will it embarrass you to have such an unsophisticated wife?" she asked.

"Sophistication can be learned."

"And if I've no desire to be taught?"

Her tone issued a definite, defiant challenge. What a contradiction she was: hiding out one moment, challenging him the next.

Obviously she would not change for him. Could he change for her? Whatever embarrassment she might cause him would pale when compared to the mortification he was on the brink of enduring.

"Then I shall adjust my thinking," he assured her.

"Tell me about your family's estate," she ordered gently.

His chest tightened with the memories of walking across the fields with his father. "Huntingdon has seen better days. The manor is grand, the land beautiful. I have two thousand acres. The tenants pay a pound per acre yearly, but few tenants are left to work the fields. Most have moved to the cities in search of employment in the various industries, work which will put more money in their pockets. The old life must give way to the new, I suppose. Therefore much of the land lies fallow. I want to restore Huntingdon to its former grandeur and I'm willing to do whatever it takes to achieve that end."

"Except work."

He clenched his jaw. How did he explain to someone who came from a new nation what it was to have his roots buried in centuries of history?

"Huntingdon defines who I am, who my family

has been. Certain expectations abound, which I'm determined to follow."

"The easy way is not always the best way."

"Believe me, Miss Pierce, no aspect of this predicament is remotely easy for me."

She turned away, and anger roiled through him. He'd come close to baring his soul, and for what? He needed neither her respect nor her kind regard. He only required her father's money to put to rights what his father had torn asunder.

"I'll agree to marry you but only on one condition," she said quietly before turning to face him.

Devon cursed the stars. Weren't enough conditions attached to this marriage? "What would your solitary condition entail, Miss Pierce?"

She tilted her chin up ever so slightly. "You must never lie to me. You must never tell me I am beautiful when I am not. You must never tell me you love me when you cannot."

"Never is a long time, Miss Pierce."

"So is until death do us part, my lord."

"Indeed it is. I accept your condition."

She seemed to breathe a sigh of relief. Then she lifted her chin up as though about to challenge him once again. "I assume my father isn't going to part with his money until we're married. How soon do you wish to wed?"

No lies, she'd said. Well, then, he'd give her no lies. "The sooner the better."

"When would sooner be?"

"I can obtain a special license. We could be married by the end of the week. There will of course be talk."

"It'll be scandalous, won't it?" She gave him a small smile. He knew it was a trick of the moonlight and that moonbeams were gentle, but for a moment she almost appeared a vision of loveliness. "I've never had my name associated with a scandal before. I think it might be quite fun."

Quite fun? Dear Lord, but he'd spent his life ensuring no scandals were associated with him. Now a hasty marriage to a foreigner would taint his efforts.

"May I call on you the day after tomorrow to apprise you of my success in obtaining our license?" he asked.

"The day after tomorrow will be fine."

She held out her small hand, and he wrapped his larger one around it, absorbing the slight tremors in hers. Theirs was a business arrangement. He needed financing. She desired a child and the respectability his title offered. A business arrangement was agreed upon with a handshake.

And if her hand hadn't been trembling, that's all he would have given her, all he'd planned to give her. Instead he lifted her hand to his lips and placed a light kiss against her gloved fingertips. "Until the day after tomorrow, Miss Pierce."

He released her hand and began to walk away.

"My lord?"

He turned back, and she was once again watching the lawn. "Sometimes things look different in the morning. I'll understand if you have a change of heart and don't call on me."

"I'll be there," he vowed quietly.

With his velvet promise lingering on the slight breeze, Georgina watched the shadows play over the lawn while clouds waltzed across the moon.

Originally she had not intended to accept his offer. In truth she had not even planned to encourage his suit with conversation. And yet she'd been unable to ignore him, to allow him to walk away. Not when he represented what she had yet to obtain. He was a gentleman. A gentleman in need of financing.

And she was a woman, a woman who longed to belong, who desperately wanted children. A little one to love who would return that affection untainted.

How could she turn away from the opportunity to live with a man who'd spoken of his home with such affection, as though bits of silver and gold threaded his voice. She did not expect him to ever extend that emotion toward her, but it comforted her to know he was capable of expressing it.

He'd said the situation wasn't easy for him. But neither was it easy for her. To give herself to a man she barely knew . . . or to never give herself at all.

What had she been thinking to accept? Here in the garden, surrounded by shadows, it had all seemed dreamlike, and she'd succumbed to the lure of at long last finding a place where she belonged. A home.

And in time a child. Someone who would love her as her father did—simply because she existed.

Dared she believe that he would keep his promise to come for her? The secret place within her that longed for all the things she'd been denied hoped that he would.

She pressed her balled hand just above her breast. The ache in her chest increased as the tears slowly leaked onto her cheeks. She knew worse things existed than a marriage without love. But was anything lonelier?

She could stand on a windswept prairie and not feel lonely. She could stand in a crowded ballroom and know a lonesome ache that defied description.

Which would her marriage resemble?

Her father's money had purchased her grandest dream: to become a wife. She could only hope his taste in men far exceeded his taste in women's clothing.

Quickly she swiped the tears from her cheeks. Although she did not need love, she dearly wanted it.

She was grateful Lord Huntingdon had approached her early in the evening. Now she could sneak away and dream of a love that would never be . . . one last time. After her marriage, she would never again dream or look back or regret what might have been. She would content herself with what was. She never wanted her father or husband to realize she was unhappy.

Her husband.

She couldn't quite wrap her mind around the possibility.

She strolled into the ballroom. Happy sounds floated toward her. Flirtations always carried such a musical lilt to them. Women blushed. Gentlemen's eyes warmed with pleasure. She'd always watched from the edge, never having been invited into the circle.

A shame she hadn't added one waltz at each ball to her list of conditions. She had a feeling that once Lord Huntingdon had his fist around her father's money, he would seldom be tempted to close his hand around hers.

Wending her way through the crowd, she listened as the gentle strains of a waltz floated across the room.

"I believe this is my dance, Miss Pierce."

She spun around, her heart thundering. The Earl of Huntingdon stood before her in his finely cut jacket that had seen better days, and his somber eyes that she was certain had seen more joyous evenings.

He extended his hand toward her. As though in a dream, she placed hers on top of his, and he escorted her onto the dance floor. Her breath caught once she realized exactly what she'd allowed. She'd never in her life waltzed. Of course, she'd never been married either, but that hadn't stopped her from accepting his proposal—such as it was.

In rhythm with the music, he waltzed with her, his gaze holding hers captive. She would look into those blue eyes every evening for the remaining years of her life. She would watch his black hair turn completely silver and the shallow grooves etched on his face deepen. She would witness the slowing of his gait and his acquisition of wisdom. Would his shoulders slump with the burden of age? Or would he stand tall against all the challenges that life would toss their way?

Slowing his step, reaching out, he grazed his gloved knuckle over her eyelashes. "You overlooked a tear, sweeting."

"It's a woman's right to cry when she accepts a proposal of marriage."

"Indeed. I find women weep over a great many things."

"I don't," she assured him.

"No, I suspect you don't."

The final refrain from the song drifted over her, around her, through her.

"I shall call on you the day after tomorrow," he said solemnly.

She nodded quickly, her throat tightening and tears threatening to fill her eyes. She refused to cry again for all they would not have—especially in front of him. "I'll be waiting."

She should have contented herself with the nod instead of speaking in a voice that greatly resembled a bullfrog sitting on the muddy bank of a creek back home.

"As you mentioned, sometimes things appear different in the morning," he said, repeating her earlier comment. "I'll understand if you have a change of heart and decide not to see me when I arrive."

She angled her chin defiantly. "I'm not one to go back on my word."

He lifted her hand and pressed a kiss against her knuckles. "Until then . . . sleep well."

She would have sworn the room became quiet enough for a prayer meeting as his long, confident strides carried him away from her.

As for sleeping well, she doubted that she would sleep at all.

Chapter 5

Lounging in a chair before the cold, empty hearth in his bedchamber, Devon studied the portrait of his wife that hung above the marble mantel. He supposed he would have to place it elsewhere. It would be bad form to leave it here where his new wife might happen upon it.

He had not expected to be drawn to Georgina Pierce. Not attracted in the classical sense, but drawn as the ocean laps at the shore. It cannot stop its momentum forward, and even after it retreats, it quickly returns.

Amazingly he'd possessed a strong desire to return to her for another dance. Perhaps it was the lure of that solitary tear clinging to her dark lash as an early morning dewdrop on the petal of a red rose might.

During the journey home, he'd constantly stroked the spot on his glove that carried the dampness from her tear. He could not prevent himself from wondering at her reason for weeping. For joy because he had rescued her from the fate of a spinster? Or from disappointment because he hadn't spoken of undying love?

He presumed disappointment was the culprit. She'd made it perfectly clear that she didn't anticipate flattery. Strange how once she'd forbidden it, he'd wanted to inundate her with it.

Not the idiotic moon pales in comparison garbage that he still had difficulty believing he'd uttered earlier. Rather something more substantial, more honest. He doubted that he would ever view her as gorgeous, but something about her that he couldn't quite identify intrigued him. Perhaps their marriage would not be as disheartening as he'd envisioned.

Yet he seriously doubted it would resemble his marriage to Margaret in any manner. Theirs had been one of passion. He had loved her with every aspect of his existence. Even when she had turned away from him. When his touch had repulsed her because his hands were no longer those of a gentleman.

This evening his gloves had hidden that disgraceful fact from Miss Pierce, but she would no doubt notice during their wedding night when he sought to fulfill his promise to give her a child. The calluses on his palms would abrade her skin.

Margaret had come to loathe the roughness of his hands. No matter how lightly he'd touched her, she'd claimed he hurt her delicate flesh. No matter how often he'd bathed, she'd sworn he smelled as though he'd rolled in the fields.

When he'd gone to her bed, she'd wept for all they'd once had and mourned all they no longer possessed. He'd lost her long before she died.

He'd been lonely for such a long time now. Lonely and alone.

He had failed Margaret, and in so doing, he had disappointed himself.

Pierce's money would help him regain his self-esteem. Would help wash away his memory of Margaret calling him a pitiful excuse for a man . . . only moments before she died in his arms.

"I want to know everything!"

Georgina squinted through the darkness as Lauren flung herself on the bed, causing it to rock. She shook Georgina's shoulder. "Wake up and tell me everything."

"I am awake." Georgina pulled herself into a sitting position and shoved the pillows behind her back.

As soon as Huntingdon had left her, she'd gone in search of the carriage. She'd come home, readied herself for bed, crawled beneath the blankets, and stared at the ceiling, mulling over the strange evening.

Lauren turned up the flame in the lamp. "I saw Huntingdon dance with you, and then you disappeared. You should have heard the murmuring and whispers that followed his departure."

"I did hear them. Why do you think I left?"

"Gina, don't you understand what he did? By dancing with you, he practically dared every other man to do the same. It didn't go unnoticed that you were the only lady with whom he danced. His attentiveness was absolutely wonderful! You'll wear out your slippers dancing at the next ball."

"I'm not going to any other ball."

"Of course you are, silly goose. Everyone's curiosity regarding you was finally piqued—"

"Lauren, I'm getting married."

Lauren's mouth dropped open, and her eyelashes began to flutter. "Pardon?"

"Huntingdon asked me to marry him. I said yes." Although he hadn't exactly *asked,* and she hadn't exactly *said yes.*

"But I only introduced you to him tonight. How could you possibly fall in love with him that quickly?"

"I didn't. I barely know him!" Georgina threw aside the covers, scrambled out of bed, and began to pace across the thick carpet. She knew many marriages were based on needs rather than love. She could accept hers would be one of those. But the litany in her mind did little to reassure her.

"I don't understand," Lauren said as she stretched across the bed and raised herself up on her elbows.

"Papa arranged it. Huntingdon needs money, and Papa wants to see me married." She dropped onto the mattress. Pleasing her father was her single greatest joy. But this latest wish of his—what would it cost her to grant it? "I've been lying here thinking about it. How can I marry a man I don't respect?"

"How can you not respect Huntingdon? For goodness sake, Gina, he's an earl."

"He didn't earn the title or his position, Lauren. An accident of birth gave him advantage, and apparently he squandered it. Respect comes with hard work, not from careless disregard of the toil of those who came before you."

"If you feel that way, then why are you marrying him?"

"Because Papa wants it so badly." She studied her hands. "And I want children."

She cast a furtive glance at her friend. "And there's a little more to it. I never told you about New York."

"What about it?"

She studied her hands. How could she explain the humiliation?

"Three years ago, Papa decided that it was time to stop our wanderings. He'd lost his fortune a couple of times, gambling, and this time, when he regained it, he wanted to make Mama happy. To make amends for some of the more difficult times. He thought New York was the place.

"But it was awful, Lauren. The city is owned by the old money. They have as many rules there as you have here, and I despise them all. Until one of the old families acknowledges you, you're no better than something to be wiped off a shoe."

"It's not that bad here."

"You don't notice, because your stepfather is influential. For all the hard-earned money Papa had, he had no influence among the socially elite. And you're nobody until a Knickerbocker recognizes you as such."

Georgina swallowed hard, buffeting the painful memory.

"One evening Mama, Papa, and I were standing in the foyer at the opera house. One of the matrons of New York caught Mama's attention. You should have seen Mama's face, Lauren. She thought she was finally being accepted. The woman walked toward us, and then she breezed right by without saying a word."

"A direct cut," Lauren murmured. "In public. She must have been mortified."

"She was such a gentle woman, Lauren."

"I remember her well. She always made everyone feel welcome."

"Well, shortly after that night, she got sick. Then the pneumonia set in. When she died last winter, Papa started making plans to visit here. I think he was hoping all along to find me a husband."

"But why an Englishman?"

"Not just an Englishman. An aristocrat. I think at the very core of his heart, he genuinely wants to see me happy, wants to see me well married and with the children that I so desperately desire. But a part of him can't forget the devastation on Mama's face when the woman walked by her and looked away. What better way to beat the old guard at their own game than through marriage, to join a club more exclusive than theirs, even if it's an ocean away? They're bound to hear of it.

"And a part of me, Lauren, thinks why not? I've yet to find a man whose interest I can hold. Neither of us would have expectations of romance or love. I can't help but wonder if a marriage of convenience would be better than no marriage at all."

Lauren shrugged. "I suppose you could do worse than Huntingdon. After all, he is deliciously handsome. He looks as though he'd be delightfully wicked in bed."

Georgina tugged on one of Lauren's blond curls. "What do you know about being *wicked in bed?*"

Lauren's cheeks blushed becomingly. "I've heard things."

"Such as?" Georgina demanded.

Wearing a mischievous grin, Lauren edged closer to Georgina and whispered, "I've heard a man kisses you all over."

"All over?"

Lauren nodded enthusiastically, her eyes twinkling. "From the top of your head to the tips of your toes—and *everywhere* in between."

"I don't believe that."

Using her finger, Lauren made a cross over her heart in much the same manner as they had when they were children. "I swear it's what I've heard."

Georgina felt trepidation slice through her. The warmth from his mouth had seeped through her glove as he'd kissed her fingers. She couldn't imagine his lips against her flesh or that a man might not expect something in return. "How is a woman expected to kiss a man?"

Lauren licked her lips. "In much the same manner, I imagine."

"Since ours is to be a marriage of necessity and

not passion, I don't imagine I'll be expected to kiss him anywhere."

Laughing, Lauren plopped onto her back. "And you said I'd become a prude."

"You're teasing me."

"No, honestly, it's what I've heard."

"Who told you?"

"Tom."

Georgina heard the wistful longing in Lauren's voice. "Did he kiss you everywhere?"

"Of course not. He said I was too young, but he promised he would on my seventeenth birthday. Then we moved here when I was fourteen, so he never had a chance." Lauren rolled over, raised herself up on her elbows, and held Georgina's gaze. "Promise you'll tell me if Huntingdon kisses you *everywhere*."

"He won't."

"But if he does . . ."

"He won't!" Because she wouldn't dare let him.

Glancing over her shoulder, Georgina studied her reflection in the mirror. She liked the way the back of the blue wool dress was gathered into puffs that went both lengthwise and across. The simple lines leading to the modest train made her look elegant.

And not a single bow in sight. She hoped as much as she dreaded that Lord Huntingdon would honor his promise and call on her today.

She'd visited a seamstress first thing that morning and ordered a gown of white. It was supposed to be completed in three days, and Georgina had no idea if that was soon enough. He'd said they'd be married by the end of the week.

Had he meant they'd be married by Friday, in which case the wedding would take place on Thursday? Or had he meant Saturday with the wedding to take place on Friday? What day did he consider the end of the week? Did he mean they would be married on that day or the day before?

And what was a special license? Would certain conditions apply to their marriage?

She thought about asking Lauren, but she was incredibly embarrassed that she'd agreed to this marriage without addressing all the particulars. Of course, she hadn't truly believed he'd honor the bargain. No lies, no love, no false flattery.

She turned away from the mirror. She shouldn't have been so quick to reveal her conditions. What would it hurt to be told just once by someone other than her father that she was beautiful—even if it wasn't true?

The rap on the door started her heart to thundering.

Elizabeth Montgomery peered into the room. Her once blond hair was now a gentle white that reminded Georgina of soft dandelions. Her blue eyes sparkled. Georgina had no doubt Elizabeth had flourished by marrying Christopher Montgomery and moving to England. She just wasn't quite sure coming here had been the best thing for Lauren, although she had to admit Christopher Montgomery seemed to be a good father.

Elizabeth smiled warmly. "You have a gentleman caller. Lord Huntingdon."

Georgina's knees grew weak. He'd come! Until this moment, she hadn't realized she'd convinced herself he wouldn't show. Nor had she realized how desperately glad she would be that he had arrived.

"I'll be right down."

"You might want to don a hat and grab your parasol. He mentioned he had an interest in taking you for a boat ride on the Thames."

"By God, you were supposed to court her!"

Standing in the foyer, Devon had barely given Elizabeth his message before Pierce pounced on him like a rabid dog. The splotchy red covering the man's face made Devon fear that he'd collapse in an apoplectic fit at any moment.

"Perhaps we should discuss this matter in a more private setting," Devon suggested.

"The library. Now!" Pierce thundered.

"I assume Ravenleigh isn't in here," he murmured as he followed the man to his cousin's lair.

As soon as he entered, Pierce turned on him.

"We had a gentleman's agreement—"

"Which I have honored."

"How do you figure that? I wanted her courted and wooed. I wanted her to feel loved. A woman should only be asked once to give her hand in marriage, and by God, that moment should be one she'll carry with her until her hair turns gray."

Devon had a feeling Georgina would always remember the moment. He knew he certainly would. "Our arrangement was based on my conforming to three conditions. I will have more success at convincing her that I find her beautiful and am in love with her if she is my wife rather than my interest.

"And I'm rather certain you'll agree giving her a child is facilitated by a hastily arranged marriage. As to my remaining faithful to her, that as well cannot be tested until a wedding has taken place."

"A shotgun wedding was not a condition—"

"Oh, Papa."

Devon spun around at the sound of Georgina's voice. How much had she heard? She knew money was a factor in their hasty marriage. She knew he was willing to give her a child. But for reasons he could not fathom, he had not wanted her to know that her father thought it necessary to demand his faithfulness or that he had been told to convince her that she was beautiful.

Both those conditions suddenly seemed cold and harsh. While financial consideration was the basis for their marriage, he'd hoped to spare her the truth of the details. A woman should not only expect fidelity from her husband, but she should feel as though he did find her attractive.

She strolled past him and placed her hand on her father's shoulder. "Oh, Papa, you're giving Lord Huntingdon a tongue-lashing for nothing. What woman wouldn't be pleased that her suitor wished to marry her as soon as possible?"

What woman indeed? She'd neither referred to herself nor confirmed that she was pleased. She'd spoken the truth, but not necessarily a truth that applied to her. He wondered if she merely wished to put her father's doubts at ease while keeping her own counsel regarding her true feelings on the matter.

If Pierce's diminishing agitation was any indication, she had succeeded. Pierce settled his gaze on his daughter. The depth of love in his eyes caused Devon to regret he didn't have time to court her properly, to make her feel as though she was indeed fortunate he had selected her.

Pierce patted her hand. "Thought I was prepared for giving you over to another man. Reckon I'm still adjusting to the thought."

Georgina kissed his leathery cheek. "I'll always be your little girl. Now, if you'll excuse us, it's my understanding that Lord Huntingdon is taking me boating."

Georgina tried to enjoy the scenery, the sight of the other boats floating along the river, but her attention kept returning to Huntingdon and the powerful bunching of his muscles as he rowed. He'd removed his jacket and rolled up his sleeves past his elbows. She was surprised by the hard, knotted look of his forearms, the veins that stood out in sharp relief beneath his bronzed skin.

Her gaze continually darted between his broad shoulders, his wide chest, his flat stomach, his hips, and then it would dip lower, and she would feel her face scald with the heat of speculation. What would it be like to kiss every inch of that remarkable torso . . . and then some?

"Is everything all right, Georgina?" he asked in that deep rumble that caused little chill bumps to erupt over her flesh.

Or perhaps it was his informality that elicited the delicious shivers.

"Shouldn't you address me as Miss Pierce?" she asked, preferring the distance such formality evoked.

"Once engaged, it is acceptable for a couple to address each other using first names," he explained. "Therefore you may call me Devon."

"Oh." She didn't know why it flustered her to think of calling him by his first name. She'd addressed boys in that manner for as long as she could remember.

Only he wasn't a boy, and each moment brought her closer to an intimacy with him for which she wasn't prepared.

Elizabeth had wanted to come with them and act as chaperone, but Georgina had refused the offer. It seemed absolutely silly that a woman couldn't trust the man she planned to marry. Besides, with chaperones around, how in the world did these people get to know each other? A person couldn't talk about personal things with someone near enough to hang onto every word.

"You didn't answer my question, Georgina."

His question, asked long ago, had slipped her mind completely. "Yes, everything is fine."

"You look warm."

Only on the inside. She could certainly use a fan

right now, a Texas fan that was good at cooling, not communicating.

"I'm fine," she rushed to assure him.

She wondered how she would manage to survive her wedding night with any amount of decorum when he had the uncanny ability to set her heart to thumping against her ribs with nothing more than his presence. She couldn't claim he gave her longing looks, the kind she read about in the romance novels she enjoyed.

Yet neither was he ignoring her. Rather she had a feeling he was taking measure of her, just as she was of him. These moments should have been shared before they'd ever broached the subject of marriage. If he looked too closely, he might change his mind. If she looked too intently, so might she.

Lauren was right. Huntingdon was devilishly handsome. He had a generous mouth, his lower lip the only portion of his face that appeared to be soft. The lines that fanned out from the corners of his mouth and eyes had not been carved by joy. Would he ever know happiness with her? Or would they simply exist side by side, going their separate ways until the need to fulfill a promise brought him to her bed?

She wondered if he would bed her on their wedding night as dispassionately as he'd proposed. Would he simply lift the hem of her nightgown or would he dare trail that luscious mouth of his over her body? How could she allow a man she barely knew to take such liberties?

Should she ask for a reprieve, a period of adjustment, during which time they could come to know each other well enough for the awkwardness to fall away?

What if that moment never came?

"If I may be beastly bold, Georgina seems a rather harsh name for a woman," he said, bringing her musing to an abrupt halt. "Although George or Georgie doesn't seem much of an improvement."

"Gina," she said softly. Only her dearest friends referred to her as such. She'd never expected him to. She'd somehow imagined in this stuffy society they would forever refer to each other in the strictest formal terms.

He leaned forward slightly, not upsetting the rhythm of his strokes in the least. "Pardon?"

"Those close to me call me Gina."

"Indeed."

Was he questioning her statement? "I wouldn't have said it if it wasn't so."

"Of course not. I was simply speculating as to whether or not you were granting me permission to address you . . . as intimately."

His eyes darkened, and his scrutiny made her wonder if she should have accepted Elizabeth's offer to serve as chaperone. Wouldn't that be something? To actually have to fend off a man's advances when all her life she'd expected she might have to lasso and hog-tie a man in order to hold him close?

"I assume once we're married, we'll be intimate—" she began.

"Indeed we shall be," he interrupted.

Her stomach quivered, and she felt her face breaking out in those unsightly blotches that announced to the whole world she was uncomfortable with her current situation. "Therefore calling me Gina is acceptable."

"I appreciate the generous consideration."

She wondered if when they were old and feeble he'd still speak to her as though they were passing strangers. She found it odd that he'd seemed to test the waters by hinting he wished permission to call her Gina and then retreated by distancing himself with so much politeness she was tempted to rock the boat until he toppled into the water.

Surely a time would come when she would be able to actually carry on a real conversation with him. Where words weren't measured, meanings analyzed, and interpretations avoided.

"I have to admit I'm amazed to see you row with such skill. With the aristocracy's penchant for servants, I'd assumed you'd have a rowing boy," she said.

An incredible, warm smile spread across his face, and his eyes sparkled with amusement. "I would have if I considered this pursuit work, but it's pleasure. The aristocracy prefers to engage in pleasure at a more intimate level."

He'd spoken the words "pleasure" and "intimate" in a low purr that made her think of flickering candles, cool sheets, and warm bodies. She assumed it was her impending marriage and her conversation with Lauren that had these carnal thoughts running through her mind. She had on occasion daydreamed about lying in bed with a man, but the visions had never taken such firm root that she couldn't shake them off.

"If I may be blunt, I don't understand your aversion to work," she said.

"A man of my standing doesn't engage in laborious acts. It's simply not done. I assume you have no appreciation for the amount of effort involved in appearing idle. It's quite tiresome."

She laughed with disbelief. "Not as tiresome as hard, honest labor."

"I take it you don't approve of idleness."

"I just figure a grown man ought to be able to dress himself."

"Ah, but I do, Gina."

He wrapped such carnality around the shortened version of her name that she almost lost her grip on her parasol. Clutching it, she strove to regain her composure, to not think about how nice it would be to have him whisper her name in that enticing manner beside her ear during the height of passion. She desperately wanted to swallow, but her mouth had grown too dry.

"Well, then, Devon—" His name squeaking out of her mouth more closely echoed fear than sensuality. She was not gifted at playing mating games, acting coy, or being sophisticatedly brazen. "My opinion of you has improved ten-fold."

"Once we are wed, I'll see to hiring a lady's maid for you."

"That's not necessary. I'm perfectly capable of dressing myself."

She'd gone years without a maid. Of course, she'd worn much simpler dresses at the time. She'd had a maid while she was in New York, and Lauren's servants had been assisting her since she'd come to London. She supposed she should graciously accept his offer to hire a maid for her. She'd spoken quickly, because she hadn't wanted him to think she was unable to manage on her own. She didn't know why his impression of her abilities mattered, but it did.

"I'm afraid I must insist. I'll not have it bandied about that my wife must do without."

"Your peers' perception of you is important to you," she said speculatively.

"Quite so. As such, I would appreciate it if you would not disclose that financial need brought us together rather than a mutual attraction. I've been quite adept at hiding my impoverished state."

Arrogant pride was carved into his features. She was only just beginning to realize that it might not have been laziness that had brought him to her father but fear of appearing to be less of a man in front of those who mattered to him. "It must have cost you dearly to approach my father."

He clenched his jaw and tightened his grip on the oars. "A price I was willing to pay."

"Wouldn't it have been easier to seek employment—"

"Of course, it would have been easier, but as I attempted to explain last night and mistakenly thought you had comprehended, people of my rank do not work. Not with our hands, not with our backs. A man does not sweat to maintain his standing among the peerage. Sweat is only allowed when he plays or makes love."

An image of tiny beads of moisture covering his flesh flashed through her mind. Averting her gaze, she watched the water ripple as he sliced the oars through the river. "I see," she replied in a strangled voice.

Did she see? Devon wondered. Did she truly understand what it was to be a peer of the realm? To be constantly scrutinized and judged? To be born into a way of life you were expected to follow regardless of your own desires or dreams?

To have obligation and duty thrust on you at an early age? To understand your place in society and to know you could never step beyond its boundaries?

"I've acquired the license we'll need and made arrangements for our marriage to take place Friday morning," he said somberly, hoping to deflect his morose thoughts.

She snapped her head around so quickly he heard her neck pop.

"You really did it, made all the arrangements?"

She appeared quite alarmed.

"Have you changed your mind?" he asked quietly. If she had, he would indeed have to woo her.

"No, of course not. I just"—she tightened her grip on her parasol—"I just never really expected to get married. I haven't quite settled my mind around the possibility."

"Around the *certainty*, Gina, for I assure you I shall not rescind my offer to marry you."

She nodded slowly, but he couldn't determine if she was relieved or disappointed.

"Regarding your attire for the wedding, something similar to what you're wearing today would be appropriate." He'd been unprepared for her elegance when she'd joined him in Ravenleigh's library. The simple lines of the dress suited her tall and slender build.

She gave him a gamin smile that took him off guard with the protective surge it ignited. "I was thinking something more along the lines of the ball gown I wore the night we met. With a few more bows, perhaps."

He lost the battle to suppress his groan. At least a wedding arranged on such short notice would garner few attendants. Family only, and if he was fortunate, perhaps they wouldn't show.

"You find the bows objectionable?" she asked.

He cleared his throat to gain precious time to consider how best to respond to her inquiry. During the courting phase of a relationship, he knew a man had to choose his words carefully for fear of offending his intended and thus losing her favor. Although their relationship more closely resembled a business agreement, he was surprised to realize he did want her to welcome the marriage.

"I hope I do not appear too forward in stating quite emphatically that bows do not suit you."

"I suppose instead of bows, I could have used feathers—"

"God, no!"

Her smile blossomed, softening the hard angles of

her face. "My father has gawd-awful taste in clothes, doesn't he?"

"Your father selects your clothing?"

"Only the ball gowns. He thinks the frillier something is, the more beautiful it becomes. I find them hideous."

"If you find them objectionable, why wear them at all?"

"Because it pleases him when I do."

"Do you not realize the unfavorable opinions you generate when you wear such garish clothing?"

"Why would I care about the opinions of people I don't know, people for whom I have no feelings?"

That attitude was going to have to change because, by God, he did care what his peers thought.

"If my father asked," she continued, "I'd ride through the streets bare-ass naked."

Devon froze, stilling the oars and his breathing as an image of her rose unbidden in his mind, her legs exposed for all the world to see, her hair loosened and cascading around her, offering only tempting glimpses of what lay beneath. He cocked his head forward. "Indeed?"

She lowered her gaze, the long sweep of her lashes resting on her reddening cheeks. "Not that he would ever ask."

"I should hope not."

She peered up at him. "It might prove scandalous."

"No doubt." He set the oars back in motion. "So for your father you wear atrocious ball gowns and agree to marry a man you've only recently met."

She held his gaze. "He means the world to me. I like to see him happy."

Devon found himself envying an old man for much more than the money he had at his disposal. "Your father is an extremely fortunate man."

She shifted on the seat as though suddenly uncomfortable with his scrutiny. "Actually I ordered a simple white gown just in case you didn't change your mind."

"I told you I wouldn't."

"I know, but . . . this has all come about so quickly, and our reasons for marrying—I'm not certain they're providing us with a strong foundation on which to build a marriage."

He set the oars aside, leaned toward her, and took her gloved hand in his. "Among the aristocracy, marriage is seldom dictated by love. More often than not, it resembles an elaborate business arrangement, but contentment is possible. I shall do all in my power to see you do not regret this joining."

"Do you resent that you have to resort to marriage in order to gain wealth?"

With every fiber of his being. He released her hand to prevent his crushing it with his frustrations. "For Huntingdon I gladly do whatever must be done."

Her gaze slowly traveled over his face, and he wondered what she hoped to see.

"Did your first wife regard your marriage as an elaborate business arrangement?" she asked quietly.

She might as well have thrust a dull knife through his heart. His stomach tightened, and his chest felt as though it was caving in on him. He swallowed hard to push down the lump rising in his throat. "No. Margaret was gravely disappointed in our marriage, in me. I thought love would sustain us. I was wrong."

"So you've just proven your words false. Your marriage was dictated by love."

"For a time."

"What precisely disappointed her?" she asked.

"Poverty that neither of us expected when we married," he murmured.

"How could you not expect it?"

"When we were first married, my father was still alive, and we enjoyed prosperity. Margaret and I were young. Margaret brought with her a small dowry. I was only just beginning to take on the responsibilities of Huntingdon.

"After my father died, I discovered that he'd made several bad investments, which began our downfall. I thought I could rectify matters rather quickly, but the next few years brought poor harvests that worsened our situation. Margaret did not take our decline well."

"Her disappointment must have wounded you."

"Wounds heal."

"But they can leave ugly scars."

Ah, yes, that they could. Straightening, he grabbed the oars and began to row with the urgency of a man striving to escape the demons that plagued him.

Chapter 6

As the carriage wheels whirred, Georgina studied the man sitting across from her. She'd lowered her lashes, hoping she wouldn't appear obvious as she peered at him. She knew it was rude to stare, but she couldn't contain her curiosity.

When he'd first helped her into the carriage, she'd sat where he was now. It had seemed only fair. He'd ridden traveling backward on the way to the spot where he'd taken her for a boat ride. She felt she should travel with her back to the horses on the journey away from the river.

However, he'd refused to hear of it. They might have even gotten into an argument over it if he hadn't ground out through clenched teeth, "It's simply not done."

She was beginning to despise that phrase. Apparently a lady was always given the honor of traveling forward. It was a small thing, but it bothered her.

She didn't know why. He wouldn't have hit her if she'd refused to move to *her* side of the carriage. Instinctively she knew that.

But neither would he have been willing to back down. He had certain expectations, rigid expectations, that governed his life. They would have waited by the river until the cows came home or until she relented.

Therefore she'd relented. She didn't feel weak for having given in. It was really a silly custom, like most of their conventions, but she was beginning to realize life with him would be a series of compromises, mostly on her part. She would have to select her battles carefully.

Women were gifted when it came to bending. Men tended to break.

Her mother had taught her that valuable lesson by example. When Georgina was younger, she would get annoyed with her mother because she never seemed to stand up for herself. She was always doing for her husband, always giving in. Georgina knew her mother had resented the constant traveling, but she'd only shed silent tears and never voiced her objections.

Georgina didn't quite understand the fine line one walked in marriage. She wondered if Huntingdon—Sheridan—Devon—Lord Huntingdon—*my lord* did.

Merciful heavens! Why did these people have to be known by so many names?

She knew cowboys who had one name only. She lifted a corner of her mouth thinking of Magpie, the one who had taught Tom all he knew. The man went by only one name. Pure and simple. She knew what to call him.

"What amuses you?" Devon asked.

She lifted her lashes to view him more clearly in the shadowy confines of his fine carriage. With its comfortable seats, it rocked gently. At one time his family must have possessed everything.

"I was thinking about all your names. Where I come from, it's not unusual for a man to have only one name."

"Ah, I see. If I were to live in Texas, I would simply be Devon Sheridan."

She shook her head slightly. "Just Devon or just Sheridan."

One of his brows shot up in a perfect arch. "Indeed?"

"I know a man and his sole name is Magpie. Not Mr. Magpie or Lord Magpie. We simply call him Magpie."

"How did he come to have such an ignominious name?"

She wasn't certain if he was amused *with* her or *at* her, but she thought he was at least interested in what she was saying. "I think because he chatters all the time."

"I assume he's an orphan."

"I don't think so. It's not uncommon in Texas for a man to simply go by one name. Especially cowboys. A lot of the men are loners. Some came to Texas to start over, and they left their names behind."

"I daresay, fearful of being found out. I suppose you find the notion romantic."

She lowered her gaze to her hands clasped in her lap. She found it difficult to organize her thoughts when those amazingly blue eyes of his were focused intently on her.

"I'm not faulting you for being of a fanciful bent," he said quietly.

She snapped her head up. "I didn't think you were. I—I can't describe it. I don't find it romantic. I find it sad . . . lonesome. I'm not sure if it takes a lot of gumption or desperation to leave everything behind, including the name your mother gave you."

"I should think it takes a bit of both. Aren't you leaving everything behind?"

"I don't feel as though I am. I mean I can always go home to Texas. I don't think these men who go by one name can return home. I'm not even sure if they have one anymore."

He turned his attention to the passing scenery, placing his profile in sharp relief, like the craggy terrain of a mountain in the farthest part of west Texas. The sun, wind, and heat sculpted the land. She couldn't help but wonder what had carved his features. It took more than handsome ancestors to create the character she saw reflected in his face. But she didn't know him well enough to guess at all that might have shaped him. She wondered if she ever would.

She watched a muscle in his jaw jerk as though he fought to unclench his teeth.

"Once we are wed, England will be your home." He'd fired each word precisely as though alerting her that she had little say in the matter.

"No."

He shifted his gaze to her, and she saw the challenging glint there. But this aspect of their arrangement she would not give in on.

"I'll live in England," she said quietly, "but Texas will always be my home."

"We shall see."

He looked incredibly smug. She should have found this unattractive. Instead she realized it was the first time he seemed completely confident of the outcome. Did he think she would come to love the land of his birth or simply forget about hers?

"Indeed we shall," she responded, mimicking his hoity-toity accent.

He chuckled low, the absolute mirth taking her by surprise. Had she really ever heard him laugh? Such a somber lot these Brits. She couldn't imagine living within the confines of their myriad rules. She wondered how Lauren's mother had ever adjusted.

"Why did you insist on sitting on that side of the carriage?" she asked.

Why indeed? Devon wondered. Now that they were engaged, it would have been entirely appropriate for him to sit beside her. He supposed, in retrospect, he should have, but they were rushing headlong into marriage, and he preferred to ease into the relationship—although he admitted the leisurely journey would come to an abrupt halt in two days' time.

"Because when sharing a carriage with a lady, a gentleman always sits so he is the one who travels backward."

"Another one of your society's rules," she stated flatly.

"Precisely. Tradition. Without it you have nothing."

She curled her fingers around the parasol resting in her lap as though she was a bit disappointed with his answer. He doubted she'd ever used a parasol before today. While sitting in the boat, she'd carried it as she might an umbrella—to ward off a deluge of rain.

"In Texas, a gentleman would have shown me deference and let me sit where I wanted," she said.

"For a woman who claims to have never been kissed, you seem to possess an inordinate amount of knowledge about the way gentlemen in Texas treat ladies."

"A man can be polite without having an interest in a woman."

"I grow weary of comparing our two societies. However, may I point out in my own defense"—as though it was needed, which he thought almost angrily it should not be—"I chose to honor tradition and place myself in the position of being the one to suffer ill effects from the journey."

Her brow furrowed, and the lines around her mouth deepened as it curled downward. "I don't understand."

"Many ladies find riding backward unsettles their stomach. Makes them queasy. Watching what has passed before us is not as pleasing as watching what lies ahead. Therefore, out of consideration for your sensibilities, I sat here."

"No, you didn't."

He stared at her, certain she had not intended to call him a liar to his face. "Pardon?"

"You didn't sit there out of concern for me. You sat there out of concern for your society's rules."

"They are one and the same."

"No, they're not. A man in Texas is a gentleman because of the way he treats a lady. You're a gentleman because you follow etiquette, more concerned with what others think of your behavior than you are with my feelings."

"What the deuce are you on about? Did I not just spend the afternoon taking you on a boat ride?"

"Why?"

She was going to drive him to the damned lunatic asylum. "Why what?"

"Why did you take me for a boat ride? Did you desire my company?"

Shifting on the seat did little to ease the tension knotting the muscles in his neck and shoulders. A tightness settling in that had little do with this afternoon's excursion and everything to do with this afternoon's conversation.

"Or did you take me because it was expected?" she asked. "Because it was the *gentlemanly* thing to do?"

He had a strong urge to plow his hands through his hair, to stop the carriage, and walk home. But such a display of frustration would be intolerable. He felt trapped, suffocating, with everything closing in.

"I thought you might enjoy an afternoon of rowing on the Thames. In two days we are to be wed, and that evening, Miss Pierce, I am going to lift your nightgown—"

She'd parted her lips ever so slightly, the tiniest of creases forming between her eyebrows. He saw the mottled blush rising to the surface of her face just before she ducked her head, averting her gaze.

He pushed out a great gust of air, swore harshly, and glared out the window. That conversation hadn't gone in the direction he'd expected nor wanted. Why should his reasons matter? Why couldn't she simply accept he'd taken her for an outing? Did she intend to question every aspect of their lives, to search for the motive behind each of his actions?

Out of the corner of his eye he saw a quick movement that caught his attention. Her fingers flew over her cheek like the fluttering wings of a butterfly gathering dew. Only in her case, it was the dampness of her tears. Had he ever known any woman who wept so easily yet tried so hard to hide it?

He removed his glove, leaned over, and with his knuckle, captured the tear dangling from her eyelash. She really did have incredibly long lashes. He skimmed his little finger across her cheek, astonished by its softness. He was accustomed to touching lily-white skin. For some reason, he had not expected golden brown to feel like velvet. "You overlooked a tear, sweeting."

"I'm sorry. I had no right to question you like that. I did enjoy the afternoon. It was very nice—"

He pressed his finger to her lips, full, warm. No

lies. He wondered how she'd accept the truth of it. "I don't welcome the prospect of bedding a woman with whom I have only spent a few hours. I thought you might share the same misgivings. I simply thought it would make things less awkward if we spent a little time together."

The corners of her mouth lifted, carrying her smile into her eyes, and he realized they were extremely expressive mahogany pools. Dark, rich, covered by a sheen of tears that only served to bring them more depth.

"Thank you."

The magnitude of gratitude in her voice humbled him.

"It was my pleasure." Surprised to discover he had, indeed, spoken the truth.

"How was your outing?"

Lounging on a chair in the sitting room, Georgina set aside her book as she heard the concern reflected in her father's voice. She knew that as much as he wanted her to have her dream of children, he also worried about her.

He was so dear to her, this man who inhabited her farthest memory. He'd worked in the fields beside her before the war had taken him away and given him opportunities to pursue. He'd been her confidant, her advisor, and her tutor.

He sat in the chair beside her. Leaning over, she cradled his ruddy cheek. His parchment-like skin was a part of aging. His eyes drooped as though he was eternally sad. She loved him with an intensity that sometimes caused an ache in her chest.

"Papa, I know you were hoping he and I would get along well, and we seemed to. Something about him reminds me of a stray dog. I can't really explain what it is."

"You always did have a soft heart where strays were concerned."

Yes, she had. She hadn't expected to feel as though Devon was a stray, though, and until this moment she hadn't realized he did have that aura about him. A man ensconced in his society who didn't really look as though he belonged. Was that the reason he diligently followed the rules? So he could feel as though he fitted in?

She wasn't opposed to rules. They had their place. She simply didn't think they needed to be followed as stringently as her fiancé did.

"So you like him," her father announced, cutting into her thoughts.

She cocked her head to the side. "He intrigues me."

A true assessment of her feelings. She found herself thinking about him constantly. She had this wickedly delightful urge to break through his reserve and force him to run through fields of clover barefoot. To laugh. She'd never heard him release the deep laughter that made a man's chest rumble and his sides ache. Laughter loud and joyous enough to bring tears to his eyes until they rolled down his cheeks.

Devon Sheridan, Lord Huntingdon, was going to be a challenge. Society would insist their marriage be dull, but Georgina thought perhaps it had the potential not to be.

"I think he's a good man, Papa."

"'Course he is, gal. I wouldn't have given him permission to call on you if I thought otherwise."

He scrunched up his face. "He's a bit stuffy, though. But you can ease him out of that. He's going to fall in love with you, Gina—"

"Papa." She separated dreams into possible dreams and unobtainable dreams. She took the unobtainable ones to bed with her to carry into her sleep. Devon loving her fell into that category. "I'm sure he'll like me, but love—"

"Can't have love without liking, gal. That's what love really is. Liking someone so much you'd give up every dream you ever dreamed just to see that she touched hers."

"Is that what you did for Mama?" she asked softly.

"My dreams changed when I met your mother. That's part of love, too. Always changing but always constant."

"It can't be both, Papa."

"It can and it is. You'll see, gal."

He pressed a hand to his chest and released a low groan.

"Are you all right, Papa?"

He nodded. "Something I ate isn't agreeing with me." He took a breath and shook his head, as though whatever discomfort he'd been feeling had passed. "I just wish the fella hadn't been so quick to ask."

"I'm glad he did." If either of them spent too

much time thinking, they might change their mind. "Doesn't give me much time to get nervous waiting for the big day."

"You're gonna be a beautiful bride, Gina."

She flung her arms around his neck, hugging him close. What she loved best about him was that he had a tendency to see beauty where none existed.

Chapter 7

Sitting astride his black gelding in a secluded spot away from the main thoroughfare, Devon watched with fascination as Gina trotted her horse along Rotten Row.

After hearing of her penchant for riding, a few coins discreetly placed in the palm of the lad who readied her beast had provided him with the time of her outings. It seemed she always rode through Hyde Park at this horrendous hour, the twilight of dawn, when night still hovered and the sun was only just beginning to break through the mist in order to awaken the day.

Unlike the more genteel women of his acquaintance, she avoided the Ladies' Mile as though she feared it harbored the plague. Neither did her morning ritual include riding a pony—favored by most women—or a mare—for those who exhibited a bit more daring. No, indeed. His Gina preferred a gelding.

And no saddle.

He'd watched in stunned enchantment as she'd stolen into the park, darted a quick glance around, dismounted, and removed the sidesaddle. With a most unladylike grace, she'd scrambled back onto the horse, her skirt hiked up past her shapely calves. At that precise moment he'd realized the woman possessed long, slender legs, legs a man could wrap around his waist three times over. The prospect intrigued him, if only because he'd gone too damnably long without nestling himself between a woman's thighs.

Obviously under the mistaken impression she was alone in the park, she hadn't bothered with decency but had left those enticing calves exposed and immediately urged the horse into a canter.

He had the distinct impression she would have selected a stallion as her riding companion if his cousin had any available in his London stables. But Ravenleigh was nothing if he was not cautious. With a house overflowing with brash females, he no doubt thought keeping stallions beyond their reach was his best means of protecting them.

An inane notion. As Devon was well aware, women were their own worst enemy. They cajoled, pleaded, and wept to distraction in order to acquire what they desired, to convince a man they relied on his strength and wisdom wholeheartedly. Yet when those ploys failed, they invariably went behind his back to achieve their goal.

A woman seldom cared whom she betrayed along the way: be it the man who loved her, the children who adored her, or herself.

Or at least that had been his experience before Gina. She did not quite fit into the mold. He wanted to decipher her moods. She was strong, determined one minute, shy, unsure of herself the next.

She hadn't a clue how to flirt, and he found that aspect of her character charming. He had not expected he would actually like her as he came to know her better. But the possibility lingered before him, resembling a beacon at the edge of a storm, drawing him toward a safe harbor.

He knew the moment she spotted him through the fog. Her body gave a little jerk before she drew the horse to a halt and glared at him, as though his presence spoiled her morning.

He urged his horse forward until he was even with hers.

"You are aware, are you not, that riding at this time of morning could be dangerous?" he asked.

"I have my gun."

He couldn't have been more surprised if she'd suddenly drawn it on him and fired. "Indeed?"

She lifted a small bag hanging from a sash around her waist. "Derringer. My own personal chaperone."

"I daresay. I've never known a woman who carries a pistol."

"Not only do I carry it, but I know how to use it."

"Indeed."

She narrowed her eyes with displeasure. "Why do you question everything I say?"

"I didn't realize I did."

"Indeed?" she snapped with such force that he was certain she'd caused the fog to swirl around her.

"Ah, I see. It's simply a comment, not an expression of doubt."

She looked contrite and subtly disappointed. "I'm sorry. I misunderstood."

"Indeed."

A corner of her mouth quirked up, and he realized something he hadn't before. She possessed an incredibly luscious set of lips. A lower lip that was full to the point of pouting and an upper one that would never totally disappear, no matter how tightly she pressed them together in anger. It would always be visible, taunting a man, reminding him of her kiss.

He also noticed she hadn't dressed in a provocative manner yet she was enticing. The simple cut of her riding habit left absolutely nothing to his imagination. She was shaped like a finely sanded plank of wood. Her hips didn't flare out nor did her waist dip in. Whatever she wore beneath the clothing was designed for comfort, not to set a man's blood to boiling. He wondered if, with her, his blood would ever heat to the point of distraction. Or would they simply go through the motions without ever eliciting the passions?

Her breasts were quite small, gentle swells that would fill his palms. Nothing more. But then why would he need more? With her, nothing would be wasted.

Perhaps because of the early hour, she hadn't bothered to pin up her hair but had braided it in one thick rope that dangled down her spine and reached past her waist. There was so much of it. Little wonder she had trouble keeping it in place on top of her head. He suddenly had an unexpected desire to see it loosened and flowing around her.

During his perusal, her eyes had not left him, but her half-smile had withered and her dark brows had drawn together, as though she feared what he might discover about her. Her brows had a fine arch to them that was easy to miss because her large, brown eyes drew a man's attention long before her brows did.

He had looked at her for so long simply as a means to an end that he'd overlooked the fact she was a woman. He'd fenced off his desires out of loyalty to Margaret, to her memory. Yet Margaret's loyalty to him had quickly withered once she'd discovered the truth of his circumstances.

But here sat a woman who wore atrocious gowns because they pleased her father, a lady who had agreed to marry him not for her happiness but for her father's. A lesson in loyalty that truly served to humble him.

"You'd mentioned that you'd never been kissed."

"That's right."

"Where would you like to experience the first one?"

She stared at him with round eyes, terrified eyes.

"What?" she asked, as though she fought for each breath.

"Your first kiss. Where would you like it to be?"

He could see the blotches of embarrassment sweeping over her face, a flustered hand patting her skirt, her hair, before coming to rest at her throat. She averted her gaze before saying softly, "I guess on my mouth."

Certain he had misheard, he leaned toward her. "Pardon?"

She took a deep breath, squared her shoulders, and held his gaze. "I'd like for the first kiss I get to be on my mouth."

He felt as though he'd walked in on the wrong end of a bad prank. "Where else might the first kiss be?"

She swooped her hand from the top of her head toward her feet. "I've heard men kiss . . . everything."

Indeed. He found that little tidbit of information interesting. He wondered with whom she'd been discussing kisses. Lauren, perhaps. Yes, indeed, these Americans were a delightful surprise on occasion.

"Did you wish for me to kiss you everywhere?"

"Depends on whether or not you expect me to do the same."

Chuckling, he cradled her face and stroked his thumb over her cheek. Ever since yesterday he'd longed for another touch of her softness. "Typical of a woman to fear giving more than she receives. I promise you, sweeting, you'll never have to kiss any portion of me you don't want to."

She ducked her head as though embarrassed. As usual with her, this conversation had not gone at all as he'd planned, but he'd found it informative to say the least. And delightful. How could a woman reach her age and remain as innocent as a young girl?

Educating her might turn into an unexpected pleasure.

"Regarding your first kiss, I was curious as to whether you wished to experience it following our exchange of vows or if you wanted me to kiss you before then."

"Oh." Horror etched itself into her features. "You were asking *when* I wanted to be kissed, not *where*."

"Yes, I suppose my question was in bad form."

"Absolutely. I misunderstood—"

"Then allow me to be a tad clearer. Do you want your first kiss to take place at the church or here in the park—at this precise moment?"

Her mouth opened slightly, a soft whisper of breath escaping into the chill of the morning. Her gaze darted quickly around, as though she expected the people of London to have lost their wits and suddenly arrive in the park.

"We're quite alone, sweeting."

Her attention snapped back to him. She licked her lips in a provocative manner that caused his insides to tighten simply because he was certain she was unaware of how alluring he found the slow movement of her tongue.

And quite suddenly he discovered he wanted to kiss her with an urgency that might have frightened him if he had been an untried lad.

"I should think your wedding day will be nerve-racking enough without having to worry about that first kiss," he prodded.

"Is it something I need to worry about?"

For some strange reason the alarm in her voice delighted him. Not because he wished to frighten her, but because she possessed the naïveté to harbor any concerns at all.

"No," he assured her calmly, "but it'll be one less thing preying on your mind."

She nodded slightly. "Then I suppose getting it over with is a good idea."

"Splendid."

He dismounted, walked around his horse, came to stand beside hers, and held up his arms.

"What are you doing?"

"Standing would work best, I should think. Horses tend to get skittish if too close."

"Of course."

She cupped his shoulders while he wrapped his hands around her waist. Dear God, but she had a tiny waist. He brought her slowly, gently to the ground. She weighed no more than he imagined a billowy cloud on a clear summer day might. She seemed to be proving false all he'd assumed about her.

"Are you certain you've never been kissed?" he asked.

"Never," she rasped in a small, breathless voice.

He could see her chest rising and falling with her short breaths. She was nervous, apprehensive, perhaps even a bit anticipatory. He couldn't explain what had prompted him to initiate this moment, why he wanted to alleviate her fears. He supposed, like her, he had a desire to get their first kiss over with. He couldn't imagine marrying a woman with whom he'd had no physical contact whatsoever.

A waltz in a crowded ballroom certainly didn't qualify.

If they had possessed the luxury of time, he would have taunted her with forbidden kisses behind those fronds for which she seemed to have a fondness. He would have arranged illicit moments in darkened corners and hallways. He would have taught her the advantage of wearing a low-cut gown to a ball. Ah, yes, he would have kissed her elsewhere and made her extremely glad he had.

But the wooing he started now would have to be finished later, after they were wed. The sun was rising, and he could hear the distant din of people getting about their day. For now, all he truly wanted was to reassure her that kissing him would not be torment.

"Then we should do it right, don't you think?" he asked.

"Is there a wrong way?"

"Hardly." He took her braid and began to unravel the plaited strands. "But some ways are more pleasing than others."

Dear God, but her hair was more glorious than he'd imagined, reaching past her bottom, a thick luxurious curtain of liquid mahogany. Who the deuce established the rule that women should wear their hair up?

Combing his fingers along her scalp, he brought her hair forward. Surrounded by a frame of dark reddish-brown tresses, the harsh planes of her face retreated, her eyes grew softer, her cheeks not so sharp. Younger. She appeared remarkably younger.

He hadn't expected the loosening of her hair to change his perception of her to such a degree. She wasn't beautiful; he didn't think she'd ever be a beauty. But neither was she stark lines. Neither was she unattractive.

He cradled her delicate face between his large hands. He hadn't realized until he tilted it toward him that it did indeed appear fragile, like hand-blown glass that could be easily shattered by carelessness. He'd deliberately not worn his gloves, wanted to give her an opportunity to demand a chaste marriage if his touch offended her, but she seemed not to notice the roughness of his palms.

Instead her eyes took on a dreamlike stare, as though she thought he was about to bestow upon her some fine gift. A part of him wished he'd never instigated this moment; another part of him was terrified of disappointing her, failing her as he'd failed Margaret.

But no hope existed for him now, no possibility of turning back. He'd set his course, suggested they get this phase of courtship out of the way. No turning back, he thought again. Even if she didn't relish his kiss or his rough hands. He would take her father's money, give her a child, and kiss her while doing it.

He lowered his mouth to hers.

The brush of his lips over hers jolted Georgina into awareness. She'd begun to think he'd never get around to it, and when he finally did . . . such a brief thing. Like a butterfly landing on a petal and then deciding it saw a prettier flower.

After all the preparation of removing her from her horse, loosening her hair, cupping her cheeks, and angling her face as though he didn't trust her to know how to meet his mouth—which she didn't, but that was beside the point—she'd expected something more.

His mouth returned to hers, the pressure subtly more as his fingers slid into her hair and his thumbs skimmed over her cheeks in slow, sensuous circles. His mouth was larger, and yet it somehow seemed to fit perfectly.

Then he parted his lips slightly and whipped his tongue along her mouth, from one corner to the other, over the top, along the bottom, across the seam, claiming territory that until this moment had belonged exclusively to her. She'd never expected a kiss to entail a man taking this much liberty. Was this what he'd meant by doing it right?

Did Lauren know a kiss involved more than lips? That a man's tongue also played? And when a man kissed a woman from the top of her head to the tips of her toes and everywhere in between, did he use his tongue then as well? Did he stroke and swirl and apply pressure—

"Open your mouth."

His voice carried an urgency that had her obeying without a second thought. His fingers clutched the sides of her head as his tongue swept through her mouth. Boldly, brazenly. Strange how the heat created by their mouths spread through her limbs all the way down to her soles. Tendrils of pleasure reached out and curled inward. He shouldn't have taken her off her horse, because her legs were growing too weak to support her.

As though sensing her struggle to remain standing, he wrapped one arm tightly around her and pressed her flush against his chest. He groaned low, and she felt the rumble vibrate against her breasts, over them, through them.

She couldn't expect him to do all the work, to keep her upright, so she wound her arms around his neck. He had such a firm neck, corded muscles she hadn't expected of a gentleman.

But neither had she expected this slow burning that promised to consume. Heated mouths, hot tongues, clutching hands. She'd always thought of Englishmen as prudes, had expected his kiss to be civilized, but the sensations rippling through her with increasing intensity bordered on barbaric. She wanted to moan, thought she might have moaned again and again as his hand slid lower and his fingers dug into her backside, pressing her firmly against him, her stomach to his hips, to the place in between. Against the startling evidence that he desired her.

She hadn't expected that. She'd hoped, of course, but she hadn't expected it to come about simply because of a kiss. But then she hadn't known a kiss would be like this: consuming, passionate, wild.

Completely uncivilized. For the first time, she felt as though they were on even ground.

Abruptly he drew back, breathing harshly, as though he fought for each intake of air. His gaze was as intense as his kiss had been. She wondered if her lips were as swollen as his, if his tingled as hers did.

She watched him swallow. He cleared his throat and swallowed again.

She felt bereft as he loosened his hold on her. He wrapped his hands around hers, moved them away from his neck, and brought them to his mouth. His hot breath skimmed over her knuckles as he studied her. She wondered what he was thinking. If he'd found her wanton, practically undulating against him, moaning. She was pretty certain a kiss was supposed to be a silent thing.

He was probably appalled by her lack of decorum.

She was grateful they hadn't waited until they were in the church to share their first kiss. She would have humiliated them both. She lowered her eyes. "We won't kiss like that in church."

"I should hope not."

Devon watched as the red splotches appeared on her face. She was embarrassed. Had he ever known a woman who was so easy to read?

Or so quick to rouse to passion?

By God, she'd been like a piece of kindling with a match held against it, quickly flaring into a full-blown inferno. Not that he'd been much better.

He'd wanted her. Here in the park. It had taken all the willpower he could muster not to drag her off to some secluded spot and have his way with her.

He hadn't expected that reaction, hadn't been prepared for the fire licking at his loins or the desire that continued to burn through him. She tasted so damnably sweet and responded with such innocence, tiny mewling moans that had only served to heighten his fervor.

He tucked his knuckles beneath her chin and lifted her face until he could hold her gaze. He'd thought her eyes a dull brown, but when ignited with passion they were a mahogany shade as rich as her hair. He was no doubt the first to discover that aspect of her. It made him feel protective, possessive even.

He had a feeling she was going to riddle his life with surprises.

"However, we shall kiss like that on our wedding night."

He grazed his thumb over the winsome smile she offered him, so apparently filled with gratitude that once again she humbled him. For the span of a heartbeat, he regretted theirs was not a love match.

He tossed aside the guilt. Since she had not found love before him, he thought it unlikely she would find it later. He would ensure she had the child she so desperately wanted. And perhaps he could offer her a bit of fondness as well.

"I shall escort you home."

She nodded shyly and reached back to gather up her hair.

"Leave it," he ordered.

The well-trained horses had wandered off to nibble on some nearby grass. Devon retrieved Georgina's saddle from the spot where she'd left it earlier. He found it difficult to believe that she preferred riding without a saddle. But he was quickly learning that she was not the most conventional of women.

He strode to the horses and saddled Georgina's. Then he grabbed the reins of both horses and walked to her.

He extended his arm, and she entwined hers around his. As he escorted her from the park, he enjoyed her hair, in wild disarray, billowing around her in the breeze.

She was as untamed as the land from which she'd come.

Chapter 8

As though she was handling a newly born baby, Georgina carefully folded her softest nightgown and placed it at the bottom of her valise. She should have been filled with anticipation and excitement at the prospect of being married.

Instead she simply felt numb, going through the motions, her stomach in knots. Tomorrow night Devon was going to kiss her as he had this morning and take the kiss farther.

If he worked such magical sensations with his mouth, what in the world would he accomplish when his entire body was involved?

"I don't know why Huntingdon had to rush into a wedding," Lauren's mother said, obviously irritated, as she placed items in Georgina's small trunk.

She'd offered to send up a servant to do the packing, but Georgina wasn't comfortable with strangers handling her intimate apparel.

"I think it's romantic," Lauren said as she sat in a chair, sipping her tea and watching their efforts.

Her mother glared at her. "It's given us no time to set up a proper trousseau."

"I have everything I need," Georgina assured her.

Lady Ravenleigh—Georgina had such a difficult time thinking of her as such; the name made her seem so unapproachable although her manners didn't—ceased her fussing over things and smiled warmly. "I think a man would be content if a wedding consisted of nothing more than a handshake, but for a woman"—she sighed—"women dream of this day. It should be special."

Georgina smiled brightly. "How can it not be special? I'm getting married."

She still couldn't believe it. What if Devon came to his senses by dawn and didn't show up? She wasn't sure if she'd be mortified or relieved.

Lauren released a tiny squeal, shot out of the chair, grabbed her hands, and swung her around as she had when they were children. Only then they'd spun until they grew dizzy and collapsed in laughing fits on a bed of soft green clover.

"I think it's splendid!" Lauren cried before they made do with the bed and landed on the thick mattress. "You're getting married! You're actually getting married!"

"Unless Huntingdon comes to his senses and doesn't show."

"Oh, he won't do that," Lauren rushed to assure her.

"Lauren!" her mother chastised her.

"I didn't mean coming to his senses. He's sensible, indeed, to marry Gina. I simply meant he won't cry off."

"He might," Georgina suggested cautiously.

"It's simply not done. You could sue him for breach of promise."

Which he could little afford. Georgina sat up. "Then I guess we can count on having a wedding in the morning."

"I should hope," Lady Ravenleigh said. "I have everything arranged. Our family will drive to the church in one carriage. You and your father will arrive in another. Gray horses, of course."

"Of course," Georgina murmured. It was as though these people lived within an elaborate play with nothing left to chance.

"Following the wedding, we shall return here for the breakfast. You will, of course, at that point travel in Lord Huntingdon's carriage." She shook her head. "I really feel as though I should have invited people."

"I just wanted a small, intimate gathering." In truth she would have foregone the breakfast altogether—but it simply wasn't done.

Lady Ravenleigh held up her hands and stepped back from the trunk. "I really must check on the wedding cake." She walked around the bed and hugged Georgina. "Your mother and I were such dear friends." She leaned back. "So, I feel I should speak to you about"—she cleared her throat and wrinkled her brow—"what you can expect when you retire tomorrow evening."

Georgina felt Lauren go perfectly still beside her.

Lady Ravenleigh glanced at her daughter. "Lauren, why don't you run and check with the cook to make sure all is ready?"

Lauren thrust up her delicate chin. "Because I want to hear what you have to say. I'm old enough."

Lady Ravenleigh's cheeks burned red as she nodded slightly. She cleared her throat again and took Georgina's hands. "Regarding the marriage act. It's a very intimate moment between a husband and a wife. And you simply have to realize it's a very natural . . . expression . . . of . . . love." She cocked her head to the side. "Have you any questions?"

Georgina fought back her smile. "I don't think so."

Lady Ravenleigh appeared genuinely relieved. "Lovely. Should you think of some, please don't hesitate to ask. I'm going to check on the status of the cake."

As soon as Lauren's mother had left the room, Lauren fell backward across the bed. "She didn't tell you anything!"

"She's not at all comfortable discussing it."

Lauren shoved herself off the bed and began to pace. "She said it was a very intimate moment. Do you think it only takes a moment, sixty seconds?"

Georgina felt the heat suffuse her face. "I don't know."

Lauren stopped pacing and screwed up her face as though it would help her decipher her mother's cryptic words. "I should think it would take all night."

"Why?"

"Well, because it's done at night in bed. Since it

has a special place, a special time, it must take all night. Don't you think?"

"It doesn't take a horse very long."

Lauren groaned. "But that's a beast! Besides, if a man is kissing you from the top of your head to the tips of your toes, it could take all night. Especially if he kisses you slowly."

Georgina nodded contemplatively. "Devon does take his time kissing."

She thought Lauren's eyes were going to pop out of her head.

"What?" Lauren fairly shrieked. "Where?"

"On my mouth."

"I know on your mouth, silly goose. I meant where were you when he kissed you?"

"At the park this morning."

"Scandalous." Lauren sat beside her on the bed and took her hand, grinning broadly. "Deliciously scandalous. What was it like?"

How could she explain it? "It was terrifying."

"My God, he hurt you?" Lauren asked indignantly. "You'll cry off, then. You don't have to marry him—"

"No, no." She wanted to laugh at the absurdity of it. Two grown women who knew so little and assumed so much. "He didn't hurt me. Quite the opposite, and that's what's unsettled me."

She darted a quick glance around the room, trying to find words that would express what she'd felt. "I could barely stand, Lauren. I melted like a pool of wax. And he was so strong, sure, confident. I felt lost and confused. All this swirling going on, drifting into a fog of . . . well, of passion. I hadn't expected that. And he said that's how we'll kiss on our wedding night."

He'd tasted heavenly. His breath mingling with hers. His tongue rough on one side, velvety on the other. She was embarrassed she'd spent a good deal of the day wondering if he might kiss her body with that tongue. How would he do it if he did, and how would it feel?

"It sounds to me as though making love definitely takes all night," Lauren said.

Georgina couldn't stop herself from grinning. "I'm fairly certain it takes more than a moment."

Lauren leaned toward her. "Are you scared?"

"I'm nervous about tomorrow, and I worry that during the long haul I won't fit in. All the rules make me feel like I've got no freedom."

"You'll have more freedom than if you married someone in Texas. There you'd be tied to the person, to the land, to struggling to survive. Here you can engage in the activities that interest you, and your husband will do the things that interest him. Sometimes husbands and wives even arrive separately at balls."

"That's not freedom, Lauren. I don't know what it is, but it's not freedom. Do you know if that's the kind of marriage Huntingdon had with his first wife?"

Lauren shrugged. "As I mentioned, we seldom saw them."

"What was she like?" Georgina asked.

Lauren hopped up and began to quickly place items into the trunk. "What does it matter? She's dead, and he's marrying you."

Georgina reached across the bed and grabbed Lauren's hand, stilling her frantic actions. "She was beautiful, wasn't she?"

Lauren sighed. "Amazingly beautiful."

"Did he love her very much?"

"Afraid so."

Georgina laughed. "You don't have to be afraid."

"I didn't mean I was scared," Lauren said.

"I know. I'm glad he loved her. I won't have to feel guilty that he's spending the rest of his life with someone he couldn't possibly love."

"He might love you, Gina."

She began folding her dressing gown. "And tomorrow morning the sun might rise in the west."

Chapter 9

Georgina thought she would forever remember her wedding day as the happiest day in her father's life.

As they stood on the steps leading into the church, she decided his beaming face was reason enough to have agreed to this marriage. She had little doubt his jaws would be aching before all was said and done.

A part of her, the portion that harbored dreams, was glad for this day as well. She wore a gown of white brocaded silk. Her veil of Honiton lace wreathed with tiny white roses fell almost to her knees. With the slight breeze wafting around her, causing the lace to flutter, she felt almost dainty. Elegant.

It had cost a small fortune to have her wedding outfit sewn so quickly, but she thought it was worth every penny. It wasn't often she splurged on herself.

Since she'd grown up with very little in the way of material possessions, even now she had a difficult time parting with money. Her father, bless his heart, had no such inhibitions.

She didn't resent his spending, but she did worry about it sometimes. Particularly here in England, where merchants preferred for their customers to shop on credit, sending bills at the end of the month. It seemed as though a person could easily spend more than he had if he didn't keep his own tally of expenses.

But this morning she didn't want to think about her father's expenses. She wanted to capture his smile, sparkling eyes, and wide grin.

He looped her arm around his and patted her hand. "You look beautiful, Gina."

She almost told him she felt beautiful. For once in her life, she wasn't worried about her gaunt features.

It was a glorious day, the sun shining and the clouds a billowy white. As though nature approved of this marriage.

She never would have thought she would have gotten married so quickly to someone she barely knew. But it somehow seemed right. If only because it was making her father so incredibly happy. She thought he might bust the buttons on his vest as he rocked back and forth on his heels.

Lauren stepped out of the church. She wore a lavender dress and a smile that rivaled Georgina's father's. She took Georgina's hands. "Remember when we were little girls and we swore we'd get married on the same day?"

Georgina nodded.

"This way is better, Gina. It's better to have your own day." She pressed her cheek against Georgina's. "Be happy, my dear friend. Be deliriously happy."

She wanted to be. She truly did. Her life had always been a challenge. Nothing had ever come easy.

And now suddenly it seemed as though a husband would.

But nothing ever did.

So even as she followed two people who grinned like fools into the church, she couldn't help but feel a sense of foreboding.

For nothing in life worth having comes without effort.

Be happy. Be deliriously happy.

Georgina knew she should be. Curled in a chair before the hearth in her bedchamber, she couldn't help but reflect that her wedding day had been perfect.

Devon had worn a wine-colored frock coat, the shade accentuating his dark coloring but bringing forth the blue of his eyes. They had repeated their vows, words of deep meaning spoken with shallow emotion.

She felt as though the entire day had been one elaborate play, everyone behaving as actors upon a stage. Lines spoken as though rehearsed for generations. Everything done according to some grand scheme; nothing spontaneous. No laughter. No gaiety.

She'd noticed that aspect of the day the most. A funeral procession had more joy to it.

It had been a stuffy wedding. Vows exchanged according to plan. Still, her father had been pleased. And that alone made the day worth it.

Now for the night.

Here within Devon's London house, in a room somewhere down the hallway, her husband's bedchamber, Devon was preparing himself for her. She couldn't help but wonder what that entailed.

She'd donned her nightgown, brushed her hair a hundred times, then two hundred. Waiting, waiting, waiting for him.

Maybe he wouldn't come.

And if he did, then what? The proper touching. Lifting the hem of her nightgown . . . She didn't want to think about it.

Marrying him was the craziest thing she'd ever done in her entire life.

But she wasn't sorry for it. She was just experiencing wedding night jitters. Tomorrow all would be well.

She rubbed her finger over her wedding ring. A circle of gold that housed a garnet stone. In the carriage on the journey to his house, Devon had told her he'd selected garnet because it symbolized truth and constancy. It would forever serve as a reminder of the promise he'd given her to never lie to her.

Standing in the bedchamber down the hall from his, Devon studied the woman to whom he was now joined according to the laws of England. Wearing a white nightgown that billowed around her in a shapeless heap, she sat in one of two large chairs resting in front of the hearth. She'd tucked her legs beneath her, but he saw her bare toes peering out. Tiny toes that somehow reflected her innocence.

She'd given him a shy, self-conscious smile when he'd first entered the room before returning her gaze to the low fire burning on the hearth, the snapping flames providing the solitary source of light in the room. Shadows advanced and retreated but never completely left the confines of the corners.

The room was designed for comfort, to serve as a woman's haven. He supposed it would in time come to reflect its current mistress. It already carried her sweet fragrance. Lilies, he realized suddenly, and wondered why he hadn't been able to put a name to the scent before.

Perhaps because here it was not competing with any outside influences. Perhaps because here their isolation narrowed their world.

After ten years of marriage, he was no novice when it came to making love to a woman. Therefore he was having a difficult time giving credence to his nerves. The entire day he'd felt as though he was merely a small-time actor in a badly written play. Now his most important scene was upon him, and he was determined to give a top-notch performance.

She was his salvation. The least he could do was grant her the gift of perceiving herself desired. Although the gift was not so distant from the reality. If he had not bartered his title, if he did not feel like a common doxy, he thought he might have cherished this moment as much as he hoped she would.

He poured a bit of wine into a glass and carried it to her. "Drink this. It'll help you relax."

She lifted her face and took his offering with such gratitude reflected in her eyes that it caused his chest to ache. Damnation, but a woman should be desired on her wedding night, this woman in particular, who had asked for nothing more than honesty between them. The one thing he could give without compromising his integrity.

He sat in the chair across from hers and stretched his legs toward the dancing flames. He did not normally indulge in a fire during the summer months, but Gina was accustomed to warmer climes apparently and had requested a small fire. Therefore he'd granted it.

Out of the corner of his eye, he watched as she slowly sipped the wine, careful not to look at him. She'd loosened her hair and brushed it until it glistened like rich mahogany with a reddish hue. Thick, it was truly quite gorgeous.

She enchanted him, prepared for bed as she was, obviously self-conscious about the fact he was here to perform his husbandly duties. And yet her careful preparation spoke loudly of her anticipating his arrival. Her hair, her gown, her fragrance . . . for him.

He'd done no less for her. He'd applied a razor to his face, a comb to his hair, sandalwood to his skin. He was as fresh now as he'd been when he'd headed to the church this morning. The only difference that he now wore a blue silk dressing gown, the corded tasseled belt tied loosely.

He'd considered remaining fully clothed, but he'd seen no point in pretending he was here for any other reason than the one for which he was.

The silence stretched between them, calming, welcome. They had rushed to this moment, and now neither of them seemed in any great hurry. He was not procrastinating, delaying the moment. He was simply allowing it to seep into him. He was once again wed, and he had a feeling this go round would in no way resemble the first.

She slid her gaze over to him then past him to the bed. "Did you make love to—to Margaret there?"

"No."

She shifted her attention back to him.

"Margaret's room is—was—next to mine," he explained. "It's common for a wife's bedchamber to be beside her husband's with a door separating the two. I thought you might prefer to have your own room rather than one that . . ." He was suddenly at a loss for words.

"Carried memories for you?"

Trust his little Texas wife not to have such a lapse.

"Quite so."

She nodded. "How many bedrooms do you have here?"

"Four. You're welcome to select another if you wish."

She shook her head. "This one is fine. I appreciate your consideration."

His consideration had been as much for himself as for her. He'd wanted few reminders of his first marriage this night.

"You're gonna have to tell me what you want," she said.

Interesting. He'd noticed before that she spoke

with a slight, charming twang, but it apparently deepened when her emotions were running high or she was anxious.

"What I want is for you to stop looking as though you expect me to ravish you."

Her now familiar blush spread over her cheeks, along her throat. Strange how he was coming to anticipate it. More unusual was the warmth it stirred within him, the need to protect her that it brought to the surface.

"I don't think you'll do that," she said.

"What are you thinking then?"

"That I just wish you'd get this over with."

Leaning forward, he planted his elbows on his thighs and grasped his hands. She pressed herself against the high back of the chair. Advance. Retreat.

"Finish your wine," he ordered gently.

She gulped it down, wiped the back of her hand across her mouth in a most unladylike manner, and set the glass aside.

A smile played at the corner of his mouth. He had not planned to seduce his wife. Bed her and be done with it. He didn't know why she made him want to give her so much more. The courtship had been hurried. No need for this night to be. He had promised her father that he would make her believe she was beautiful. He didn't think he could accomplish that undertaking, but he could ensure she experienced beautiful sensations.

"Come here," he rasped softly as he unclasped his hands and held one toward her.

The tip of her tongue darted out and touched her

upper lip, leaving behind moisture that glistened in the firelight.

"You mean we're gonna . . . in the chair?"

"I mean come here."

She hesitated before slowly rising and walking toward him as though approaching a guillotine. He didn't know why his heart went out to her. On his first wedding night he'd been eager to get his wife out of her clothing. But he'd been younger then and thought the strength of its physical aspect defined love.

As Gina stopped in front of him, her bare toes peering out from beneath the hem of her gown a scant distance away from his, he wondered if he'd known love at all. He patted his thigh. "Sit."

Her eyes widened a fraction before she darted a glance toward the bed. "I haven't sat on a man's lap since I was six. I just thought we'd"—she flapped her slender hand in the air—"beneath the covers."

An hour ago, half an hour ago, he'd harbored the same delusion. "We shall—eventually. Are you in some great hurry?"

She met his gaze. "I'm nervous as all get-out."

Smiling warmly, he wrapped his fingers around hers. "I know you are, Gina."

He tugged gently, and she eased slowly, provocatively onto his thighs as though she feared she might hurt him.

"I won't break," he teased.

She nodded and studied her hands, folded primly in her lap.

He heard her breath catch as he slid his hand beneath the curtain of her hair and cupped the nape of her neck. With his thumb, he turned her head until they were looking at each other. "I'm nervous as well."

Her mouth opened slightly. "Why? Surely you know what to do."

Ah, yes, he knew. He knew how to tease, taunt, and titillate. He knew where to place his mouth, when to be gentle, when to be rough, when to move quickly, and when to proceed slowly. But his knowledge didn't guarantee her pleasure. Not when he was under the impression she'd bolt at any minute.

He stroked his thumb over her bottom lip. "I know exactly what to do."

He pulled her forward at the same moment that he moved toward her. He watched as her eyes slid closed just before his lips touched hers as lightly as twilight brings forth the night.

He felt her relaxing against him, sinking into him, as he drew her closer until her head was nestled in the crook of his shoulder. He settled his mouth more firmly against hers, coaxing with his tongue until she parted her lips and allowed him entry.

She tasted of wine and sweetness. Incredible sweetness and innocence. Her tongue danced around his with increasing sureness. Her fingers clutched his lapels, and he heard a little purr vibrate within her throat.

Unexpected raging desire speared him.

She was so giving, open, and candid with her thoughts, her emotions, and her physical sensations.

A man did not have to guess where he stood with her. She was refreshingly forthright. He could be no less.

He glided his hand to the buttons at her throat and nimbly loosened them, parting the material before trailing his mouth along the golden column of her throat. He dipped his tongue into the hollow at its base. She shivered within his arms and dug her fingers into his shoulder. She tasted of the outdoors, his wife, and he imagined them walking over rolling hills together, riding at dawn and twilight.

As though she was a taut bow, he bent her backward over the chair, nudged the soft cloth of her nightgown aside, and closed his mouth around her nipple, not surprised to find it already pearl-hardened. Her straightforwardness would not allow her to hide what she felt, thereby increasing his enjoyment.

Dear God, her lack of demureness served as an aphrodisiac, heightening his pleasure even as it lured him to increase hers. He suckled gently, swirling his tongue over the sensitive bud as shudders rippled along the length of her.

Whimpering, she combed her fingers up into his hair, holding him in place—or perhaps she sought to keep herself tethered—as her hips undulated in his lap. His body reacted as though she'd poured molten passion over him. Every nerve ending leaped to attention. Blood thrummed between his temples and rushed to his loins.

With a low growl, he swept his mouth across the valley between her breasts, latching his lips around the darkened center of the other pliant orb, tugging, nipping, biting gently. She nearly shot off his lap.

His breathing grew labored while hers quickened. With an awkwardness he hadn't experienced since his youth, he pulled her gown off her shoulders, along her arms, and over her hips. With a tiny mewling sound she buried her face in his shoulder and drew her knees up toward her chest as much as she was able.

"Don't hide from me, sweeting," he croaked as though his voice had yet to change into that of a man.

But she did hide, refusing to face him, so he watched the play of firelight over her bare narrow hips and the manner in which it danced over her hair, which cascaded down her back to pool at the curve above her backside. How had he ever considered the vibrant tresses to be dull?

He felt as though he'd been observing her through a mist of resentment—she was the salvation he wished to God he did not need, he had not wanted to want her, and so he had blinded himself to her attributes. Her giving nature revealed itself in each shudder, each twist, each sigh.

Placing one arm around her back, sliding the other beneath her knees, he pressed her against him and stood. He couldn't recall ever carrying a woman to bed, but somehow it seemed the most natural movement, as though nothing else would do.

Gently he laid her on the soft linen sheets that awaited them after an attentive servant had turned down the coverlet earlier.

When Devon's arms were no longer encircling

her, Georgina opened her eyes. The darkness of the night cast shadows over him as the firelight failed to reveal him.

She watched with stunned fascination as he slowly worked free the knot holding the corded belt at his waist. The silk robe fell open, the fire's glow only daring to caress the defined muscles of his chest, as she longed to, leaving the remainder of his body in obscurity. His skin looked as silky as the cloth had felt beneath her fingertips.

With little more than a slow, masculine roll of his shoulders, he caused the robe to slither to the floor, taking the shadows with it. Her breath backed up in her lungs at the sight of his naked magnificence, from the top of his head to the tips of his toes . . . and especially in between.

He looked as though he'd been sculpted from Texas red granite: solid, substantial, firm. He was quite simply breathtakingly beautiful. She thought she should be afraid of his immense size and hardened muscles, but she could only stare in wonder with the realization he intended to share his glorious body with her.

To have and to hold suddenly took on a whole new meaning for her.

The bed dipped beneath his sturdy weight as he stretched out beside her and skimmed his fingertips from her collarbone down to her hip. A light grazing of roughened skin against soft. Then up until he cradled her breast within his palm. He lowered his mouth to her flesh, and the incredible sensations that had abated were brought back to life with amazing swiftness, as though her body had simply gone into hibernation waiting for the heat of his mouth to reawaken it.

And how he stirred it. Amazing. Incredible. With his hands, his mouth, his tongue, the hard length of his body. Responses rippled through her. Acute. Hot. Swirling deep. Rising. Had she not agreed to this marriage, she might have never known that a man's touch caused a woman's body to hum.

Tentatively, she reached out and touched his chest, much more intimate a gesture than cupping her hand around his neck. He stilled, and she wondered if she'd committed a grave mistake.

He lifted his head, his gaze traveling over her features as though he was searching for something unfamiliar. With the greatest of care, he combed her hair off her brow and tucked it behind her ear before giving her a haunting smile. "I should have known you wouldn't be content to simply take."

Beneath her palm pressed against his flesh, she felt the thundering of his heart. "Is it all right if I touch you?"

"Quite all right, I assure you."

She licked her lips as her gaze dipped to the dark shadows between their bodies before darting back up to his. "Is there anyplace I shouldn't touch?"

He slowly shook his head, his eyes darkening to the blue of midnight. "None at all."

Raising herself up on an elbow, she leaned forward and flicked her tongue over his nipple, as taut as hers. He issued a guttural groan as his fingers clutched the back of her head. A small thrill of intoxicating victory shot through her with the knowledge she had power over him, perhaps not as much as he had over her, but enough to lead her to believe if they could become partners in lovemaking, they could eventually become partners in all things.

She returned her mouth to his distended flesh, licking, fascinated by the differing textures, the dampness her touch caused, his hardness that remained. He trailed his hand along her spine, and she guided hers along his ribs and lower.

He cradled her hip at the same moment she cupped his. He inched his hand lower. She glided hers up toward his heart.

"Chicken," he purred in a low, sultry voice.

She snapped her gaze to his, expecting mockery. Instead she was greeted with desire, yearning. She absorbed the heat of his stare, even as she nodded slightly, acknowledging his claim.

He wrapped his hand around hers and carried it to his mouth. He pressed a kiss to the heart of her palm, his breath coating her skin in dew. Holding her gaze, he moved her hand lower, lower into the shadowy crevice between their bodies, to the torrid heat that stood at the ready.

She furled her fingers around the velvety length of him. She watched as he closed his eyes and swallowed, his Adam's apple slowly sliding up and then down, mimicking the movement of his hand over hers as he patiently taught her how best to fondle.

Then his hand drifted away, leaving her to explore while he once again took up his tender ministrations. He nuzzled her neck, nipped beneath her chin, grazed his mouth across her collarbone, while his hand skimmed across her stomach and sought its own darkened crevice.

With his knee he nudged her thighs apart and wedged himself between them. She might have known fear then if he hadn't gazed down on her as though he thought she was, if not beautiful, at least pleasing.

His mouth swooped down to capture hers, his arms tightened around her, and she felt the sureness of his long, deep push. She stiffened. He stilled. Beneath her hands his back was slick, his muscles tense.

"The pain will ease, sweeting, I promise," he whispered near her ear before beginning to move slowly against her.

The discomfort did subside as the sensations began to swirl through her again, more intense than before. His mouth took hers again and again after each quick sojourn to her throat, her breast, her shoulder. A nip here. A kiss there. And then the thrust of his tongue as sure as that of his hips.

Beneath him her body curled from the pure pleasure of each stroke. She dug her fingers into his bare buttocks as the tempo quickened and he dove deeper and deeper into her.

With a cry, she spiraled over the edge at the same moment that he drove himself as deeply as possible and with a guttural groan stilled, his arms trembling, his breathing harsh, his breath skimming across her shoulder as he buried his face in her hair.

For all that had come before and during, she

hadn't expected to savor this moment. She felt as though her body was unfurling, as though she'd simply been a bud waiting for the sun to coax it into full bloom.

"Are you all right?" he asked quietly.

"Oh, yes," she whispered breathlessly.

"Good." Easing off her and onto his side, he rolled her toward him and tucked her in close against his damp side, her head coming to rest near his heart where she could hear its rapid pounding.

Her smile of contentment withered as she lifted her gaze to his and found him unsmiling, staring at the ceiling, obviously lost in thought. He absently skimmed his fingertips up and down her arm, but she could sense him drifting away, going someplace where he wouldn't allow her to follow.

Was he thinking of his first wife or his present bargain?

He rolled his head to the side and looked at her. He combed strands of her hair behind her ear before leaning over and kissing her brow. "Go to sleep now."

Standing, he tucked the blankets around her before walking to the window. He drew the curtains aside, and moonlight spilled into the room. He appeared to be such a lonely figure, standing with his arm braced against the pane. As lonely as she was.

She wanted to call him back to bed, to beg him to hold her for a moment longer . . . but she wanted all he had to offer without having to ask for it.

Even their glorious lovemaking had come at a price: her father's wealth. Without his money and

Devon's great need for it, she would have never known about the beauty that could pass between a man and a woman.

She swiped at the tears dampening her cheeks, closed her eyes, and sought whatever comfort she could find in dreams.

Devon stared at the fog rolling in, swallowing the street lamps' lights until their soft glow was all that was faintly visible. He'd never in his life left a woman in bed so beastly abruptly, but he'd needed to distance himself, wanted to gain control of his raging emotions.

He'd expected to perform his duty, bed her dispassionately, and dread the next mating. Instead he'd been consumed with an intense desire. As in all things, she was incredibly easy to please, to arouse. So frightfully giving. Why couldn't she be content to simply take what he offered?

Because it was her nature to please, the very heart of her, which allowed her to marry him in order to gladden her father, worrying little of the consequences to herself. He'd never known a woman such as she.

She scared the hell out of him.

On rare occasions, since Margaret's death, he'd bedded women, but he'd never felt unfaithful to her or her memory, as he did now. Always before, he'd sought and found the much needed physical release. Tonight he'd come close to achieving emotional release.

The manner in which Gina had writhed beneath

him, whimpered his name—was she even aware she'd called out to him as she'd reached the pinnacle of pleasure or that he'd trapped her name behind his clenched jaw?

He rubbed the stiff nape of his neck. What was it about her that affected him so? He didn't want her love, and he had none to give. Their relationship was based on her need for a child and his for money.

With a sigh he turned away from the window and walked to the bed. With feathery fingers the moonlight limned the lone teardrop clinging to her lashes. Reaching out, he captured it with his knuckle. "You overlooked yet another tear, sweeting."

His chest ached as he wondered why she'd wept this time. He considered returning to his room.

Instead he slid beneath the blankets and wrapped Gina within the cocoon of his arms. Perhaps they both needed more than the original bargain dictated.

Chapter 10

Georgina awoke to the heavenly weight of a man's leg draped over hers, his open hand resting against her breast, his mouth puckered against the nape of her neck.

She hadn't expected him to return to her bed. She hadn't thought she'd spend the remainder of the night wrapped in his embrace. She was surprised she'd slept soundly, deeply, with him sharing her bed.

It was uncanny, the manner in which their bodies would shift to accommodate one another. For a time they'd slept front to front, then his back pressed against her front, finally her back curved to his chest. She wasn't certain which position she preferred. Each had something to recommend it.

The fire in the hearth had burned itself out long ago, but the man in the bed had held the early morning chill at bay. She supposed in time she'd consider these days as hot as the English did, but she was still too accustomed to heat with the ability to cook an egg dropped on the boardwalk.

The sunlight barely peered through a parting in the heavy drapes that hung over the floor-to-ceiling windows.

Devon began to rub his thumb lazily along the underside of her breast. Through the night she'd discovered he had the ability to stroke her in his sleep, to squeeze her breast or her backside, and to bury his fingers in the wiry curls between her legs. To press against her, moan low, then snore softly.

She'd awoken with each touch only to discover the caress was not a prelude to lovemaking, but simply an unconscious motion on his part. Yet his actions endeared him to her for their possessive nature and their sweetness.

In the end he hadn't left her to sleep alone. She was fairly certain Englishmen did leave their wives alone in their beds. Why else would they have two bedchambers joined by a door?

Did the husband always come to his wife's bed? Or was the lady permitted to seek out her man?

She'd have to check with Lauren and discover if some sort of book on bedchamber etiquette existed. The Brits had books on every other aspect of behavior. Surely she could find one that went into detail regarding what happened behind closed doors.

His fingers joined his thumb, kneading, shaping, gently pinching, tenderly tugging. Insistent. Not quickly drifting into stillness as they had through the night.

The bed rocked as he rose up on an elbow.

"Awake?" his deep voice rumbled, scratchy with its first use of the day.

How intimate it seemed to have his first words of the day fall on her ears. She twisted her head slightly, smiled at him, and nodded. His hair swept across his brow. His beard was as shadowy as the corners where the sunlight had yet to reach.

Since he hadn't objected to her touch last night, she lifted her hand and touched his jaw. The whiskers were thick, rough, creating a raspy sound as she trailed her fingers along them across the defined edge of his chin.

He placed his hand over hers, holding it in place as he lowered his mouth and kissed her palm, his eyes never leaving hers. Her body tingled with the memories of the night, stirred to life as though the fires had merely been banked, waiting for dawn.

"I missed my morning ride," she said inanely.

He smiled with such warmth, a smile that traveled up to touch his eyes, a sparkle there she'd never before seen, a joy almost, a teasing glint.

"If we go slowly and take care, keeping in mind you might be a bit sore this morning, you should be able to ride me."

Her breath rushed out with an unexpected *oomph*, as though he'd snaked an arm around her chest and given a crushing squeeze. "R-ride you?" she stammered.

If at all possible, his smile grew. "You were all for experimenting last night."

"No, I was just curious."

"Then be curious still," he dared. "Unless you are experiencing great discomfort this morning."

He'd offered her an honorable out, which she had no wish to take.

"I'm not hurtin'," she assured him.

He traced his finger around her cheek, along her jaw, to the tip of her chin. "But you are nervous. Do you know how I know? Because you speak with a charmingly slow drawl when you're nervous."

He pressed a kiss to the corner of her mouth. "Utterly charming. As are you."

He sounded baffled, as though he hadn't expected to be beguiled, and having been, wasn't quite certain he approved of her wiles. Only she'd given him nothing but honesty, because she'd learned in the long run it served her best.

People always knew where she stood, and if they knew, then so did she.

"My morning ride?" she reminded him.

His eyes darkened, his gaze dropping to her lips. "Ah, yes."

He rolled onto his back and lifted the blankets, making a tent, inviting her to join him on his side of the bed—on top of him.

She turned onto her side, running her gaze up and down the magnificent length of him. "What do I do?"

"Straddle my hips."

"Then what?"

"Go as slow as you like, as easy as you need to." With his free hand, he cupped her cheek and stroked his thumb over her lower lip. "You can plod along, trot, or gallop." He brought her mouth to his. "You control the reins, sweeting."

He kissed her with a lassitude born of the dawn, a reluctance to begin the day. With the heel of his hand, he moved her head more in line with his, her body following as she sat on top of him, a sense of vulnerability mingling with an unfamiliar fleeting feeling of domination.

He draped the blankets over her shoulders before moving his hands to her breasts. She could see an advantage to this position. It gave him more freedom of movement, while she could do as she wished.

She traced the indentations of his chest, every muscle, every dip, every flattened plane. She welcomed the power, rejoiced in the endowment. She had not expected to feel so amazingly comfortable with her body so soon and certainly not with his.

And yet the touching, the positioning, the closeness seemed remarkably natural, as though they'd known each other a lifetime instead of merely a week.

As her hands traveled over him, she felt him tensing beneath her between her thighs. His breath came in harsh little pants as she explored slowly with her mouth, lapping up the salty dew coating his flesh.

He dug his fingers into her hips.

"Who would have thought you were one to torture?" he rasped. "Be quick about riding me or you'll miss your chance."

He lifted her and then eased her down inch by incredible inch. Initially she did experience discomfort, a slight burning, as she took him deep inside her body. For all his threats, all his eagerness, he guided her cautiously, watching her face.

"Halt me if you need to," he ordered.

But she had no more ability to stop than he did. He released a low shuddering sigh that rippled through him as she sank down completely, enveloping all of him, absorbing his fullness.

Leaning forward, she planted her hands on either side of his shoulders and braced herself above him. A fine sheen of sweat coated his brow, his neck, his chest. Each breath he took seemed more labored than the one that came before it.

With his hands guiding her, she rocked slowly against him, increasing the tempo until she rode fast and furiously, the sensations mounting, her body growing as taut as his.

With one hand maintaining its vigil at her hip, the other moved to her breast, his nimble long, slender fingers massaging as he rose up and latched his mouth onto her nipple. She dropped her head back, riding him for all she was worth.

The intense pleasure spiraled upward, outward, inward, ebbing, flowing. He grabbed her hips, pumping into her as she peaked with rapture. Tiny jerks continued to ripple through him as he otherwise lay still beneath her, breathing harshly, his eyes closed, his beautiful mouth opened slightly.

Reaching up, he cupped her head and directed her down to his chest, her limp, sated body sprawling over his. She thought she might never move again.

She'd just remain here for the remainder of her life, reliving that glorious moment of release, a pinnacle she realized they'd reached simultaneously.

She smiled with the wonder of it, that two people could be so in tune with each other's needs and desires. Merciful heavens. If only every aspect of their marriage could be as satisfying as the physical part, the years stretching out before them would hold incredible promise.

He took a deep breath, and a hard shudder vibrated through him, through her.

"When I watched you in the park, I was under the impression you would have preferred riding a stallion. I'm rather pleased to learn I judged you correctly."

She pressed her fist to her mouth to stifle her giggle. Were people supposed to laugh during or after lovemaking?

He rubbed her head, his fingers circling her scalp. "I daresay I make a fine stallion, don't you think?" he asked lazily.

She nodded, and he laughed low, a rumble beneath her cheek.

He fell into silence, and she relished the comfort of it, of not having to speak, of simply lying in bed with a man who seemed in no hurry to move, except for his hand, threaded through her hair, scraping her scalp.

"This is nice," she said softly.

"So it is."

The quiet wove around them. Peaceful. She would have this contentment for the remainder of her life. Of all the things she'd expected of her marriage, she found this revelation the most pleasing, because it spoke volumes.

"Unless you have a burning desire to remain in London for the Season, I have some matters at Huntingdon to which I must attend," he said. "I thought we would leave on the morrow."

She lifted her head. He watched her through half-lowered lids, as though at any moment he would drift back off to sleep.

"What about my father?"

"He's welcome to join us. The manor has an abundance of chambers. Why, he could have an entire wing to himself if he wished."

"I'll ask him. I'd like to spend the afternoon with Lauren." She gave him a wry smile. "She's the reason I came to England to begin with, to visit with her."

He cradled her face between his hands. "If you'd prefer to stay, we shall stay."

Stay. Attend boring balls and monotonous dinners where she wouldn't be allowed to sit beside her husband because husbands never sat next to their wives. She didn't like the rules here. They should be less evident and confining in the country.

"I'd like to go to Huntingdon."

"Splendid."

He wrapped his arms around her, hugging her close before flipping her onto her back and landing on top of her, raised up on his elbows to keep the bulk of his weight off her. He gave her a deliciously wicked grin. "What say before we begin making social calls, you take your stallion for another ride?"

* * *

Standing before the window in Ravenleigh's library, Devon gazed out on the garden and watched his wife strolling beside her father. He envied the old man's ability to put her completely at ease.

The wind carried her laughter while the sunlight brightened her smile. He imagined her eyes sparkled with joy and her voice reverberated with the love she held for the man who had sired her.

He could hardly fathom he'd made love to her three times this morning. He'd thought twice had done him in until he'd gone to his bedchamber and begun to dress. He couldn't remember what he'd thought he needed so urgently to tell her when he'd returned to her chamber and caught her rolling a stocking up that impossibly long, slender leg of hers.

Her foot had been perched on a stool, her petticoat slung back over her knee, and the only urgency of which he'd become acutely aware was the necessity to bury himself in her up to the hilt and then some.

In the last two years of his marriage to Margaret, he'd barely been able to work himself up for a weekly romp. He'd blamed his lack of interest on his schedule, on her disappointments, on his failings as a husband.

He'd certainly never expected to again feel as randy as a schoolboy, as eager as a young man in his prime. Nor had he expected to tease in bed, to enjoy her so damned much.

"Cognac?"

"Yes, I believe I shall." Distractedly he reached for the glass his cousin offered. "Thank you."

Ravenleigh pressed a shoulder against the window casing. "Am I to deduce since you've been staring at your wife for the better part of two hours that you are not finding marriage to Gina quite as objectionable as you feared you might?"

"You're welcome to deduce anything you wish." He sipped the cognac before shifting his gaze to his cousin. "I will admit she has turned out to be quite an unexpected boon."

A treasure, actually, although he was loath to admit it so soon after the vows had been spoken. He dared not trust that she would continue to be as giving once they arrived at Huntingdon. Yet why should she find fault with him there when she hadn't here?

With her father's money in his hands, he could make certain that she never discovered the unpleasant side to his life that had so turned Margaret against him. The baser part of him that had caused self-loathing.

"Indeed?" Ravenleigh asked.

"I would not say so if I did not mean it." He swirled the liquid in the glass. "Tell me. How does Lady Ravenleigh address you?"

"As Christopher."

"And your first wife?"

"The same."

He nodded speculatively. "Margaret always called me Huntingdon. Even in the throes of passion."

"I doubt that's unusual. After all, you and I are first cousins and yet we call each other by our titles rather than our given names."

"Perhaps." But he could not help but be haunted by the realization that Margaret might have considered herself married to his title more than married to him. She'd never called him Devon. He found it endearing, the manner in which Gina cried out his name as though he'd carried her into a realm of such magnificent beauty she could hardly believe it.

Damnation, but he liked the way she said his name, a slight hesitation as though not quite certain it was acceptable. As though she cared about acceptability. Not his wife. Not a woman who went without a chaperone and rode bareback at dawn.

But she did care that she pleased him and that made him care all the more about pleasing her.

Georgina sat on the cool stone bench and drew her shawl more closely around her. With a heavy sigh her father dropped beside her and took her hand. His was like ice.

"You need to wear gloves, Papa," she reproved softly.

"I'm tough, gal."

She wrapped her hands around his arm and leaned her head against his shoulder. He loved her as no one else ever had, probably as no one else ever would.

"Was your husband kind to you last night?" he asked gruffly.

She felt the heat suffuse her face. They'd strolled

the gardens speaking of everything except her marriage.

"Papa—"

"Don't Papa me. Did he hurt you? Because if he did, by God—"

"No, Papa, he didn't hurt me."

She still couldn't believe how attentive he'd been or that he seemed to be insatiable. The expression on his face when he'd walked into her room while she was putting on her stocking . . . She'd been surprised she hadn't burst into flames on the spot. By the time he left, she'd felt lethargic.

"Good." He patted her thigh. "Good."

She was so aware of Devon that even now she knew he was watching her within the shadows of the window. Not possessively. She knew she gave him no reason to be jealous, but she was flattered he had more of an interest in her than she'd expected him to have. She actually had hope for their marriage.

"He mentioned we're going to go ahead and return to his country estate and not wait until the end of the Season. You'll come with us, won't you?"

"What's in the country for me?"

"Lauren mentioned her father goes foxhunting. I'm sure Devon would let you hunt on his property."

"Foxhunting," he scoffed. "Gal, I've hunted renegades, outlaws, and to put food on the table. Where's the sport in going after a little critter just to kill it?"

"You could keep me company, then."

He slid his gaze toward her. "Your husband's supposed to do that."

He shifted slightly and cupped her cheek. "And

he will, gal. You're as beautiful to him as you are to me."

She smiled warmly. "Oh, Papa, you always see beauty where none exists."

"I see with my heart, not with my eyes. You're like your mother with a beauty so deep a man has to be willing to look long and hard. I miss her something fierce."

She squeezed his arm. "I know you do."

"Everything I've ever done I've done for you."

"I know, Papa."

"This fella, this husband of yours, I know he ain't wealthy, but life is much more than money. It can slip through your fingers without you even knowing. But love, once you've got hold of it, it never lets go. That's the way it was with your mother and me. That's the way it'll be with you and this fella."

She thought of her wedding night. "He respects me, Papa, and he has a care for my feelings."

"As he damn well should." He grimaced.

With concern etching her brow, she cupped his face between her hands. His cheeks were a bright red. "Are you all right, Papa?"

He nodded briskly. "Something I ate ain't agreeing with me, that's all."

"I don't understand why the food isn't agreeing with you. Most of it is so bland."

He shook his head. "My digestion isn't something I want to discuss with a lady."

She laughed lightly. "You can discuss it with your daughter. Do you want me to brew you something to ease the discomfort?"

He waved her away. "No. I want you to be happy. Everything I've ever done I've done for your happiness, because I love you more than life. I want—" He grabbed his left arm, his face contorting.

Alarmed, she dropped to her knees in front of him. "Papa?"

"No matter what happens, know I loved you . . . more than life."

In his eyes she saw love that knew no bounds, but she also saw pain, incredible pain.

"Papa!"

He toppled off the bench, gasping and clawing at the collar of his shirt. In spite of the cool weather, beads of sweat popped out on his brow as he curled into a ball.

"Oh, my God! Papa! Papa!"

Frantically she worked to free his buttons while she yelled for help, for the servants, for Devon. Anyone!

She heard the pounding of hurried footsteps. Her father stilled.

"Papa!" Her father stared straight at her, but she didn't think he saw her.

She barely noticed when Devon knelt beside her.

"Oh, dear Lord," he whispered.

Clutching her father's hand, she watched as though from a great distance while Devon ran his hands over her father. Her father didn't object to the intrusion, didn't move, didn't blink.

Devon took her in his arms and rocked her gently. "Sweetheart, I'm sorry. He's gone."

Chapter 11

Wearing her nightgown, Georgina sat in a chair, her feet tucked beneath her. How could a person who felt incredibly numb hurt with such ferocity? Her chest ached with each breath she drew into her lungs. Her eyes constantly stung from the tears she'd shed.

She'd never considered a life without her father. He'd doted on her as though she was the one who hung the stars in the night sky. He'd purchased her gaudy jewelry, atrocious gowns, and a husband.

Because he'd loved her.

He'd never cared that she possessed gaunt features. He'd never been bothered by the fact she didn't walk as though she had a book balanced on the top of her head. He'd never been concerned she'd been more interested in climbing trees, exploring caves, and riding horses than stitching handkerchiefs.

With him she'd never been afraid to be herself. He'd embraced both her strengths and her weaknesses. He'd loved her simply because she existed. She was his, and he was hers.

Now she had nothing but the memories to sustain her. In the blink of an eye, he'd left her alone. So alone.

Not physically alone. She had Devon, a few friends, and the servants. But emotionally alone, because she knew no one would ever love her as deeply as he had.

She lifted her gaze to dark sky. She longed for the vastness of a Texas night. "I hope Mama was waiting for you when you arrived," she whispered.

A tear leaked onto her cheek, and she brushed it away. She wondered how long it would be before tears no longer accompanied thoughts of her father.

She didn't turn when she heard the door open. Servants knocked. Devon didn't. It was his house after all. And she was his wife.

Her father's last gift to her—a husband who would give her children to fill the emptiness in her heart.

Devon crouched before her and took her hands, running his thumbs over her knuckles. Her father's hands had been callused and rough. Although Devon's were strong and comforting, they weren't her father's. Reaching up, he grazed his knuckle against the corner of her eye, causing her eyelashes to flutter.

"It's late. Why don't you try to get some sleep?"

Sleep. How could she explain that sleep only increased the loneliness, a loneliness that seeped deep within her bones, chilled and frightened her? She had Devon and therefore no reason to be lonely.

But loneliness had nothing to do with the number of people who surrounded you. Only acceptance and love could hold it at bay.

Blinking back her tears, she shook her head. Her throat tightened. "I just miss him so much."

With gentleness he tucked her hair behind her ear. "I wish I could tell you that time eases the yearning for their presence, but it doesn't. The hollow ache will always be there, and I suspect with you, so will the tears." He gave her a sad smile. "I shall do all in my power to ease the burden of your grief, and you need not worry that I shall take advantage once your father's wealth is absorbed into my estate. I shall give you adequate pin money, and you shall never do without anything you wish."

She angled her head slightly, studying him at his reminder that their marriage was grounded in money, not love. "That's the last thing I'd worry about."

"Good." Standing, he lifted her into his arms. "Now, come to bed."

She felt small and fragile within his strong embrace. He laid her on the bed and drew the covers over her before removing his clothes and slipping in beside her.

She snuggled against him, relishing his warmth and sturdiness. He held her close, his fingers skimming lazily up and down her back.

Nice. Pleasant. She thought she might easily become accustomed to having a husband who offered comfort with such finesse.

"Relax and go to sleep, Gina. We won't make love tonight."

Disappointment surfaced, but she was also grateful for his concern. She had little doubt most husbands put their own needs first. Her father had obviously chosen well.

She closed her eyes and amazingly began to drift off.

"Everything will be all right, sweeting," he murmured. "You'll see."

Mr. Ludlow reminded Devon of a ferret. Slender body that might have been tall, although it was difficult to tell, since his stooped shoulders detracted from his height. Black, beady eyes peered through the spectacles perched on the bridge of his long, narrow nose.

Nathaniel Pierce's solicitor. The man who, along with Devon's own solicitor, had overseen the drawing up and signing of the settlement papers. The Monday morning following the wedding, the morning of the day that he died, Pierce was to have placed fifty thousand pounds into Devon's account at the bank.

Devon was not overly concerned that the man had failed to do as he'd agreed. After all, the entire bulk of his holdings would be transferred to Gina and thus to him.

Ludlow had arrived, satchel in hand, an hour earlier. He'd spent his time sipping tea and patting Georgina's hand, telling her not to worry, all would be well.

"Mr. Ludlow," Devon announced.

The man snapped his head around as though only just remembering Devon was in the library. Ludlow raised his thin brows.

"You came to discuss my late father-in-law's estate," Devon reminded him.

Ludlow set aside his teacup, grabbed his satchel, and stood. "I came to discuss his leavings, yes, my lord." He tilted his head toward the desk. "May I?"

"By all means."

While Mr. Ludlow removed papers from his satchel and meticulously sorted and arranged them, Devon led Georgina to a plush chair in front of his desk. He sat beside her and took her hand, not at all surprised to find it chilled. It had to be incredibly difficult to listen to her father's life shrunk down into assets and liabilities, to hear a value placed on all a man had accomplished in his lifetime.

Mr. Ludlow finally stilled, his eyes blinking rapidly as he read the document that rested on the top of the pile. He cleared his throat. With his forefinger, he shoved his spectacles up the bridge of his nose. He cleared his throat again. Then he lifted his gaze.

"My lord." He cleared his throat yet again, his Adam's apple sliding up and down. "My lord, regarding Mr. Pierce's leavings, the sum total comes to roughly twenty thousand pounds."

Devon felt as though he'd been poleaxed. "Twenty

thousand pounds? I assume that amount does not take my wife's dowry into consideration."

Georgina's hand flinched within his, and he regretted his abruptness. He could only be thankful the settlement ensured they would have a livable income.

Mr. Ludlow's shoulders rose to his ears, as though he wished to hide. "I fear, my lord, there is no dowry."

"But we had a signed settlement."

"Yes, my lord, so I am aware. But it appears Mr. Pierce did not set aside any money before visiting the gaming hells, where it appears his luck deserted him."

"What the deuce are you talking about?"

"I am speaking of his debts."

"Debts?" he forced out.

"Yes, my lord." Ludlow riffled his thumb through the stack of papers. "I have bills from every London establishment to which he owed money."

Devon heaved a sigh, striving to rein in his impatience with the man's apparent ineptitude in handling the transfer of an estate. "I am not concerned with what he owed his creditors. I shall make good on all. I would, however, appreciate your giving me the sum total of his assets."

Ludlow blanched. "I apologize, my lord. Apparently I'm not being quite clear. There are no assets."

Devon shifted his gaze to Georgina. She looked as confused as he felt. He came up out of the chair and planted his palms on his desk. "What nonsense is this?"

"No nonsense, I'm afraid. Mr. Pierce came to see me the morning of the day of his demise. He was quite distraught. It seems he had frittered away a substantial amount of his holdings in an unbelievably short amount of time. Wagering on one thing and another. Unsuccessfully, I'm afraid.

"He knew that he was to hand over a sum of money to you, and he no longer had it at his disposal. He feared you would be able to nullify the marriage. I assured him that was not the case. He felt confident that in time he could make restitution to you. Unfortunately, it seems he misjudged the amount of time he had as well."

Georgina shifted in the chair. "But my father hadn't gambled in years."

Devon jerked his attention to her. "You knew of this?"

"I knew of his penchant for gambling, but as I said, he hasn't gambled in years."

"Apparently, my lady, in celebration of your wedding, he gambled to excess." Ludlow cut his gaze to Devon. "He seemed to have no restraint where wagering was concerned, my lord, as you'll no doubt discover once you've reviewed his debts."

"My father had amassed a fortune. You can't tell me that in the space of a few days he lost it all," Gina said softly.

"I fear, my lady, that is exactly what I'm saying."

"What of his holdings in America?" Devon asked.

Gina looked up at him, dazed, and slowly shook her head. "We never put down roots long enough to own a house. He sold off all his business ventures.

He didn't want to worry about business. He brought all his money here because he didn't know how long we'd stay, and he contemplated traveling elsewhere."

"He must have left something behind," Devon insisted.

"No," she said.

"Debts," Ludlow murmured.

Devon glared at the man, who quickly drew his head in, his chin touching his chest.

"Are you quite certain there is nothing?" Devon stated, surprised by the calmness of his voice.

"No assets, my lord. Of that I am certain. Mr. Pierce had given me an accounting of his assets before we drew up the settlement papers. I have verified that nothing remains available to you or his daughter."

Devon walked to the window and stared out. Damn Pierce. What had the man been thinking to gamble everything away?

He stiffened as Ludlow shoved the chair back across the wooden floor.

"My lord, may I notify those to whom Mr. Pierce owed funds that you will make good on his debts?" Ludlow asked.

Devon swallowed hard as thoughts of all he was losing swirled through his mind. He was under no legal obligation to hold himself responsible for the man's debts. Of that he was certain. But moral responsibility was another matter entirely. "Of course."

"Thank you, my lord. I shall see myself out."

Inwardly he cringed as Ludlow snapped closed his valise. His retreating footsteps echoed loudly through the library. The man was considerate enough to close the door in his wake.

Devon heard the rustle of his wife's skirts, and then she was standing beside him, a hazy reflection in the window.

"Father promised you a dowry?"

"Fifty thousand. Then of course upon his death whatever you inherited would have come to me. It's English law, and you, my sweet, are now English."

"You must feel as though you had no reason to marry me," she said quietly.

An affirmation hovered on the tip of his tongue, but the devastation ringing in her voice held his anger in check. What good could possibly come from lashing out at her?

"You have to believe me, Devon, I had no idea Father was gambling to such an extent that he would lose everything."

"How could you not know?" he asked.

"I didn't follow him around London. As for the creditors, Father always told me to have my purchases placed on his accounts and he'd take care of the bill at the end of the month."

"Well, he damned well took care of it, didn't he, *Countess*?" he ground out before turning to glare at her.

"It's been years since he gambled. Why now?"

"He wanted you to have respectability, the old-world affluence that his new world dollars could never purchase. A title, *countess*, steeped in tradition and honored by society. You can snub anyone and get away with it. He moved you into the most elite echelon of society. Having achieved his goal, he obviously no longer cared if the damned money was there or not."

"I can't believe he'd gamble it all away."

He wanted to rail at his wife, but she seemed frail and lost, as devastated by her father's chicanery as he was himself.

And she had that tear clinging to her lash. She'd no doubt wept a few silently before approaching him. Why did that knowledge have the power to undo him as nothing else could?

"The solicitor's wrong," she said beseechingly.

"I'll have my own man make some discreet inquiries."

He turned away from her, fearing all the inquiries in the world wouldn't make a bit of difference. He possessed less now than he had before.

"I simply don't understand exactly what Papa was thinking."

Strolling through Hyde Park with Lauren, Georgina was surprised to discover the sun still shone, flowers continued to show their colors, and the elms retained their leaves.

Her frustration mounting, she glanced at Lauren. "When we were in the garden, he kept telling me that he loved me—and the entire time he knew that he'd dishonored his pact with Devon. This is so unfair. You should have seen the absolute disbelief on Devon's face when he realized Mr. Ludlow was speaking of debt. He looked as though Papa had slit his throat with a bowie knife."

"Yes, I can see that might well have been his initial reaction, but in time surely he'll come around and realize he gained so much more from marrying you than he would have gained with your father's money."

Georgina shook her head. "I don't think so."

For a time their marriage had held the promise of being glorious, and she'd forgotten that his quest for funds had motivated his actions. He'd treated her kindly not out of consideration, but from an overwhelming desire to receive her father's money.

"In order for him to divorce you, you'd have to commit adultery," Lauren said.

Now that Gina had fully experienced the intimacy of making love, she couldn't imagine herself ever being in bed with another man. Although she and Devon were little more than strangers, she'd still felt comfortable with him after the initial awkwardness had drifted away. She couldn't imagine allowing a man who meant nothing at all to touch her.

"I don't see that happening," she muttered.

"You could divorce him if he raped you."

She thought of the gentleness of his touch, the heat of his mouth, his calming, murmured words. "He'd never force himself on me."

"He might abandon you. Then you could divorce him."

She couldn't see Devon leaving her behind, not physically anyway. But emotionally . . . She wondered if emotional abandonment was possible. She'd felt as though he'd erected a wall of ice between them as the solicitor had explained the dire situation.

"Why are you searching for ways for us to divorce?" she asked.

"Because it would get you both out of a situation that neither of you wants."

A week ago she might have agreed she didn't want this situation, but somewhere between his first kiss of her fingers and the comfort he'd offered immediately after her father had died—before her father's poor judgment had become evident—she'd discovered she liked having Devon around.

She had an incredible urge to delve beneath the stuffy layers and discover the man beneath.

"I feel as though I owe it to him to stay. To be loyal. To right Papa's wrong."

"You're not responsible for your father's failure."

"How can I not feel responsible, Lauren? Devon was willing to marry me, to give me children in exchange for money so he could rebuild his estate. The very least I can do is stand by Devon and help him out the best way I can."

"What if he doesn't want your help?" Lauren asked.

"I'm not sure men ever really know what they want. Besides I do have some feelings for him. There are times . . ." Her voice trailed off. How could she explain?

"What? Finish your thought," Lauren urged.

"Times when he looks at me that I feel as though he might care for me a bit."

"Of course he cares for you—if he has a lick of sense. Why do you persist in believing a man couldn't love you?"

"Perhaps because no man ever has."

The loneliness ate away at Georgina like a sore. She hadn't seen Devon in three days, not since the solicitor's hasty retreat.

She'd sat in her bedchamber, waiting for him to pay her a visit. She'd waited in vain.

Night after night at midnight she'd hear him pacing the hallway before withdrawing into his bedchamber. How fortunate they were to each have their own room.

Glancing in the mirror, she was not at all pleased with her appearance. Dark circles rested beneath her puffy eyes. She wore the blue dress that Devon seemed to favor. It would do well for this meeting.

Gathering her courage around her like a finely sewn cloak, she left her room and wandered to the library.

Pale light spilled out from beneath the closed doors. She considered knocking, but she wanted to give him no opportunity to rebuff her. Wrapping her fingers around the cold handle, she jerked it down, marched into the room, and froze.

Her husband, her dear husband, looked like hell.

He gazed at her through eyes that were as swollen and red as hers. A heavy beard shadowed his face.

His hair—usually every black strand in place—stuck up at odd angles, deep furrows indicating that he might have repeatedly plowed his fingers through it. Several buttons were loosened on the white billowy shirt, which was wrinkled enough to have been slept in.

Papers were strewn over his desk in disarray.

With a heavy sigh, he leaned back in his leather chair. "What do you want, *countess?*"

The weariness in his voice kept her temper in check. Quietly she closed the door and approached. "We need to talk."

"Yes, I suppose we do."

As calmly as possible, she sat in the chair across from him. "What did you learn?"

"That your father did indeed somehow manage to lose *everything.*"

Her heart sank. How could her father have returned to gambling when he knew the misery it had brought them before? Why risk it? She clearly didn't understand his obsession. All it took was one turn of the card, and he became completely lost.

Devon bowed his head and rubbed the back of his neck. She eased up in the chair. "Can't you explain that you aren't responsible for his debts?"

He lifted his gaze and pinned her with an icy glare. "I would have gained his wealth from you, sweeting. I can't very well turn his debts aside."

"But if you tell those to whom he owed money that you haven't got the means to pay—"

He slammed his fist on the desk, and she jerked

like a puppet whose strings had just been yanked.

"No one is to know I haven't the means," he said in a tightly controlled voice.

"If we weren't married, you wouldn't have to concern yourself with his debt, would you?"

"But we are married."

"We could get a divorce."

His gaze hardened. "The men in my family do not go through the scandal of an expensive and time-consuming divorce."

"My father did you a disservice. He failed to honor his word. Surely people will understand if you explain everything that happened and the reason you cast me aside."

"My God. Each sentence that comes out of your mouth is worse than the one that came before it." He slowly, menacingly stood, planted his hands on the desk, and leaned toward her. "As long as I breathe, no one is to ever know of this debacle. I shall find a way to rectify our dire financial situation."

"If you knew of a way, you wouldn't have resorted to marrying me in the first place."

His defeated mien made her regret her words, but he had to understand that they could not remain together.

"Don't be so proud," she pleaded. "We can find a way to turn this disaster so it falls on me, and you won't have to accept his debt."

"Trust me, sweeting, your father's debt is the least of my troubles. Pack your things. We'll leave for

Huntingdon in the morning. I've instructed my solicitor to place this house on the market."

Disbelief coursed through her. "I can't have everything in this huge house packed by morning."

"Not everything. Only your things. If you've taken a fancy to some small item, you may pack it. Everything else stays." He walked to the window and gazed out. "Everything else is to be sold."

She thought her heart might crack at his despondency. "Oh, Devon. I am so sorry." She slowly rose to her feet. "My father—"

"Your father did not uphold his end of the bargain. Therefore neither shall I uphold mine. I shall never again warm your bed."

Her breath backed up painfully in her lungs with the realization he would disregard her feelings, her dreams, as though they possessed no more substance than a whisper in the wind. "What?"

He turned from the window. "My arrangement with your father. In exchange for his wealth, I agreed to give you a child."

He waved his hand dispassionately, as she imagined kings had done just before they regretfully sent someone to the chopping block.

"I believe you'll agree he left to me no wealth."

He considered her no asset at all. Yet her father had spoken true words. Life was more than money, and suddenly she found herself with a desperate desire to have him see *her* as worthy of his affections. "I can offer you more than wealth. I can give you an heir."

"I have an heir."

She felt as though he'd jerked the Aubusson rug she was standing on out from beneath her. The room spun, and she grabbed onto the back of the chair. "You have a child?"

"Two. A son and a daughter. You'll no doubt meet them when we return to Huntingdon."

"No doubt? We'll be living in the same house."

"But in separate wings. Besides, they have a governess who looks after them. You need not bother yourself with them."

He made them sound as though they were pets, not children.

"But what of a spare? I thought the aristocracy was keen on having two sons."

"I shall make do with what I have. It seems to be an acceptable punishment for having acted in haste."

"In greed. You acted in greed, Devon."

"Arguing over semantics, my dear countess, will gain neither of us anything. Accept that you are the wife of an impoverished nobleman and be done with it. We can at least live together civilly if not luxuriously."

She considered simply packing her bags, walking out on him, traveling back to Texas, and making her own way in the world. She still had the ticket her father had purchased for her guaranteeing her passage back to Texas before he'd made arrangements for her marriage.

But she couldn't quite get past the notion that he

had children. Children. Children who had a governess but no mother.

She angled her chin defiantly and nodded. "Very well. I'll abide by your wishes for the moment. I owe you that much at least."

Chapter 12

As his coach journeyed along the road toward Huntingdon, Devon strove not to notice how his wife took delight in the rolling hills. She often reminded him of a child discovering the world and awed by its magnificence. Her high regard humbled him. He couldn't remember the last time he'd taken a moment to appreciate the beauty of England.

Yet she was no child. She was a woman with a woman's desires and needs. That she had so readily accepted his conditions for their continued association made him feel like a cantankerous curmudgeon. If she'd thrown a tantrum, as Margaret had often done, he might not have been sitting here feeling as though he was completely unworthy.

In his own defense, he'd held certain expectations regarding this marriage, and while his more gentlemanly self acknowledged she was not to blame for her father's failure, the part of him struggling to survive had lashed out like a cornered animal on the brink of madness.

He'd been surprised to discover she'd managed to pack all her belongings in one small trunk. He'd not been present at his London home when her things had been brought over. Still, he'd assumed she'd have several trunks, boxes, and bags.

She assured him she'd left nothing behind. He couldn't imagine Margaret traveling abroad with only one trunk. He'd always hired two wagons to cart her belongings from Huntingdon to London and back. He'd arranged the same hauling services for Gina, only to discover he didn't require them.

He really needed to learn to stop expecting his current wife to behave as his former wife had. He couldn't recall Margaret ever peering at the countryside and showing an appreciation for it. Perhaps that was the reason she'd come to hate his land. He could only hope that Gina would not find it as loathsome.

"I've been thinking," she began unexpectedly.

"And here I thought you'd been enjoying the scenery."

She gave him a wry smile. "I can do both."

She twisted the wedding band on her finger, studying it a moment before lifting her gaze to him. "I was thinking you should return my ring to the jeweler."

He'd purchased it when he'd expected riches, when generosity was an easy matter. Necessity would turn him back into a miserly creature.

A miserly and fearful creature. He'd banned himself from her bed because he knew that once she understood the true poverty of their existence, she'd toss him out on his arse. His pride couldn't handle another exile. It was much easier to attack than to defend.

Margaret had taught him that lesson well.

"It's not necessary that you sacrifice the ring," he said quietly.

She intertwined her fingers and pressed her hands together as though to protect the ring. Her hands were not soft like a lady's. He remembered the callused tips digging into his buttocks after the roughened palms had skimmed over his damp back. Her touch, unlike any he'd ever felt before, had enamored him. He shouldn't have been so hasty to deny himself the pleasure of it.

"I have some jewelry that belonged to my mother. I have no idea what it's worth, but it might pay off a few of my father's debts," she offered.

It had been a long while since he'd felt the stirrings of humanity. Taking money from her father was one thing, to take a precious item from her unthinkable.

"I doubt it would make enough difference to truly matter."

She gazed out the window again. If she was anxious about arriving at her new home, she didn't allow it to show. In profile, her long, slender neck reminded him of a graceful swan's. There were aspects to her person that when he took the time to notice them he found remarkably appealing.

But it seemed he was always rushing through life, striving so hard to put his situation back on an even keel that he missed the finer moments of simply being. Idleness had always seemed contrary to his nature. With a great deal of concentration, he'd learned to master sitting for hours, giving the appearance of doing nothing.

But even a carriage ride tested his patience. He would be more content to be walking alongside. Although he was traveling a great distance, sitting here made him feel as though he was wasting his time.

He needed to do *something.*

If her fidgeting was any indication, Georgina experienced the same impatience. An Englishwoman would sit perfectly still no matter how badly she wished to move. She understood decorum and all its subtle nuances.

His wife knew little about playing the game.

"How is it that you'd never been kissed?"

She snapped her attention away from the countryside, her dark brows furrowing. It was strange how the more he gazed at her, the less unattractive she seemed. Her features didn't change, but his perception of them did.

"What?"

And his perception of *her* was altering. He now realized her question didn't indicate that she hadn't heard him, but rather she was having a difficult time believing he'd asked what he had.

"You heard me," he said, a challenging edge to his voice. "It's not as though you're hideous."

"Well, thank you for that backhanded compliment."

She turned her head and stared out the window.

"I meant no insult. I simply can't fathom that a

woman could go through life and never have known a kiss."

The furrows grew shallow, and the harsh lines around her mouth softened. He didn't think she was seeing the trees and land that spread out before them. Instead she seemed to be gazing inward.

"I was nine when the war started. Thirteen when it ended. There weren't many fellas around during those years."

"No men, certainly, but there would have been children."

Slowly she shook her head and looked at him with sad eyes. "Not many boys stayed behind. As soon as they could beat a drum, they joined their father or older brother on the battlefield. The fellas from a town fought together, which meant if the Yankees were victorious, a town could lose most of its men. That's what happened to Fortune."

She glanced back out the window. "The few who did return . . . Defeat haunted them. When you've survived hell, it's hard to trust in the existence of heaven."

She lifted a shoulder slightly. "Those who might have shown an interest in me before the war had grown into men surrounded by blood and death. They weren't quite comfortable around girls. Besides, so few returned, they could have their choice of girls. Why settle for tin when you can have gold?"

He contemplated telling her that he didn't consider her tin, but then neither was she gold. She hovered somewhere in between—common, yet precious. Why in God's name did he think that?

"Your eyes carry that haunted, defeated look," she said softly.

Her gaze was trained on him now, and he had the uncomfortable feeling she was looking down the sight of a rifle, getting a good bead on him, searching for his vulnerable spot so she could destroy him with one well-aimed shot.

"I don't see how that can be, *countess*, when I've never gone to war."

"Battles aren't always fought over land or between nations."

"I assume you speak from experience."

She gave him a soft smile before turning her attention back to the countryside.

"We are not engaged in a war, you and I," he announced.

"I'm glad you feel that way, *my lord*, because if we were, you'd lose."

There it was again. The obstinate part of her nature that she kept hidden, as though she wasn't quite certain if it belonged to her or not.

He didn't want to be intrigued by her, and yet he was. What baffled him was that he was actually pleased he did not have to return to Huntingdon alone.

Georgina fought desperately not to gawk as she stepped into what she supposed was the main foyer. To her embarrassment, her mouth had dropped open when the driver—she was relatively certain a groom should have accompanied them on the trip, but it seemed Devon had a smaller staff than Ravenleigh—had helped her out of Devon's carriage and she'd caught her first sight of his home.

His home. Heavens! From what she'd been able to see as they approached, she could have fitted almost every store that lined the main street of Fortune inside it.

But once inside, she noticed the evident signs of deterioration. The floors were not polished to the same sheen as those in London were. The draperies were faded.

Since guests here were no doubt few and far between, Devon had not needed to keep up a front, as he had in London, where people could easily drop by. Still, the place came close to being a palace as far as she was concerned.

Gilded chandeliers, statues, paintings. She lifted her gaze to the ceiling. Someone had painted cherubs frolicking in fields. She slowly turned, resisting the strong desire to lie on the floor so she could study the artwork without straining her neck.

"Milord, you've arrived," a stately voice announced.

She jerked around and watched as the butler approached. His jacket was frayed at the edges, and his shoes had seen better days, yet he stopped before them with a haughty dignity and bowed slightly.

"Winston, please see that the east wing is prepared for my . . . wife," Devon commanded in a strained voice. "And see that she is made to feel at home there."

She didn't think Winston could have looked more shocked if Devon had aimed a loaded pistol at him.

He recovered quickly and tilted his head slightly. "Milady, if you'll allow me to escort you to the east wing."

"What about the children?" she asked, turning her attention to her husband.

"I'll introduce you to them later. At present, I have important matters to which I must attend."

"What could possibly be more important than your children?"

Fury flashed in his eyes, and a jaw muscle contracted. "Winston, where are the children?"

"In the day nursery, milord."

"Countess, if you'll honor me with your presence, I'll make introductions, after which you may retire to your wing."

He crooked his elbow, a courtesy gesture he might not have made if the butler hadn't been standing nearby. She slipped her arm through his, surprised by the firmness that greeted her—a hardness caused more by restrained anger than arduous work.

"Winston, see to her ladyship's accommodations."

"Yes, milord."

Devon led her down the long, wide expanse of the hallway and up the grand sweeping staircase.

"Never question my actions in front of the servants again," he warned through clenched teeth once Winston was no longer within hearing.

"Forgive me, *my lord*. I was under the impression that I was about to be banished to the farthest regions of the house, and I wasn't certain if I'd ever see hide nor hair of you again."

He snapped his head around. "You are my countess. Our spending some time together will be unavoidable."

She slipped her arm free of his. It took him two steps to realize she wasn't following like an adoring pet. He glared at her.

"Devon, this arrangement is asinine."

"Lest we forget, allow me to remind you this arrangement came about as a result of your father's inability to walk away from a gaming table."

"You're not the only one he hurt."

He averted his gaze, his hand gripping the banister until his knuckles turned white. "He did not hurt me. He failed to uphold his end of the bargain, and for his weakness I am forced to pay an extremely steep price."

He'd promised Devon wealth and given him nothing. She couldn't even claim to have a husband after the journey they'd taken for the most part in complete, absolute, infuriating silence.

"Although I must admit it does not seem he did well by you either. However, he could have done worse. At least I am not in the habit of striking women."

"You think blows can only be made against flesh?"

He blanched. Civilized Englishmen seemed to have no way to release their anger. Back home she would have ridden a horse hard, galloped him until they were bone-tired.

She placed her hand on his arm. "Devon, we're both weary from the journey and disappointed. Introduce me to the children. Then we can part company, and with any luck—in this massive structure—you'll never set eyes on me again."

He began walking up the stairs. "As I mentioned, Countess, there are times when we'll be unable to avoid each other's company. Dinner, for one. I'll not have the servants whispering about our failure to dine together."

He was exiling her to the farthest regions of his home, and he was worried about meals? She considered pointing out his flawed logic, but she thought it might be best if they did indeed live at opposite ends of the house. Their wedding night had given her unexpected memories to cherish. He'd thought he was getting something out of the bargain then.

She dared not contemplate his bedding her when he knew his only prize was her. She didn't think he'd be as thoughtful, as considerate. The act would be cold and leave her feeling emptier than she felt now.

The hallway at the top of the stairs was as remarkable as the foyer, although she also noticed signs of its decline. How hard it must be for Devon to witness such grandeur aging ungracefully.

At the end of the wide corridor, he opened a heavy mahogany door. She preceded him inside to what she instinctively knew was a day nursery. A rocking horse stood unused in a corner. Books lined a tiny set of shelves. A large dollhouse dominated a section of one wall.

And children. Children sat at a small table with a woman who looked as though she had one foot in the grave and was gingerly lifting the other one to join it. Her bones creaked as she stood. "Milord."

The children snapped their heads around. "Father!" they yelled in unison.

The children stood and with their arms raised, they dashed across the room.

The harsh rumble of Devon clearing his throat bounced off the high ceilings.

The children staggered to a stop, their little chests heaving, their eyes once bright with joy now downcast in shame.

"That is hardly the manner in which children take leave of a table," Devon said sternly.

The children spun on their heels, their tiny shoulders slumped forward in dejection as they trudged back to the table and straightened their chairs before turning to face their father as though they were soldiers about to be inspected by a general.

Devon offered them a curt nod and they marched forward.

Georgina wanted to slam her fist into her husband's handsome face. For all of her father's shortcomings—and she wasn't blind enough not to realize that he had possessed many—he'd always loved her unequivocally.

She remembered all the times he'd returned home from a long day at work only to scoop her up in his arms as soon as her churning legs got her close enough to him. He'd hold her high above his head, his grin so wide that she'd been able to see the gaping hole at the back where he'd once had a tooth knocked out by a kicking mule.

"You're my sunshine!" he'd yell for the whole world to hear.

And she'd known it was true. They'd been poor for much of her life, but she'd always felt rich.

"I'm glad you're home, Father," the boy said.

With his hands clasped behind his back, he was a small replica of the man standing rigidly in front of him. The sunlight easing in through the floor-to-ceiling window stroked his black hair, making it seem almost blue in places. But not nearly as blue as his eyes, which reflected the calmness of a placid lake. They no longer sparkled with joy but sought acceptance.

"Yeth, Father," the little girl lisped. "We're tho glad you're home." She smiled tentatively, her fingers fiddling with the bow on the front of her dress.

Devon nodded curtly. "Lord Noel. Lady Millicent. May I introduce my wife, Lady Huntingdon."

Since smacking their father was out of the question, Georgina dropped to her knees and smiled warmly. "But you may call me Gina."

"They may not," Devon said curtly.

She angled her head toward him and flashed him a sickly sweet grin. "They may indeed."

"Milady, it's simply not done," the governess stated, her hands primly clutched in front of her.

"And you are?"

"The governess, milady. Mrs. Tavers."

"Then you must forgive me, Mrs. Tavers. I'm not yet familiar with all the British etiquette. I assumed that since I am the countess and this is my home, I could establish some rules outside of societal constraints."

"It would confuse the children, milady, to have two sets of rules to follow."

"Are you saying that my lord's children are dimwitted?"

Devon paid attention to the exchange with interest. Christopher had warned him about Texas ladies. The night he'd proposed, Gina had first shown him some of her stubbornness. He'd not expected her to bring it into his home, however.

He watched Mrs. Tavers's cheeks burn bright red. He feared the woman might swoon on the spot.

"Of course not, milady. My lord's children are exceedingly bright."

"Then I would think they could well comprehend that when it is only us, they may call me Gina, and when we are in the company of others, they are to address me with the stilted name of Lady Huntingdon." She arched a delicate brow. "Are you smart enough to know the difference?"

Devon was hit with unexpected pride as his son thrust out his tiny chest.

"Yes, my lady, we are," Noel answered.

Devon did not miss that his son included his sister in his answer. He felt his throat tightening with an emotion he couldn't quite put a name to, something that went beyond fatherly satisfaction.

"How old are you, Lord Noel?" Georgina asked.

Noel darted a glance up at Devon, who gave him a brusque nod.

"Eight," he answered.

"And you, Lady Millicent?" she asked.

"I'm five." Her eyes widened. "I have a loothe tooth." She opened her mouth and flicked her tongue over a lower tooth.

Before he could scold his daughter for such inappropriate behavior, Gina had eased down to the floor, latched onto Millicent, and pulled her onto her lap so she could inspect the tooth more closely.

"How exciting!" Gina crooned. "It looks like it'll come out any day now."

Apparently not at all uncomfortable that she was sitting on a stranger's lap, Millicent nodded quickly. Devon was certain that the late afternoon sunlight streaming through the windows was responsible for softening the lines of his wife's face.

He crossed his arms over his chest and leaned against the wall. Not even on her wedding day had she looked that radiant. As though she'd suddenly discovered the moon and stars had been placed in the heavens for her pleasure alone.

"Are you our mother?" Millicent asked.

"No," Devon said brusquely as he shoved himself away from the wall, regretting the harshness in his voice as his daughter's face fell and she scrambled off Gina's lap. Regretting more the disappointment that swept through Gina's eyes before she worked her way to her feet.

"Mrs. Tavers, I apologize for interrupting the studies. We'll leave you to the children now." He extended his elbow toward his wife. "Countess, you and I need to talk."

With a swish of her skirts, she spun on her heel and strode from the room. Judging by the wide-eyed stares of his children, they had not missed the fact she had snubbed their father.

Ah, yes, they needed to talk quite badly.

Chapter 13

"You're determined to make this entire situation as difficult as possible, aren't you?"

Sitting behind the desk in his study, Devon studied his wife as she stood in front of the window. Sunlight glimmered in a halo around her, but she did not appear angelic. With her hands on her hips, she more closely resembled a warrior goddess. She almost looked magnificent.

"I allowed you your freedom to establish rules of behavior for the day nursery—"

"Freedom?" she said. "You *allowed* me my freedom?"

She moved forward, planted her palms on his desk, and leaned toward him. "My freedom is not yours to give. I own it—lock, stock, and barrel."

No woman had ever dared to speak to him so defiantly or look at him with fire shooting from her eyes. Certainly Margaret never had. For a time she had worshipped the ground upon which Devon had stood. Then she'd simply whined and sulked.

"Madam, you are my wife—"

"But not your slave."

He felt a muscle in his jaw jump. He was in danger of grinding his teeth down to nothing.

Sadness touched her eyes as she straightened. "You didn't even hug them," she said resignedly, as though all her anger had eased away. "You're their father, you've been gone at least six weeks, and you never once touched them."

"It's simply not done."

"They're your children."

"There are expectations that must be met by the children of an aristocrat—"

"Damn the aristocracy, its expectations, and its rules. Noel and Millicent are *your* children!"

He didn't know what shocked him more, her immense anger or her use of profanity. "Madam, there are also expectations of the wife—"

Shaking her head, she returned to the window.

"Never turn your back on me," he warned her through clenched teeth.

"We've been intimate," she said quietly. "We've caressed each other. You've heard me cry out during the height of passion." She glanced over her shoulder at him. "Yet you speak to me as though I'm someone you've just met on the street."

"What passed between us beneath the blankets was the result of my fulfilling an obligation. Make no more of it than that."

"What in God's name possessed my father when he decided you were the best catch in London?"

What indeed? He held her gaze and decided it was time to change the subject and get down to the reason he'd wanted to have this meeting to begin with.

"Regarding your duties. The staff here is small, but you will oversee their efforts with decorum and dignity. They will *not* address you as Gina. You shall not become their friend or their confidant. They are our employees. We cannot afford to hire any more. We must make do with what we have and hold no grudges when they leave."

"You expect them to leave?"

He leaned back in his chair. "In time. It is only their loyalty that has kept them here this long. They have gone without wages for some time. It's unfair to make them feel that they are obligated to stay."

"I assume, with the exception of your bedchamber, that I can have full run of the house."

"Yes."

"I assume, then, that there is to be no affection between us."

Had he not stated as much in London? Why was she questioning him now?

"I thought we had agreed to civility."

She visibly shuddered. "Your house is almost as cold as your heart."

With that parting shot, she once again turned her back on him and strode from the room.

* * *

He did not have a cold heart.

He had been wronged. Her father had disregarded his obligations in exchange for a night of folly, and now they were both paying the price. To make matters worse, his new wife irritated the devil out of him.

He stared at her as she sat at the opposite end of a massive table that had been in his family for generations. Beneath the linen cloth it was hideously scarred, but it represented tradition.

With a curt nod he signaled the butler to begin serving.

Gina's head came up with a snap as the man ladled soup into her bowl.

"Aren't the children joining us?" she asked.

"They have their meal in the day nursery."

Even from this great distance, he could see her brow furrow.

"Always?" she asked.

"Always."

"When do you visit with them?"

He sipped his wine while he was served his soup. When the servant had quit the room, he reminded her, "I visited with them this afternoon."

"That was hours ago. Aren't you at all curious as to what they've been doing between then and now?"

"Mrs. Tavers will give me a report."

"A report?"

With a heavy sigh he shoved his bowl away. His appetite had deserted him. Why couldn't his wife?

"Countess, the children are not your concern.

We've managed quite well until now without your interference."

She lowered her gaze to her soup and began to spoon it up and sip quietly.

"My apologies," he murmured. "I know you mean well. It is simply that English children are not reared in the same manner as American children."

"So I'm learning."

It was not until dessert that he dared risk another conversation. "Did you find your chambers satisfactory?"

"Yes, they're fine." She met and held his gaze. "Does Millicent favor her mother?"

His throat tightened with the memories. "Very much so."

"She's beautiful."

"As was Margaret."

"How did you meet?"

He moved aside what remained of his pudding, snatched up his glass, and took a sip of wine before saying, "I gained an introduction at a ball."

He swirled the liquid in his glass, contemplating how much more to reveal. Speaking of Margaret had the advantage of shoring up the wall around his heart, and so he decided to continue. "It was not an easy task to gain an introduction. Gentlemen flocked around her. Her dance card was filled within moments of her arrival. She was quite the toast of London during her first season."

"And by the next season?"

He smiled wryly. "She was my wife."

He lifted his glass in a mock salute. "I seem to have a penchant for marrying hastily."

"But you didn't regret your first marriage."

"I regretted that I could not give Margaret all she deserved."

With typical brashness she planted her elbow on the table and cupped her chin. "I can't imagine that she wanted for anything of importance."

"Because you do not view the world through the eyes of an aristocrat." Wishing to end the thread of this conversation, he added, "If you are quite finished with the meal, you are welcome to excuse yourself."

"I'd like to go with you when you say good night to the children."

His initial reaction was to explain that he didn't tuck the children into bed. Their governess did. But after her earlier chastisement regarding his failure to hug them, he decided that for tonight at least he could break with tradition.

She was exquisite. He wasn't certain he'd ever noticed. Certainly the day she was born his chest had tightened into an unbearable but heavenly ache. The first time he'd held her, he'd thought his heart would burst.

But he couldn't remember ever gazing upon her small body, lost within the massive canopied bed in which she slept. Her head was nestled against the pillow, the blankets tucked beneath her chin. Her expressive blue eyes were filled with rapt wonder as she listened intently to Gina's story of an Indian maiden named Serena who loved a man who failed to love her.

Equally entranced, Noel sat on top of the comforter, his back resting against the carved headboard.

Before she began the tale, Gina had taken her place on the edge of the mattress, and throughout the telling—as a wily fish worked his magic and transformed the maiden into a mermaid—she constantly touched his children. Millicent's hair. Noel's leg. Her hand. His chin. With each caress, their eyes softened more and their lips curled higher.

Standing at the foot of the bed, watching, he felt as though he was an intruder. A stranger to his own children. He had no idea what their nightly rituals entailed.

He was fairly certain stories were not involved, since Mrs. Tavers had protested that delaying their bedtime would spoil the children.

"They're children for such a short time, Mrs. Tavers. They should be spoiled," Gina had replied.

Apparently another rule the countess intended to put into play in his household. He couldn't bring himself to object, not when his children had perked up with such delight.

Her story ended with betrayal and the maiden's tears flowing through a river somewhere in Texas. Within Gina's voice, Devon heard a lilting sadness. But in his children's eyes, he saw their amazement that a fish had the power not only to turn a woman into a mermaid when the moon was full, but to cause the man she loved to love her in return.

"Can you believe it, Father?" Millicent asked, her eyes round.

"It does seem quite remarkable," he replied.

"Does that mean it isn't true?" Noel asked.

Gina looked at him, and he wasn't certain if it was her faith he didn't want to shake or his children's.

"It's a legend, Noel," he said quietly. "All legends have at their center the seeds of truth."

Gratitude softened the lines of his wife's face much as the late afternoon sun had earlier. For so long he'd been absorbed with the greater goal of finding a way to improve Huntingdon that he was beginning to realize he may have overlooked the importance of the details.

Leaning over, she kissed Millicent's forehead. "Good night, Millicent."

Devon knew a pang of regret as Millicent's face lit with joy. He was fairly certain Mrs. Tavers didn't kiss her good night. Millicent had been only two when her mother had died. Did she have any memories of her mother's tender kisses?

He searched the recesses of his own memories and couldn't locate a solitary image of Margaret kissing their daughter. At least not after she'd been moved from the bassinet.

Gina stood and stepped back as though she fully expected him to follow her example. He wasn't about to let on that he had no remembrance of kissing his child since her mother's death.

Stiffly he moved to the head of the bed and bent over slightly. Millicent flung her tiny arms around his neck, clinging to him as though he were her favorite doll.

"Good night, Father," she whispered sweetly in his ear.

His throat clogged with emotion as he closed his arms around her and inhaled her innocent fragrance. "Good night, Kitten."

Working himself free, he straightened and tucked the blankets around her. With a wink, he touched his finger to the tip of her nose.

Turning, he caught sight of Mrs. Tavers's stern visage. He almost felt guilty that his daughter would carry that austere image with her into her dreams. "Mrs. Tavers, you'll stay with Millicent until she falls asleep."

"Yes, milord."

It was only then that he realized Gina and Noel had slipped out of the room. He glanced at his daughter again. The flame flickering in the lamp beside her bed played over her delicate features. Millicent had inherited his eyes, his hair, but the rest of her delicate attributes had come from her mother.

When Millicent was a baby, he'd spent long hours watching her sleep. She was a marvel to him. He loved both his children, but a little girl had the power to wrap her father around her tiny finger.

He felt a need to protect her that he didn't experience when he thought of Noel. Naturally he wanted no harm to ever befall Noel, but he knew his son would be adept at looking out for himself. Upon what sort of man would he bestow the honor of looking after his little girl? No matter how much she grew or how many years she acquired, he would always think of her as his little girl.

Had Nathaniel Pierce felt the same way at one time regarding Gina?

The man had certainly done a lousy job of seeing after his daughter's welfare. Marrying her off to an impoverished nobleman and then squandering his own wealth without setting any aside for his daughter. What had the man been thinking?

He should have foisted her onto some unsuspecting man of wealth, regardless of title or position in society. Devon's title certainly didn't have the power to keep Gina warm, her stomach from growling with hunger, her body clothed in the finest of gowns.

Her body. Dear Lord, but she did have a sweet body. Swells, curves, and hollows that had driven him mad on their wedding night. He'd always shown such regard for Margaret in the dark beneath the blankets, respecting her modesty and only lifting her gown.

But with his Texas wife, he'd revealed every inch of her flesh, feasted on the sight of it.

His aching hand brought him to his senses. It was gripping the bedpost so hard he was surprised he didn't see indentations in the wood when he loosened his fingers.

He gave Mrs. Tavers a curt nod before striding from the room. He'd only bedded Gina because of the bargain he'd struck with her father. He certainly wasn't attracted to her, didn't want her in his bed.

Theirs had been a marriage of convenience, and the convenience had come to an abrupt halt with the death of her father. Or so he repeatedly tried to convince himself.

Perhaps, in retrospect, his canceling the conditions of the bargain had been a bit rash. But he had not gained the wealth her father had promised. It was only fair she not benefit beyond the title, of which he could not deprive her.

He stepped into Noel's room. The boy's eyes were fastened on Gina in a manner that could only be described as heroine-worship.

Did Mrs. Tavers normally tuck the lad into bed, or did he see to himself? If their situation were not so dire, the lad would have a valet. Perhaps Devon needed to speak with Winston. Surely one of the remaining servants would provide the service.

His eyes growing more round, Noel sat up and smiled so brightly that Devon feared his son might damage his jaws.

"Father, did you know that cousin Kit was a marshal? And that he fought in a duel with a bunch of outlaws?"

A *bunch* of outlaws? What sort of English was his child speaking? A bunch of grapes, perhaps—

"And he shot them all dead?"

Devon quirked a brow. His wife's cheeks grew rosy as she avoided his gaze.

"And he's a hero! He saved the whole town! I think it's splendid! I wish to travel to Texas when I grow up."

Devon cleared his throat. Kit had been sent to

Texas because his disreputable ways were distressing his father. He hardly wanted his son behaving in a similar manner.

"Did you know cousin Kit?" Noel asked.

"Of course. He is Lord Ravenleigh's twin brother. We played together as children, and while he was quite daring, I hardly think he was one to kill a *bunch* of outlaws."

"But he did," Gina said quietly. "His exploits are legendary."

"Another legend, countess?"

She gave him a beguiling smile. "At the center of which you'll find the truth."

"I wish we had legends," Noel said, fairly bouncing his bottom on the bed.

"We do have legends," Devon said, distressed to realize his son wasn't aware of them.

"What are they?"

"King Arthur and Robin Hood for starters."

"I didn't know they were legends. I thought they were only stories! Do you know them, Gina?" he asked, his eyes wide.

Devon ground his teeth together. They really were going to have to come up with a more appropriate name for her. The informality was beyond bearing. What sort of example was she setting for the heir apparent?

"No, I don't," she told Noel.

Noel bounded upright with such enthusiasm that Devon thought he might actually come off the bed.

"I can tell them to you. Shall I?"

The smile she bestowed upon his son as she

combed her fingers through his hair was almost breathtaking. He couldn't quite comprehend where it had come from. He'd certainly never seen it before.

"How about tomorrow? I think it's time we all went to sleep now."

Noel plopped back onto his pillow, and she brought the blankets up to his chin.

"I shall tell you about King Arthur first. And Merlin. He was a sorcerer. He knew magic!"

"He sounds very interesting." Bending over, she kissed his brow. "I look forward to hearing his tale tomorrow night."

She stepped back, as she had earlier in Millicent's room, a subtle movement of her eyes indicating that Devon could give no less to this child than he had to the other.

He strode forward, leaned over, and stilled. His son watched him with eyes the same shade as his. With his toothy grin, he seemed incredibly innocent and remarkably trusting. Trusting his father to ensure he would have a worthy estate to inherit.

Pierce's reckless gambling had ensured that Devon never could. Resentment rose like bitter bile. He brushed a quick kiss over his heir's brow. "Sleep well."

"I will, Father."

Noel bounced over onto his side. Devon lowered the flame in the lamp before striding from the room. He turned back in time to see Georgina bring the blankets up to Noel's chin.

She walked slowly from the room, as though she

loathed leaving it. He hadn't expected her to show such remarkable interest in his children. Although he supposed he shouldn't have been surprised. After all, the bargain had revolved around his willingness to give her a child.

She joined him in the hallway. "They're wonderful children, Devon."

He agreed wholeheartedly but found himself at a loss for words to express his sentiments. "I'll escort you to your chambers."

Her laughter tinkled around the hallway like a thousand bells at Christmas. "That's not necessary. I'll admit your house is about as big as the town I grew up in, but I can find my way to my room. Good night."

She headed for the stairs. He had this uncomfortable need to have her tuck him into bed. With long strides, he caught up to her. "I insist on accompanying you."

She shrugged and floated down the stairs.

"I find it difficult to believe you've never heard of Robin Hood or King Arthur. What sort of schools do they have in Texas?" he asked.

She gave him a sly glance. "I know all about Arthur, Lancelot, and Camelot. Not to mention Robin Hood and Little John."

"You lied to my son?"

"The truth would have removed the sparkle from his eyes. That'll happen soon enough as he gets older. Besides, what harm can come from allowing him to have the joy of believing he is the first to share with me stories of magic and good deeds?"

"None, I suppose. Still, I do not wish their lives disrupted overmuch. They have a routine, a schedule. Children need constancy."

"They need love."

"Which they have," he ground out.

They reached the bottom of the stairs, and he escorted her through the grand foyer. He grabbed a lamp from a nearby table and followed her into the east wing and up the stairs that led to the next level. A musty odor assailed his nostrils. This part of the house had lain dormant since Margaret's death.

Without her, he'd had no desire to host parties, to invite guests, to share his life with anyone. He could not remember the last time he had walked these halls.

Georgina came to an abrupt stop beside a door. He tried to envision what the room on the other side looked like, but he had no recollection of it. He was certain he'd seen it at some point in time. When his father had died, he'd taken a careful inventory, so he could determine what, if anything, he could part with.

She opened the door and peered inside. Then she turned to him with a smile. "It seems the servants have been busy. I have a lamp, a low fire, and the bed is turned down."

"Is there anything else that you require?"

"I need you to forgive my father."

"That's not likely to happen."

"Good night, then."

She slipped through the door and out of sight. He

briefly wondered if her request meant she had forgiven the deceitful bastard.

He strode back toward his study. He needed a good, stiff drink.

Chapter 14

Wearing her nightgown and wrapper, Georgina sat in a chair before the hearth. Even with the fire, the room held a chill that she associated with abandonment. She thought some time had passed since this section of the house had been used.

How appropriate that her husband would exile her here.

She didn't mind the loneliness. She'd lived with it long enough and thought of it as more of a companion than an enemy. She understood it, could almost reason with it.

She did, however, resent that Devon had no plans to allow her into his life or that of his children.

She was here in this decrepit old house that chilled her to the bone. Yet she could not help but feel that it possessed much potential if she was only willing to look below the surface.

Somewhere in the house, a clock began to chime. She counted each *bong* that echoed between the walls. Twelve. Midnight. The magical hour.

She should tuck herself into bed, as she had Devon's children. What a delight they were!

Watching Devon, she'd been struck by the various emotions playing over his features. At times he'd seemed almost in awe of his children, as though he was only just discovering they existed. At other times the love reflected in his eyes had caused her chest to ache.

Had her father known he was capable of such intense feeling? Her father had always placed love above all else.

"As long as I have your love, Gina, I'll die a wealthy man."

She'd almost forgotten his words. Glancing around her, she sighed. "Ah, Papa, what were you thinking when you started gambling again, knowing that Devon had married me expecting to share your wealth?"

And what was she thinking to remain in this situation when she still possessed a ticket that would provide her with passage back to Galveston? But there was the rub, as they said in these parts. Until she knew for certain that leaving was what she wanted, she'd forever look back and wonder.

Devon was not surprised that he'd awoken earlier in a grumpy mood. He'd not slept soundly. He did not like it one bit that Georgina was making him doubt his fatherly devotion. His children were happy and well cared for. They went to bed neither hungry nor cold.

He supposed his first thought upon arriving should have been to visit with them. He hadn't planned to see them right away simply because he trusted his staff to look after his children's welfare. He'd not needed to reassure himself that they were fine, because he'd had no reason to believe they would be otherwise. He'd had several things on his mind, but in hindsight he grudgingly acknowledged that Gina had made a valid point: Looking in on his children should have been at the top of his list of things to do.

As for tucking the children in at night. Well, again, he trusted Mrs. Tavers to make certain they were comfortable. Perhaps he would speak with her to ensure she shared a story with them before they went to sleep.

They'd certainly seemed to enjoy Georgina's tale of a fish with the power to turn a maiden into a mermaid. An enchanting legend. As for her tales regarding Kit . . .

Devon had heard his cousin had taken up enforcing the law in Texas. A strange undertaking for a man who had once taken pleasure in snubbing society's code. Devon had certainly not heard Kit was having duels with outlaws. He'd have to consult with Christopher regarding that matter.

It was one thing to share time-honored legends with his children. Quite another to fill their heads with fanciful stories about members of the family.

He had expected Gina to content herself with her wing of the house, a wing that did not hold his children. After they finished eating breakfast, he would have another meeting with her, so he could spell out her duties more precisely.

He walked into the large dining hall and stumbled to a stop. What the deuce was going on here?

A woman in a tattered dress stood at the top of a ladder, cloth in hand, dusting cobwebs. A red triangular scrap of material covered her head and hid her hair. She was swaying her hips with such enthusiasm he feared she might topple off the ladder at any moment.

He didn't know who she was, couldn't get a good look at her face, but he knew she wasn't anyone he'd ever had in his employ before now. Had his wife not understood when he'd explained yesterday that he had no funds with which to pay his servants?

Now she was hiring more?

He spun on his heel and strode from the room. He spied his butler in the foyer. "Winston, locate my wife and inform her that I wish to speak with her in my library immediately."

"Yes, milord."

His heart hammering against his chest, Devon stormed into his library and crossed to the window. Jerking the draperies aside, he stared at the forlorn landscape.

Margaret had asked his counsel on every household decision to be made, and here was Gina, after only one day, hiring servants, upsetting the natural order of things.

"You wanted to see me?" she asked.

His blood was thrumming through his temples so loudly he hadn't heard her arrival. "Did you not understand that you were not to hire—"

He spun around and froze, unable to believe his eyes. His wife stood before him in the tattered dress with the red cloth covering her hair and dirt smudged across one cheek and the tip of her nose.

"What the deuce are you wearing on top of your head?"

She snatched off the offending object to reveal the thick rope of her braid coiled around her head.

"A bandanna. Cowboys have a hundred uses for them. And I *did* understand that I wasn't to hire any servants. Is there anything else you wanted to discuss, because I have quite a list of things I want to accomplish this morning and—"

"What in God's name do you think you're doing?"

She gave him a gamin smile and waved the cloth in the air like a white flag. "I decided your house could use a little spit and polish."

He thought the top of his skull might explode. "Madam, my wife neither *spits* nor *polishes*."

Her smile withered. "This house is huge. You're short on staff, and those who are here are overworked. I wanted to help out."

He took a step toward her. He wished she'd rub that damnably distracting dirt off her face so this urge he felt to gently wipe it away himself would leave him. "You help out, madam, by delegating chores, determining which tasks are essential to the upkeep of the manor—"

"Gina!"

His daughter flew into the room and wound her arms around Gina's legs. Millicent wore rags and one of those abominable bandannas over her head as well!

She tilted up her smudged face and looked at Gina with evident joy. "I finished duthting the flowers. Now what?"

"Now you may go eat breakfast," Devon said succinctly.

Millicent snapped her head around, her eyes sparkling like jewels placed before the sun. "Father, I've already eaten."

"The children and I ate our breakfast together this morning," Georgina told him.

"I see."

Gina smiled at Millicent and cradled her tiny chin. "Go ask Winston what's next on the list while I finish speaking with your father."

"Are you going to give him chores ath well?" Millicent asked.

Gina cut a quick glance his way. "I don't think so. I imagine he probably has enough to do."

"I'll tell Noel what to do when he's finished with his chores." Millicent skipped out of the room as though she hadn't a care in the world.

"Tell me the heir apparent to Huntingdon is not wearing one of those abominations on his head," Devon ordered.

"Of course he isn't."

"Thank God." He started to turn away, then jerked back to face her. "You have my children doing manual labor?"

She rolled her eyes. "A little dusting and polishing. I'd hardly call that labor."

"Madam, there is a hierarchy in England of which you are obviously unaware. An earl's children *do not* dust. Nor do they dress in rags or cover their hair with scraps of cloth. You will put an end to this nonsense now!"

"They just wanted to help."

"They can help by remembering their place in society."

"There's nothing wrong with hard, honest work."

"Is that something your father taught you?"

He regretted his words the instant he saw the flash of pain cross her face. She'd loved the man, and he'd not meant to remind her of her recent loss. "I apologize. That was uncalled for."

She shook her head. "I don't know why he was unable to stop himself from gambling away everything he'd worked so hard to obtain. It had happened before, and I'd assumed he'd learned his lesson. I'll explain to the children that it's beneath them to help the servants."

She pivoted and walked from the room, back erect, shoulders squared. He dropped down into the chair behind his massive desk and wondered why she'd left him feeling as though he was the one who'd acted improperly.

* * *

In the end Georgina hadn't explained any such thing to the children. She knew children had a habit of speaking from the heart and not the head, which meant that at any moment, in their innocence, they could blurt out that they were too good to lift a finger to help.

Instead she praised them for the tasks they'd completed and asked if they'd like to escort her on a walk about the grounds while she decided what else needed to be done. But then Mrs. Tavers had appeared, and the children had been whisked away to do their lessons. Therefore Georgina was left to wander the grounds on her own.

And her imagination took flight. She'd never seen such lush greenery. Even though it was obvious gardeners were no longer employed to keep the grounds tidy, the land's wild disarray possessed an untamed beauty. Devon no doubt would say it had gone to ruin, but she appreciated the naturalness of all that surrounded her.

She enjoyed walking in England. Unlike Texas, where the heat was suffocating and the air often heavy, the weather here was usually pleasant. Even the rain was more of a mist than a deluge.

If her cleaning offended her husband, then perhaps she would garden. Not the lovely roses Lauren's mother was dedicated to, but something a bit more substantial, something useful. Corn, beets, peas, beans. She could section off some of the land, rig up a plow. Kneeling, she dug her fingers into the dirt, relishing the texture of good, rich soil.

By the time Devon realized her hobby didn't revolve around flowers, she'd have vegetables on the table.

She was determined not to be a woman of leisure. Unlike her husband, she was willing to work in order to gain a better life. She saw no merit in idleness.

Here more so than in London, their differences would stand out, but no one would see, so where was the harm?

For the first time since leaving Texas, she'd actually felt deliriously happy. She'd been doing something that made a difference. She'd been able to see the results of her efforts.

Damn him! He had no right to take that feeling of self-worth away from her. She would polish. She would dust. She would scrub. She just wouldn't do it in the main rooms, where he might happen upon her. But she would do it.

He couldn't expect her to sit on a pedestal all day. She shook her head. Of course, he expected it, but that didn't mean she had to oblige him.

She would have to plant her garden away from the house, so he wouldn't come across it in his wanderings. If he ever left the house. She had no idea what his day entailed. But if he didn't work, what *did* he do?

He excelled at rowing. His firm muscles indicated he did something more. But what?

In the distance, she caught sight of the stables. Since neighbors were as rare here as they were in

Texas, she assumed those were Huntingdon's stables. Wonderful. He'd mentioned he had two thousand acres. With a horse at her disposal, she'd be able to locate an out-of-the-way spot for her garden. The possibilities seemed endless.

Fisting her hands around her skirt, she raised it slightly and trudged toward the stables, the tall grasses snatching at her hem. She was grateful she hadn't worn one of her nicer dresses this morning.

It would be a while before she wore anything fancy. She was in mourning, and she would wear black to reflect her grief—not only for the loss of her father, but for the deprivation of her husband as well.

She'd been a fool to think the physical aspect of their relationship somehow reflected the emotional aspect. Devon had no doubt been reacting to his baser instinct. That he'd been considerate, taking the time to stir her passions to life, had been a blessing. But in his mind he'd probably been no more than a rutting stallion. He could turn her aside with the wave of his hand.

As much as she tried, she couldn't consider him cruel. He'd expected to receive funds as a result of his marriage to her, not debt.

Bending down, she plucked an errant yellow flower from its mooring in the rich soil. She imagined the field had been awash with color in the spring, but now only this tiny bloom remained, determined, holding on. She didn't know its name or its origin. She knew bluebonnets, Indian paintbrush, and an occasional cactus.

She hadn't bothered to learn much about England, because she hadn't planned to stay. She might still leave, once she'd determined the best way to make up for her father's fiasco.

She figured her father, loving her as he did, probably thought he was doing the man a favor by hitching him to his daughter.

But he hadn't walked in Devon's shoes, as she was doing now. Everywhere she looked, she saw his heritage, steeped in tradition. The generations that had come before stared at them from portraits hung on the walls. The manor house carried their fragrance, each adding to the one who'd come before. They'd all slept in the hand-carved beds, sat at the heavy mahogany table, and gazed through the windows at the rolling hills and fertile fields the Crown had bestowed upon them and placed in their keeping.

Her father couldn't have possibly understood Devon's desire to do right by those who'd come before him. Until she'd arrived here, she hadn't understood. She still didn't. Not really.

As she neared the stables, she saw four horses prancing in the corral. Only the large fenced enclosure probably wasn't called a corral here.

The dark bay coats of all four shone in the morning sunlight as though they'd recently received a good brushing. Their black manes glistened. They were beautiful creatures, no doubt bred for their sleekness and haughtiness.

Ah, yes, they knew they were gorgeous, tossing their heads, elegantly lifting their black tails. Just like their aristocratic lord, they weren't expected to work, as a cow pony would. Class distinctions in this country even extended to the animals.

Still, she appreciated good horseflesh and wondered what it would take to gain permission to ride one of these beauties.

She caught sight of a tall man, the sleeves of his white shirt rolled up, his black vest stretched taut across his shoulders, dumping oats into a wooden trough. As though she was back home, she stepped on a bottom slat of the fence, lifting herself off the ground, and crossed her arms over the top railing. "Excuse me, sir?"

The man jerked around, his face revealing a deep scowl. "What the devil are you doing out here?"

Georgina fought not to stare at her husband or display any measure of surprise at his performing such a menial task as feeding the horses. "Since I'm not allowed to clean the house, I decided to take a walk."

He narrowed his eyes and clenched his jaw before returning to his task. "The stable boy has been negligent in his duties," he tossed over his shoulder, as though to answer her unasked question as to what he was doing here.

She was surprised he was making right what the stable boy hadn't. She would have expected him to give the boy a good tongue-lashing and then to stand over him while he worked.

"The horses are beautiful, Devon."

He set the half-empty bag inside the doorway leading into the stable and strode toward her, his long legs quickly cutting the distance between them. "Indeed they are. Their papers are in perfect order. Aristocratic horses. Good bloodline."

"Am I allowed to ride them?"

She could have sworn a smile touched his eyes before he looked away from her. "Certainly."

"Is the stable boy around? I'd like to go for a ride now."

"I can saddle one for you." He crossed his arms over his chest and leaned back against the fence. "I should think Midsummer Moon should do well by you. She's a bit feisty but eager to please."

"I like her name. Do you plan to breed them?"

He shook his head, his gaze never leaving the horses. "No." He faced her. "I have to go into the village. You can ride with me, if you like. It's preferable to your riding alone and risking getting lost."

She smiled enthusiastically. "I'd like to see the village."

He gave a brisk nod. "Go change into your riding habit. I'll saddle two horses and bring them up."

She hopped off the fence, turned to go, then stopped and glanced back at him. She held up the tiny flower she'd discovered. "Do you know what this is?"

"Cowslip. In the spring you'll find them in abundance, along with bluebells and primroses. They're usually gone by now."

"It was the only one I saw." She backed up a step. "I have so much to learn about your country."

About him. She'd certainly never expected a proclaimed man of leisure to be pouring oats or saddling horses.

Hiking up her skirts, she ran back toward the manor, wondering if there was more to her husband than the civilized veneer he'd revealed to her in London.

Chapter 15

Devon decided he was undeniably insane, placing temptation within his reach. And Gina was certainly a temptation as she rode beside him.

He'd been unwise to invite her to go to the village with him. When she was nearby, he could easily forget that it was only a matter of time before she learned about everything he'd been reduced to doing in order to survive. With that knowledge would come thorough and complete disgust for him. Then she would avoid him as Margaret had.

He would experience much less pain if he were the one to put the distance between them. It would be easier to endure her disappointment in him if he grew accustomed to her aloofness and absence now, when she meant frightfully little to him. He needed them to spend as little time together as possible, because he could not risk allowing his fondness for her to grow.

And it would grow, because, God help him, she'd somehow managed to enchant him already.

"Papa will forgive me," she'd said when she'd stepped out of the manor house wearing a deep red riding habit edged with black.

Hardly mourning attire, but if he'd learned one thing about his wife, it was that she'd seldom stand on ceremony. He gave her a week, a fortnight at the most, before she did away with black altogether and began wearing whatever she pleased.

As he guided his horse alongside hers he readily admitted part of her appeal was her disdain for the rules. He had spent his life adhering to them, down to the letter, had never considered casting them aside even when they seemed archaic or inconvenient. They were the mortar that held his world together.

Of late, as his world was crumbling around him, he could count on the mortar remaining, providing him with the means to rebuild. He honored the rules she despised, because they provided constancy in an ever-changing world.

He glanced at his wife. With her hat poised at a jaunty angle, her back straight, her riding crop in hand as she properly sat her horse, she appeared to be a woman who easily fitted into his society. Further proof that looks could be deceiving.

He himself still looked to be a lord, although he'd tumbled off the pedestal long ago. Marriage to her was supposed to have helped him clamber back on. Instead he'd fallen farther down.

Nothing to be done about it now except to make the best of it. Although he hadn't a clue how he was going to manage that feat.

He watched as joy lit her eyes, and he realized it was that specific emotion that had caused him to turn his attention to her. He'd wanted to witness her expression when she first saw the village that had served his family's estate for generations.

"Is that the village?" she asked.

"Yes. Farmingham."

Grinning, she looked at him. "The houses are pink."

"Since medieval times, pink has been the preferred color for half-timbered buildings."

"Half-timbered?"

How differently she pronounced "half," harshly, as though someone had asked her to stick out her tongue and make some retched sound.

"They split logs in half and use them to form the frame for the houses."

"The village is quaint."

"Quite so. It's a peaceful place. You'll be quite safe coming here on your own. You should find a dressmaker, shoemaker, blacksmith, butcher, just about anything you might desire. Whenever possible, I prefer to support the villagers rather than the merchants in London. I would ask that you not purchase excessively. They keep a tally of our purchases, and I make payment at the end of the month. None of these people is in a position to wait long for debts to be settled."

"I'd hardly call myself extravagant."

Ah, he'd managed to offend her, if her tone of voice and the narrowing of her eyes into darkened slits were any indication.

"I meant no offense. I simply have no desire for these good people to suffer because I am not currently in a position to make good on all debts."

She studied him thoughtfully. "Are you here today to make payments?"

"Yes. Winston and Mrs. Cooper, the cook, made purchases for Huntingdon in my absence. I'm here to settle the accounts."

"I see." She glanced back toward the village. "I think I'd like to take a walk here."

Georgina had never felt comfortable in London, teeming with its people and conveyances. If the noise wasn't bombarding her, a putrid odor was. She never felt clean.

But here. Dear Lord, she thought she could easily fall in love with this place. The shops were small, beckoning, and the people were friendly. Word had quickly spread that she was "her ladyship."

"Ever so glad to see his lordship has taken a new wife," the butcher's wife had said. "High time, if you ask me, him bein' the good man that he is."

Unfortunately she couldn't stop herself from asking, "Did you know the first Lady Huntingdon?"

"Ah, that I did. Lovely woman. Absolutely lovely. And his lordship adored her."

Of course he had. Affirmation of his regard for his former wife was not exactly what she wished to hear. The woman was apparently perfect.

Georgina tried not to wonder how she might compare to Devon's former wife, and yet she could not help but feel inferior.

Comments made by others as she passed their shops reinforced her opinion that her husband was well liked by these people. As Margaret had been. She'd apparently purchased an abundance of items from them, which, considering their financial situation, had surprised Georgina. She would have expected the woman to show restraint, especially in light of Devon's earlier admonishment that she not spend excessively.

Perhaps he felt that rule did not apply to a woman he loved. She hated harboring the unkind thought about him or his deceased wife. Yet she could not see him taking his Margaret to task regarding any matter.

He'd excused himself to take care of his business, leaving her to wander the streets, peer into the shops. She'd been with him when he'd made payment at the butcher's, whom he called by name. He seemed to know everyone's name.

She didn't mean to spy on him, but he stood out, dressed in his frock coat with his top hat. A gentleman. His lordship. Lord Huntingdon. Her husband.

She couldn't help but feel proud watching him. He cut an exceptional figure whenever he stopped and spoke to one of the villagers. He never smiled but always appeared incredibly serious, as though his worries were many.

Her little vegetable garden wasn't going to do much to hoist his burden.

She watched, mesmerized, as he strode toward her, tugging on his gloves as though he'd removed them, though she knew he hadn't.

"I'm finished here," he said as soon as he reached her. "Are you ready to return to the manor?"

"Yes."

He extended his arm, and they strolled toward the blacksmith's, where they'd left their horses tethered earlier.

"I noticed several straw objects decorating windows, hanging over doors—cornucopias, dolls, horseshoes—do they have some meaning to the villagers?" she asked.

"How astute you are, countess. They're corn dollies. The villagers weave them out of straw to preserve the spirit of the corn and ensure a good crop next year."

"They grow corn around here?"

He gave her a wry grin. "Wheat and barley."

"Then where does the spirit of the corn come from?"

"When we refer to corn, we're discussing all grains."

"When I think of corn, I think of ears of corn."

"We don't grow your American corn here."

"Your tenants, then, those that farm, they grow wheat and barley?"

"Yes. Another month, and they'll be harvesting it."

"And then?"

"They'll begin preparing the soil for next year's crops. It's a constant cycle."

"For a man of leisure, you seem to know a lot about the process."

He gave her a pointed look. "I daresay I have discovered that one can gather an abundance of information while engaged in a casual morning ride. I should think you could attest to the same experience. Besides, I have years of watching tenants toil in the fields. I've managed to acquire a bit of knowledge regarding their labors."

Devon slipped his watch from his pocket, snapped open the cover, which bore his family's crest, and glared at the time: seven-thirty. Dinner was to be served precisely at seven.

He vividly recalled explaining that fact to his wife the day before. He scraped his chair back from the table, and the servant who had been standing at the ready to begin serving the meal flinched.

"Give me a moment to locate Lady Huntingdon, and then we shall begin."

He fought to walk calmly from the room. He hadn't seen Georgina since they'd returned from the village. He was hesitant to admit how much he'd welcomed her company. Although they'd spoken little, he'd still managed to find some comfort in her presence.

How different she'd appeared on horseback then. She'd been poised and confident. While she might not have known her way around a ballroom, she was comfortable around horses and the villagers. Her interest in the people was apparent. She never looked down her nose at anyone as Margaret had been prone to do.

Although he had to admit that she'd been equally confident with a dust rag in her hand. He still couldn't quite get over the fact that she'd been instructing his children in the art of cleaning.

In truth his children were not her responsibility. That they seemed to have taken an instant liking to her was understandable. They were children, eager to open their arms to affection, and Gina certainly seemed to have a penchant for bestowing affection. She was more giving than he cared to recognize.

He strode into the hallway, where Winston suddenly appeared. Thank God, someone in this household could be relied upon. "Winston, have you any notion where I might find my wife?"

"Yes, milord. She is dining this evening with the children in the day nursery."

He couldn't have heard correctly. He cocked his head. "Pardon?"

"Indeed, milord. I assumed her ladyship had discussed this change of plans with you and received your permission to dine with the children."

Winston had been in Devon's service too long to let on that he realized Devon had no earthly idea what his wife's plans were. "You're quite right. I seem to recall that indeed she did."

"As I thought, milord. With all the burdens you carry, it is little wonder you are not more forgetful."

"I shall just . . ." He considered returning to the

dining room to eat alone, but he had done that for the past three years. Solitary meals with his own thoughts echoing through his mind served as his only distraction.

It was not that he enjoyed dining with his wife, with her outrageous ideas concerning what was proper. It was that he preferred company, and as she was the only one available, then she needed to make herself available to him, not the children.

He realized Winston stood at attention, patiently waiting for him to finish debating his course of action. By God, if his wife wished to dine with the children, she could jolly well eat two meals then, because he wasn't dining alone.

If she couldn't provide him with money, she could provide him with conversation.

Taking them two at a time, he bounded up the stairs. He was completely unprepared for the sight that greeted him when he walked into the day nursery.

His children sat in small chairs at a short table. Gina also sat there, her knees close to touching her chest, as she listened intently to Noel rambling about Merlin's powers. Holding a glass of water, she was so focused on Noel she'd obviously not heard Devon's entrance.

He cleared his throat.

Georgina screeched. Her arm went up, as did the glass in her hand. The water sloshed around her, over her arm, her gown.

The children giggled. Devon swallowed his laughter, knowing from ten years of marriage to

Margaret that a startled woman's recovery included a dressing down.

But Georgina merely peered at him impishly while she carefully patted the moisture from her arm and bodice. Her eyes held no anger. She didn't scold him. On the contrary, she seemed glad to see him. He wondered how much longer it was going to take for him to realize that Georgina was completely unlike Margaret.

"I'm incredibly pleased you could join us, my lord."

Before he could respond that he had no intention of joining them but had merely come to fetch his wife, Millicent was out of her chair, her eyes wide, her hand tugging on his.

"Oh, Father, are you going to eat with uth?"

His gaze darting between his daughter and his wife, he knew he could not utter his true intent without harming his daughter's gentle heart—and he knew his wife knew that he knew it. Blast it!

The woman had a true gift when it came to manipulation. And a way of paying him back for startling her that made him want to throw his head back and laugh. He couldn't remember the last time he'd laughed with absolute impetuosity—or more to the point, had possessed any desire to.

He turned his full attention to Millicent. "You must forgive me for my tardiness, Lady Millicent. I seem to have misplaced my invitation."

She placed her tiny hand over her mouth and giggled.

"Here, Father, you must sit at the head of the table," Noel said, abandoning the chair in which he'd been sitting.

Devon had no idea that a square table could possess such an exalted position. Still, he sat beside Georgina and found his knees dreadfully close to touching his throat. Millicent sat across from Devon. Noel removed the doll from the last chair, a bowl of soup in front of her, and took her place.

"We're eating son-of-a-gun stew, Father," Noel explained.

"Son-of-a-gun?" he asked.

"Yes, sir. Cowboys eat it all the time."

"And we made it!" Millicent boasted.

Devon quirked a brow and looked at Georgina. "So not only have you taught my children to clean but to cook as well."

"I thought they would enjoy it."

"Taste it, Father," Millicent prodded.

With skepticism he studied the conglomeration of items surrounded by the thick juice in his bowl. Cautiously he spooned up a helping and brought it to his lips. One taste later, he was surprised cowboys didn't expire on the spot.

"Don't you think it's deliciouth, Father?" Millicent asked.

"Who wouldn't think that, Kitten?" he hedged.

"We made sourdough biscuits and fried apples," Noel added.

"Fried apple dipped in thugar," Millicent explained.

"Ah, now that sounds tasty indeed," Devon said. "I look forward to sampling dessert."

"We've already eaten them," Noel said.

"I would think dipped in sugar meant they were dessert," Devon mused.

"They were, Father, but since we were the cooks—" Noel began.

"We got to eat them firtht," Millicent finished.

Devon glanced at Georgina. "Are there no rules in this world you inhabit?"

"Only to make the most of each day."

"Am I to gather then that we do that by eating dessert first?"

"Sometimes."

"I'm not at all certain that's wise," he murmured.

He dropped his gaze to her mouth. He was incredibly tempted to feel her smile against his lips. He'd been a fool to taste her sweetness and then deny himself further enjoyment of it.

He should have bedded her as dispassionately as he'd originally planned. Perhaps then his body would not ache with his need for her.

He turned his attention back to his bowl of stew only to discover that his appetite had disappeared.

Chapter 16

Georgina drank her coffee, relishing the bitter brew. As mistress of the manor, she could dictate exactly how she wanted it prepared. As far as her husband was concerned, that's what she did.

Mrs. Cooper, however, knew differently. Georgina prepared it herself and brought it into the breakfast room before Devon arrived.

Sitting at her place at the table, she watched as her husband filled his plate with food from the sideboard. The offerings were not as abundant as they were at Lauren's house, but the variety was nothing to scoff at. Devon seemed pleased with the assortment, if the amount he piled on his plate was any indication.

She had a feeling in later years he was going to become as rotund as her father. He had an immense appetite for a man who did nothing all day.

She had yet to determine exactly what an earl did.

And her husband was as elusive as a shadow. Their paths seldom crossed except during meals. He had insisted she honor him with her presence during the morning and the evening meals.

She'd eat with the children in the late afternoon, then join him in the evening. If he knew she was spending time with the children, he voiced no objection and he went with her when she said good night to them, a silent sentinel standing at the foot of the bed while she regaled them with stories.

She found it odd that the longer they were here, the more distant he became, as though he was strengthening the wall he'd begun building between them in London. Lauren had mentioned he was reclusive, but Georgina didn't think he should feel uncomfortable in his own home.

He set his plate on the table and took his chair, barely casting a glance her way. He unfolded *The Times*, which Winston set at his place each morning. She'd been horrified to discover the butler actually ironed the newspaper "to set the ink for his lordship," he'd explained.

As though ink on fingertips was a crime.

She had no idea where he went when he left the table. A few times she'd searched for him, certain he was somewhere in this vast house, but she'd never been able to locate him during the day.

In the evening, after they'd put the children to bed, he'd retire to his library. She could find him there, going over his ledgers. But what he did with the remainder of his time was a mystery.

She planted an elbow on the table and cupped her

chin with her palm. "What do you do all day?"

He stilled, glaring at her over the edge of his newspaper, a forkful of eggs halfway to his mouth—a mouth framed by lips that had brought her immense pleasure. She'd never expected to miss the days and nights in London that they'd had together before her father died. Who would have thought they would be more like strangers the longer they were married?

"How I spend my day is not your concern." With precision, he shoved the fork into his mouth and then dabbed at his lips with his linen napkin.

"But how I spend mine is your concern?"

Glowering, he set his fork aside as though he feared he might bend it with his anger. "Impertinence does not become you."

"And you think being mad enough to spit nails might?"

He leaned forward slightly. "Pardon?"

She sighed in frustration. "Devon, I need something to do."

He straightened, studying her as though he couldn't quite determine what language she spoke.

"You are responsible for managing the household, overseeing the servants," he said.

She scoffed and rolled her eyes. "Which takes very little of my time. They know their duties. They don't need me poking my nose into their business."

"But you feel a need to poke your nose into my business?"

She slapped her palms on the table. "I don't know what your business is! I seldom see you. Surely there is something I can do around here to feel more useful."

"I daresay some sort of needlework is acceptable for your position."

"Needlework?"

"You are familiar with needle, thread, cloth, are you not?"

"Of course I am. Do you need something mended?"

He briefly slid his eyes closed, during which time she thought he might be counting. "The servants would mend my clothing. You would apply needle and thread to some sort of artistic endeavor."

"For what purpose?"

"To occupy yourself, as Margaret did. You might also read, pen letters, practice the piano. Genteel pursuits."

"Is that how Margaret spent her day?"

"Quite so."

"And you feel this is a worthwhile use of my time?"

"I daresay as much as possible you should give the appearance of being a lady of leisure."

"Why?"

"Because it is tradition, and without tradition you have nothing."

Before she could inform him of her opinion regarding his harrowing suggestions, Winston walked into the room and stood beside Devon's chair. He waited patiently to be acknowledged. Everyone was so polite that sometimes she wanted to scream.

"Is there a problem, Winston?" she asked, unable to stand the suspense a moment longer.

Only his lips moved as he responded, "I do not perceive a problem, milady, but a missive has only this moment arrived for his lordship."

Devon shoved back his chair. "I'll take it here."

"Very good, milord." Winston passed the letter to him and stood at attention, waiting for whatever else his master might require.

She couldn't determine Devon's emotions as he read. Why did everyone here have to keep such a stiff upper lip? Why hide their feelings?

"Alert the driver to ready the carriage. I need to travel to London immediately."

"Yes, milord."

Devon turned his attention to her. "The missive is from my solicitor. Someone has an interest in the London house. I need to see to the paperwork."

"Did you want me to go with you?"

She didn't think he could have looked more surprised if she'd suddenly stood and removed all her clothes, but he quickly banked down his astonishment.

"I assure you that your presence is hardly necessary."

"I know it's not necessary," she said quietly, "but I thought it might be welcomed. I'm sure this moment can't be easy for you."

"I think it would be best if you stayed here." He stood. "I shall be gone a few days."

He turned to leave.

"Devon?"

He faced her, his eyes devoid of emotion. For the briefest of moments during their wedding night, she'd thought he'd let down his guard and revealed the man behind the title, but now, standing before her, he was a stranger, keeping his emotions and thoughts in check. She desperately wanted to comfort him, but she didn't know how to reach him.

"I'm sorry things turned out as they did."

He nodded brusquely before striding from the room. She shoved her plate aside.

She didn't like the lurid thoughts entering her mind. She'd begun to wonder if his absences were an indication he had a mistress. He had to do something with his days. She was fairly certain he didn't take needle and thread to cloth.

If there wasn't a mistress here, was there one in London?

Georgina was surprised to discover that with Devon gone, she felt lonelier than ever. She shouldn't have even noticed his absence. After all, it wasn't as though they spent their days enjoying each other's company or their nights locked in a passionate embrace.

Yet the high-ceilinged rooms seemed to echo a bit more deeply, and the faces in the portraits seemed to glare down a bit more sternly than before.

As a rule, she preferred solitude. She'd been overwhelmed by the balls to which Lauren had dragged her. Enthusiastic, outgoing Lauren simply hadn't understood how Georgina could prefer the quiet of an afternoon or find contentment in sitting and talking with one person. Lauren was like a rose in full bloom gathering busy little bees around her. The more, the sweeter the honey.

Georgina more closely resembled the dandelion in the garden, clinging to the brick wall, hoping not to be noticed for fear of being plucked.

She didn't know why she felt as she did. Her parents had been kind and generous. She'd always known they loved her. But they had been older than the parents of most of the children her age.

Her father had often not been at home. He'd always been searching for the best get-rich scheme. She'd thought he'd found it, only to discover riches didn't last.

Her mother had ached from the years of picking cotton, her joints stiff. She'd preferred staying at home, and Georgina had spent much of her time in her mother's company. She was glad of it, because she had stories and memories, but she'd hardly been prepared for the swirl of social life in London.

She wandered through the house, surprised to discover that within some of the rooms she couldn't hear the rain at all while in others its steady downpour was a comfort.

She drew her shawl more closely around her. This drafty old mausoleum was cold. Marble floors and statuettes didn't draw in any warmth. She thought of her house in Texas—the one in which they'd lived before her father had decided to travel with the wind—so small that she could stand in its center and see every room. Her home possessed warmth that had little to do with the Texas heat. Cozy. Comforting.

As she entered the foyer, she spotted Winston talking with a young serving girl, Martha.

"Winston?"

He turned and approached her. "Yes, milady?"

"While the first Lady Huntingdon was alive, was the house always this cold?"

"Quite so, milady. I believe the chill is a result of all the marble, which has a tendency to absorb and reflect the cold."

She shook her head. "I'm not talking about the cold in the air. I'm talking about the atmosphere, the . . ." She waved her hand in frustration. "This house just doesn't seem to invite a person to kick off his boots and relax."

"I should be quite glad that it doesn't."

"Don't you ever feel as though you're walking through a museum where you're not allowed to touch anything?"

"There are many valuable pieces here. Touching them would risk destroying them."

"Quite right. We wouldn't want to destroy anything, now, would we?" she asked with a sarcastic edge to her voice. Heaven forbid that she should manage to wipe out the stuffiness that surrounded her.

"No, milady, we would not."

"Thank you, Winston."

"Anytime I might be of service, milady, do not hesitate to call upon me."

Leaving her frustrated, he walked away, while she headed for the stairs. How could she explain to these people what it was she wanted to create? But maybe what she was looking for came only from the warmth of love.

She stepped into the day nursery. The children were unnaturally quiet, busy at their studies. Young children should romp and play.

"Lady Huntingdon." The governess greeted her without emotion.

The children's heads bobbed up, hesitant smiles playing at the corners of their mouth. Thunder resounded, and Millicent's eyes rounded, her smile completely withering.

Georgina turned to the governess, who sat in a rocker with a book on her lap. "Mrs. Tavers, how are you this afternoon?"

"Quite well, milady."

"I'll be glad to watch the children if you'd like to get some tea for yourself."

"Milady—"

"I know. It's simply not done, but since his lordship is in London, I think it will be all right."

Mrs. Tavers set her book aside. "A spot of tea would be nice. Thank you, milady."

She waited until the woman had left the room before dropping into the rocker and holding out her arms. Millicent immediately popped up from her chair, hurried across the short distance separating them, and clambered onto her lap.

"Are you afraid of the rain?" Georgina asked.

Millicent bobbed her head.

"She fears the thunder," Noel provided. "At night, I sneak into her bed to protect her."

"Do you?" Georgina asked.

He nodded, although he didn't look all that brave himself. She held out her free arm. "I'm afraid of storms. Do you think you could sit on my lap?"

He was curled against her in the blink of an eye.

She began to rock back and forth, enjoying the slight weight of the children.

"When will Father be back?" Millicent asked.

"I'm not sure," Georgina confessed. "How would you like to go on a picnic when the rain stops?"

"A picnic? What's a picnic?" Noel asked.

"You've never been on a picnic?" Georgina asked.

Both children slowly shook their head.

"Do you ever go outside?" she asked.

"Oh, yes," Noel answered quickly. "We take a stroll in the morning and then in the afternoon."

A stroll? "Do you ever run?"

"We're not allowed to run," he said. "It's unseemly."

Georgina was horrified. "Have you ever climbed a tree?"

He shook his head.

She hugged them close. "As soon as the weather clears, I'm going to take you on a picnic. We'll run and climb trees."

"Will you climb trees?" Noel asked, obviously not certain whether he should be delighted or affronted at the thought of his stepmother hiking up her skirts and scrambling from limb to limb.

She smiled wickedly. "Of course."

"Will Mrs. Tavers?" Millicent asked.

"No, I think for our first picnic we'll leave her here."

Devon was barely aware of the speed with which the coach traveled over the rough country road toward his estate.

Selling the London townhouse—a house his grandfather had purchased as a young man—and allowing strangers to inhabit it had left a gaping hole in his chest. He had not expected it to be so incredibly difficult to apply his signature to the papers turning his home over to someone else's keeping.

An American no less. An American with three daughters, whom he wished to see married to someone of rank.

A *wealthy* American, who had paid the initial installment with cash. If Devon had not been already married, he might have found himself a suitable match with one of the daughters.

Instead he had a bit of the man's money to replenish his coffers—but for how long?

He'd paid off the debts Georgina's father had accumulated, because he no longer wanted those hanging over his head. He'd used a portion of the remaining funds to make good on his own London debts. It was unconscionable to force a shopkeeper to wait any longer than necessary for what was owed him.

As they did with most of the nobility, shopkeepers had all extended Devon credit in good faith. He did not want it bandied about London that he was not a man to whom credit could be offered. It was bad enough that news of it would be bandied about the countryside soon.

He glanced out at the passing scenery. The dwindling sunlight of late afternoon added to his melancholy. Life as the peerage had once known it was drifting away like smoke rising from an open fire.

If Christopher had not been investing in some of Kit's ventures in Texas, that branch of the family would no doubt be in as dire straits as Devon was.

Even with the selling of his London home, Devon felt as though he was only one breath away from drowning.

A sudden flash of waving arms in a tree and a high-pitched yell caught his attention. He stuck his head out the window for a clearer look.

Was that a child dangling from a branch in the tree?

By God! Was it *his* child?

He banged on the roof of the carriage, and his driver brought it to an immediate halt. Devon shoved open the door and climbed out.

"M'lord, what is it?" the driver asked.

Hands on his hips, Devon stared at the trees. How far had they traveled since his sighting?

"Did you see a child in the trees?" he asked.

"No, m'lord. My eyes were trained on the road ahead. It's been a bit bumpy, and I was working to avoid the ruts."

Devon took two steps forward. "I saw something."

"Probably one of the little farm urchins, m'lord. I'm sure he knows what he's about."

His driver was no doubt correct in his assumption. Still the hairs on the back of Devon's neck prickled with unease. "Wait here."

"Yes, m'lord."

With each step he took he felt his muscles slowly knotting from his calves all the way to his neck.

He saw bare arms as skinny as the twigs in the trees and almost as brown from the dirt that had gathered on them. He forced himself to take a deep breath as he neared the flailing arms that were reaching toward the ground instead of the sky. It would not do to startle the lad with an eruption of temper if what he suspected was true.

The child was dangling with his legs hooked over a branch. His chest was bare, and some sort of red markings marred his face, painted across his brow, cheeks, and nose like those on the Scottish heathens of old.

The boy's blue eyes widened. "Father, you're home!"

Devon's heart nearly stopped when his son swung up and shoved his legs off the branch, falling to the ground and landing with a heavy thump.

"Father! Father!" Millicent cried as she came scampering around the tree. Georgina followed closely behind her.

Was that the quill of a pen sticking out from behind his daughter's head and held securely in place by the abominable red bandanna?

Some of his irritation with the situation must have shown on his face, because both she and Georgina staggered to a halt. Devon jerked off his jacket and tossed it around Noel's bare shoulders.

"Get into the carriage," he ordered in a tightly controlled voice.

"But Father—" Noel began.

"Now," Devon stated flatly in a voice that brooked no arguments. His gaze alighted quickly upon the female members of his family. "All of you. Into the carriage *now.*"

Standing in the library, Georgina knew beyond a doubt that Devon was furious. More furious than she'd ever seen him. Angrier than he'd been when he'd discovered her father had gambled away his wealth.

The fury had been evident in the cold, hard stare he'd fixed on her once he'd followed her into the coach. As though she was a mother hen guarding her chicks, Georgina had wrapped her arms around the children, nestling them against her sides with the absolute determination to protect them from the consequences of his wrath.

Tiny Millicent had buried her face against Georgina's breast while Noel had fiddled with a button on his father's jacket.

Georgina had angled her chin defiantly, but she'd found it difficult to display righteous indignation with any success when war paint decorated her face. As soon as they'd arrived home, Devon had insisted she join him in his study.

She had refused, indicating her need to ensure that the children were seen to. She'd also wanted a moment to scrub her face.

She'd won that argument.

She had a feeling she wasn't going to win this one, regardless of what it was.

Devon had the look about him of a man who'd suffered far too many defeats of late and would do whatever it took to ensure victory this go round.

With her back as stiff as a poker, she stood before his desk, grateful her skirt hid her quaking knees.

He loomed on the other side of the desk, gripping the edges as though he feared if he released his hold that his hands would find their way to her throat. Anger darkened his eyes. The veins in his neck stood out in stark relief, and the tenseness in his face served to sharpen the angles that usually provided him with a handsome visage.

She could see his chest heaving. It was evident he was striving to tether his anger. She simply wished he'd release it and be done with it.

"What in God's name were you thinking to have my son, the heir apparent, the future Earl of Huntingdon, running about the countryside half-naked?" he asked in a tightly controlled voice.

"Half-clothed," she answered, grateful her voice didn't tremble.

His dark eyebrows shot together as quickly as a fired bullet. "Pardon?"

She swallowed hard and cleared her throat as quietly as possible. "It depends on how you look at him. You saw him as half-naked. I saw him as half-clothed."

"It depends on how *I* look at him? Madam, it is not *my* looking at him that concerns me. It is how our tenants may have seen him! How the villagers may have seen him! How someone from the peerage might have viewed him! I'll not have him referred to as the insane heir apparent who runs about the countryside half-naked—"

"Half-clothed."

"With paint smeared on his face and skinny chest." His gaze darted to the small stand where his pen usually rested beside the bottle of ink. "My daughter had a bloody quill pen stuck in her head!"

"It wasn't actually stuck in her head—" She quieted as he jerked his uncompromising glower to her.

"What in God's name were you thinking?"

"That they could use some fresh air and fun. I'd never heard them laugh, seldom seen them smile—"

"Do you not comprehend the gravity of your actions? Have you no concept of what it is to constantly be looked upon to set an example? Do you not understand the burden we carry upon our shoulders to be better—to always make the right decisions—to do what is best regardless of the consequences to ourselves?"

It wasn't fury she saw in his eyes, but fear mingling with disappointment and perhaps even a bit of self-loathing.

"This has nothing to do with my taking the children on a picnic." She placed her palms on the desk and leaned toward him beseechingly. "Devon, what's happened?"

"Everything is bloody well caving in on me!"

She leaped back as he swept his arm across the desk and sent everything crashing to the floor.

He stormed to the window, banged his fist against it, and bowed his head. His defeated mien caused a surge of compassion in her.

His harsh breathing began to lighten. "Leave, Gina. See to the children. I'm certain the terrifying journey with me in my carriage has left its mark on them."

"I've already seen to them. They're fine. Children recover quickly. Adults not as fast." She braved a step toward him. "Devon, tell me what's brought all this on?"

She watched the subtle shaking of his head, could see his throat working as he swallowed. "Please tell me," she said gently.

He released a long, slow, deep breath.

"It was harder to let go of the house in London than I expected. Three generations have lived there. I sold it to an American who paid me in cash. In cash. He has three daughters whom he wishes to marry off to a man who has a title. Three daughters with ample dowries."

"And you're thinking maybe you could have secured one as your wife if you hadn't settled for me."

If at all possible, he bowed his head farther and his shoulders slumped. "Please leave before I say something we'll both regret."

His unwillingness to voice his thoughts was as

devastating as if he'd said what he feared they'd regret. Why she would want to comfort this man, who always seemed to look to the darkness instead of the light, baffled her, but she did possess a strong desire to ease his burden. That he didn't want her help was painful. Why did he have to be unbearably proud?

"If you want a divorce—"

"Don't be ludicrous," he stated.

"But you'd be free to marry—"

"What heiress would want a man who sent his first wife to an early grave and could not hold on to his second? Besides, a divorce is a lengthy process. By the time you were rid of me, his daughters would be long wed."

She almost informed him that he'd misunderstood. She didn't want to be rid of him, rather she expected he would welcome being rid of her. Instead she said, "You're not responsible for Margaret's untimely death."

"Shows what you know," he muttered.

What she didn't know, what she'd never thought to ask was how the woman had died, although she was relatively certain he had nothing to do with her demise.

"Did you use a knife or a gun?" she asked.

He snapped his head around and glared at her. "Pardon?"

"You said you were responsible for her death. I was trying to determine what sort of weapon you used."

"I didn't murder her, but neither was she happy with this life."

"She took her own life then?"

Shaking his head, he turned his gaze back to the window. "She fell ill one winter. Lacking the will to live, she succumbed to the disease. Had I managed to ensure her happiness, she would have fought more valiantly."

"You can't possibly believe—"

"I disappointed her, countess, beyond measure. There are aspects to our life of which you are not aware. Suffice it to say that Margaret was a genteel woman and I failed her."

Dear Lord, but he'd placed the woman on a pedestal from which she should have long ago toppled. How could he not see that? Margaret had his love, his children, and their love. She'd been wealthy beyond measure, taking for granted all the things that Georgina dearly desired.

It was hardly fair that she found herself caring for a man who would never care for her, who was so blinded by his first love that he could not see that Margaret had been undeserving of him. He would defend her to the death.

Georgina knew she could never compete, could never convince him that the woman hadn't deserved him, and so she retreated.

"About dinner—"

"Serve whatever you wish," he interrupted.

His voice carried no emotion, and she thought she might have preferred him angry. It was unsettling to hear the emptiness.

"While you were away, I invited the children to eat in the main dining room with me. I'd like for them to continue eating with us there."

He waved his hand in a gesture that seemed to take all his strength. "Do whatever you wish. Nothing matters any more."

She considered arguing everything mattered and mattered to a far greater extent, but she didn't think he was in the mood to listen or heed her words of wisdom. As quietly as she could, she left the room, left him to his misery, to his demons, to the memories of his dead wife.

Chapter 17

Georgina was grateful Devon did not appear to be inclined to inflict his foul mood on his children any more than he already had.

She was surprised he'd shown up for dinner at all. He looked beleaguered, sad, embarrassed.

As they all sat at the dining room table, quietly eating, she contemplated his earlier outburst. She had assumed poverty carried with it a certain burden because one never knew from where the resources for providing food, warmth, and housing would come.

She'd never considered living up to expectations as a burden. She'd always wanted to please her father, but she'd always seen her actions as more of a gift, not a requirement of his love.

She wished she knew how best to help Devon. Even when he'd thought he was going to have her father's funds in hand, he had not seemed happy.

What was the value of money when there was no happiness?

Even when her family had been as poor as dirt, they'd been happy. Certainly life was easier when one had money. But joy was something that came from inside a person, not from the things surrounding him.

Devon was right. There was so much about his way of life that she simply couldn't comprehend.

During the third course of the meal, Devon cleared his throat, and both children jumped in their chair, giving him sideways glances. He visibly relaxed, allowing the scowl he'd worn all evening to drift into oblivion.

"I presume you children were pretending to be Indians this afternoon," Devon said drolly.

"No, Father," Noel answered. "We were acting out the Boston Tea Party. Do you know the story?"

Georgina saw his fingers tighten around his fork as he cast a quick glare her way before turning his attention back to his son. "I am well versed in that tale of traitors—"

"Heroes," Georgina interrupted.

With precision, he lifted his napkin from his lap and wiped his mouth. She was almost willing to bet he was attempting to hide a smile.

"I suppose it depends upon your perspective," he said.

She angled her head. "Exactly. Had England won, no doubt history would have shown them to be traitors. Since the colonies were victorious, they were rebels fighting in a just cause."

He cleared his throat and returned the napkin to his lap. "I see."

She wondered if he really did understand her explanation or if he was merely placating her. Either way, his mood seemed to have lifted, and she much preferred to look at him when he wasn't scowling.

Millicent shifted on the pillows in her chair. She'd needed a little boost to be able to eat properly at the adult table as she called it. Georgina wished Devon had been here to see the delight in his daughter's eyes the first night she'd been granted permission to eat in this room.

"Father?" Millicent asked hesitantly.

He gave her an indulgent grin. "Yes, Kitten."

She jutted out her lower jaw. "I lost my tooth."

Along with her lisp.

"You certainly have. Splendid."

"Gina told me to put it under my pillow. I did. And guess what?"

He shook his head. "I can't imagine."

She placed her fist on the table and slowly uncurled her fingers. "A fairy brought me a ha' penny!"

"I've never heard of such a thing," he said.

"Gina said the fairy must have followed her from Texas, and perhaps when I lose my next tooth, it'll pay me a visit as well," Noel told him.

Devon sat back in his chair. "Perhaps I should knock out a few of my teeth," he murmured.

"The fairy only visits those who believe in magic," Georgina said, "and you, my lord, are too cynical."

"Cynicism protects the heart."

"No, my lord. It imprisons it."

"Once again, my sweet, one's perspective seems to come into play."

She was close to believing he was actually beginning to enjoy the conversation.

The grandfather clock in the hallway struck midnight. Devon shoved the ledger aside and rubbed his stinging eyes.

He'd perused accounts since dinner and had been unable to find a shred of hope for salvation in the entire mess.

Perhaps he *would* knock out a few of his teeth and place them beneath his pillow.

He was exhausted and disappointed. But more, he was ashamed of his circumstances, which had forced him to marry for money alone—although, he reluctantly admitted, Georgina was turning out to be a bit of a gem.

He had little doubt she could match angry retort for angry retort, and yet she'd seen through his anger and probed for its cause.

He'd never displayed his bad temper in front of Margaret. The very thought was inconceivable. She'd been a lady of the highest regard, sheltered, protected from the harshness of the world.

He could not help but believe the shame of his poverty had destroyed her as effectively as her illness. She'd simply had no desire to continue on in the only world he could provide. So he carried the burden for her death, held himself accountable, and was often overcome when the guilt reared its ugly head at the most inopportune moments.

Yet Georgina took their situation in stride, as though it was merely an inconvenience instead of the rapidly approaching demise to a way of life. He knew no other.

And that scared the hell out of him.

She'd seen that as well. It was frightening how well the woman was coming to know him, even though he kept her at a distance. What in God's name would she discover if he allowed her to get close?

And what would he discover about her?

She had seemed tough when she'd laid out the conditions that accompanied her agreement to marry him. He had not suspected then that she was as soft as a goose down pillow on the inside. The manner in which she'd hugged his children against her as they'd driven home—by God, she'd been a lioness fiercely protective of her cubs.

Her delicate nostrils had flared in warning, and he'd dared not utter a word during the journey for fear he might imperil his life. His anger should have increased. The very notion that she expected him to direct his fury toward his children! Instead he'd admired her determination to shield them.

When he married her, he'd expected her to have little interest in the children. Although her father had indicated she wanted her own, Devon had not considered that his would intrigue her and that she would want to spend as much time with them as she did.

He hesitated to admit that he'd enjoyed having his children present during dinner. They brought sunshine into the dreary room. And God knew he could use all the sunshine he could muster.

With a deep sigh he stood and stretched. The clock had stopped its *bonging* some time ago. It was time he turned in for the night. No amount of staring was going to bring him a solution this evening.

He ambled into the hallway, not in any particular hurry. He regretted the tantrum he'd thrown that afternoon. Regretted so many things.

He was surprised to notice the candles in the chandeliers were still alight. He would have to instruct Gina that her wifely duties entailed ensuring that the servants extinguished all flames before they went to bed.

Then he spotted her.

Lying on the floor in the middle of the foyer, a blanket spread beneath her, her head cushioned by a pillow.

He was unprepared for the warm pleasure that flowed through him and the easing of the loneliness that seemed to be such a part of him these days. Not wishing to startle her, he softened his step until he was near enough to see her more clearly. She was staring at the ceiling.

He crouched beside her. "What are you doing?"

She smiled gently. "I've been intrigued by the paintings on the ceilings since I arrived, but I get a crick in my neck when I look at them for too long." She shrugged. "I decided to indulge myself and stretch out here so I can gaze on them for as long as I wanted."

Chuckling, he sat beside her, raised his knee, and

draped his wrist over it. "You're unlike any Englishwoman I've ever known."

"Thank you."

"I'm not quite certain that I was offering you a compliment."

"I am."

She appeared incredibly smug. She wore a wrap over her nightgown. He could see the buttons that ran up the front and came to a stop just beneath her chin. His stomach clenched as he remembered loosening those perfect pearls until they revealed the velvety softness of her skin beneath.

He swallowed hard in order to free his voice. "Why these particular ceilings?"

"Because they were next."

"Pardon?"

She slid her sparkling gaze toward him. "I've spent some time on the floor in all the hallways in the east wing. The foyer was next before I moved on to the other areas of the house."

"The floor must make for an uncomfortable bed."

"I don't sleep here. Usually I don't even study the paintings for very long, but these seemed sort of sad. I wonder what the artist was thinking."

He lay down beside her, rested on his elbow, and squinted at the painting of cherubs and unicorns in a mystical garden. "I imagine he was thinking, 'I hope I don't jolly well fall off this scaffold.' "

Her soft laughter wove around him, through him. A delightful lilt that drew his attention back to her. She fell into immediate silence when he tucked behind her ear a stray strand of hair that had escaped her braid. "What do you think he was thinking?" he asked quietly.

"I think he thought it was a shame unicorns no longer existed."

Their faces were incredibly close, her eyes amazingly large.

"I suppose you believe in unicorns," he murmured.

She nodded slightly. "I believe in all good things."

"So innocent." He heard her breath catch as he trailed his finger along her chin, her first weapon of defiance. "I owe you an apology for my outburst this afternoon. It was totally inappropriate under the circumstances. You were merely taking the children on an outing, and I—I overreacted."

"I have to apologize, too. I haven't been very understanding about my father's failure to uphold his end of the bargain. I knew you were angry, but I didn't realize the extent to which he had harmed you."

"I was searching for a quick solution to a long-term problem. With the money I made from the sale of the townhouse, I was able to pay your father's debts."

She furrowed her brow. "You paid off my father's debts?"

"As well as a goodly portion of my own. If we are frugal, we should be all right for a short time."

She rolled onto her side and tucked her hand beneath her cheek, an incredibly innocent pose.

"You strike me as a clever man. How did you find yourself in this predicament of near financial ruin?"

"*Near* financial ruin? Sweeting, I'm in the depths of it."

"How did it come about?"

He retrieved the strands of hair he'd placed behind her ear earlier and began to toy with them. "The world has grown smaller. Crops that were once ours to produce are grown elsewhere and shipped in. The product is cheaper. The tenant farmers can barely make their rent, even though I continually lower it."

"Then kindness has made you a pauper."

"No, my father made me a pauper."

"How so?"

The light from the flickering flames burning in the candles overhead danced over her features, softening the sharp lines of her nose and chin, making her cheekbones less prominent. Just as the firelight in the hearth had on their wedding night.

She was a woman who belonged in a bedchamber, shrouded in shadows, writhing on satin sheets, calling out his name. How easy it had been to cast himself from her bed when her father's breach of faith had sliced his pride to ribbons. How difficult now to cast his pride aside and ask to be welcomed back into her bed.

"My father took little care in anticipating future needs. He married for love. My mother brought little to the family coffers." He hesitated, wondering how she would handle the remainder of his tale.

"And you did the same," she said quietly. "With your first marriage."

"Yes," he rasped. "I was young and too full of myself to put the greater good ahead of my own desires."

"I think you're wrong. Nothing is more important than love."

"You don't understand our society."

"Were you happy with Margaret?"

"For a time. Until she realized the truth of our situation and accepted the ghastly prospect it might never improve. My love did little to ease her misery. It is better not to have it, I think."

She looked at him as though he was daft.

"Given the choice between love and money, you would choose money?" she asked.

"I have already proven my current preference, have I not?"

He knew he'd spoken too freely, revealed too much when pity touched her eyes.

"Don't look at me like that," he ordered as he shoved himself to his feet. "I do not desire your pity."

But as his strides carried him away from her, he feared pity was all that remained for him to receive from any woman.

Georgina galloped the dark bay mare over the lush countryside until its sides were heaving from the exertion and her body was aching. Unable to locate the stable boy, she'd simply taken matters into her own hands and saddled the horse herself.

While she contented herself with a stroll most days, today she'd felt a driving need to ride, to travel farther than she ever had . . . she'd have gone all the way back to Texas, if only an ocean hadn't stood in her path.

Drawing back on the reins, she slowed the mare to a plodding walk.

A week had passed since Devon had returned from London. She saw less of him now than she had before. He joined her and the children for breakfast and dinner.

But he was "out and about" during the day. To her continual inquiries regarding what he did with his day, he'd simply respond, "I have things to which I must attend."

Those *things* kept him away from the house. She didn't want to contemplate that one of his activities might involve a mistress. Yet he arrived home as immaculate as he appeared at breakfast. Too clean. Too tidy.

He was hiding something. She'd gamble her life on it.

And the only thing she could conceive of a man wanting to hide was his mistress.

Perhaps he had a woman in the nearby village.

She considered confronting him with her suspicions, but he'd made it clear they no longer shared a life. He remained with her because of a document and his desire not to have scandal surrounding his name.

As for her reasons for staying, they were more difficult to explain, to understand. She couldn't fathom why she hadn't already packed up her things and returned to Texas.

She'd survived hunger and cold. And a Texas

winter wasn't nearly as frigid as marriage to a man who wanted nothing more from her than money.

On their wedding night she'd actually held out hope that his feelings for her would grow. Not enough to include love, but fondness at least.

He'd been kind and gentle. And passionate. She'd almost believed he wanted her in his bed.

A notion that had died along with her father.

Indebtedness had prompted his solicitousness.

Yes, indeedy. She ought to gather up her belongings and head home, where she knew how to play the game.

Here the apparent rules and rigidity of class distinctions confused her.

Sometimes she thought Devon looked at her with a bit of caring. At least she'd thought that as he sat beside her in the foyer at midnight, studying the paintings on the ceiling. He'd appeared amused, maybe even glad to visit with her. And a little lonely.

He seemed to carry a heavy burden, and she didn't know how to help him when she understood nothing about it.

He had proclaimed that gentlemen didn't work.

Then what in God's name did he do all day, and why in tarnation couldn't he do it at the house?

Her musings came to an abrupt halt when she spotted the workers in the field. A longing for the familiar had her guiding her horse toward them.

Several men were swinging scythes, cutting what appeared to be wheat. Or corn, she supposed with amusement, was how they would refer to it.

One man in particular caught her attention. His

clothes, a tight fit, were more worn than the others. Sweat dampened his broad back as he wielded the scythe as though he thought to cast out demons.

He was obviously the leader of the group, working with more determination and fury than the others did.

She wondered if this land belonged to her husband and if he was aware he had such an extraordinary worker in his employ. He certainly needed to be told.

One by one the other men stopped, removed their hats, and crumpled them against their chests. But this one man continued on, as though nothing could deter him from getting the crop harvested.

Suddenly he stilled, and obviously catching sight of his comrades, slowly turned.

The battered brim of his hat cast a shadow over his eyes, but she still felt the intensity of his gaze as he strode toward her.

When he neared and lifted his face toward her, the utter and complete mortification etched into his features almost unseated her.

"What are you doing here?" Devon demanded.

She couldn't take her gaze from the beads of sweat coating his throat, the dirt pressed into the tiny lines fanning out from the corners of his eyes, the rope of muscle in his forearms as he held the scythe in a white-knuckled grip.

"I . . . uh, I wanted to see the countryside." She looked out over the land before returning her attention to him. "This is where you spend your days."

She watched the muscles in his throat work as he

swallowed. "Go home, countess. We'll discuss this matter after dinner."

"My riding or your working in the fields?"

He looked as though she'd just cut him off at the knees. Her heart restricted. "Devon—"

"Go home, countess. *Now.*"

He spun on his heel and strode back toward his men. He shouted an order, and the men immediately returned to work.

She urged her horse into a lope. Obviously her husband did have a mistress. A very demanding one.

The land.

Chapter 18

Standing at the window in his library and staring at the moon, Devon considered lying to his wife. He contemplated explaining that what she'd witnessed today was an aberration. But in the end, he decided she deserved the truth. And if what little respect she might have held for him deserted her, so be it.

Dinner had been a beastly uncomfortable affair. The children had rambled about their day, lessons taught, stories told. Gina had listened intently, giving her usual delighted praise. But she'd seldom glanced at him—as though she found him as disgusting as he found himself.

Each morning he arose while the moon still cast a faint glow and went to the fields. He changed clothes in a barn when he arrived and before he left. He worked for an hour or two before returning home. Breakfast. Then back to the fields.

Until today only those who worked beside him had known what he did. Their silence bought them their positions.

Now the whole county would know.

Turning from the window, he met and held his wife's gaze. "I had hoped to spare you the shame of learning your husband is little more than a common laborer."

Obviously in stunned astonishment, she sat on the edge of the chair, her hands folded in her lap, her lips slightly parted, her brow furrowed, and her eyes blinking rapidly.

"In light of my confession, if you find it intolerable living here . . ." What? What could he offer her? A divorce? Separate living arrangements? Passage back to Texas? Each suggestion seemed wholly inadequate, only worsening the situation.

He plowed his hands through his hair and dropped his gaze to the floor. "Christ, Gina, I don't have anything to offer you that could begin to make up for this deception."

"You think I'm upset because I saw you working in the fields this afternoon?" she asked.

He lifted his gaze to hers. "How could you not be? Your father thought he'd arranged for you to marry a gentleman. A gentleman does not work until his hands bleed and his back aches in agony. He doesn't awaken before the sun in hopes of getting in additional hours that might make a difference. He doesn't pore over his books until midnight, hoping he'll discover something he missed that might better his plight."

Gracefully she rose and approached him. She took his hand and trailed her fingers over the calluses, which had grown more prominent since his return to the fields.

"A gentleman is supposed to have soft hands?" she asked.

"Of course. I was surprised you didn't notice on our wedding night that my hands weren't . . . as they should be. Since you didn't mention the fact, I thought perhaps I'd succeeded in distracting you."

A warm smile played across her lips. "Oh, you did indeed distract me."

Lifting her gaze to his face, she brushed his thick, black locks from his brow. "Your face reflects its battle against the wind and the sun. It makes you stand out in a ballroom."

"Should anyone ask, I attribute it to hours spent hunting instead of days spent toiling in the fields."

"I thought you had a mistress, that you were spending your days with her."

"Dear God, where would I find the energy?"

She smiled fully then, and it hit him that she wasn't responding with a tantrum, as Margaret had when she'd noticed his hands losing their softness and the lines in his face growing deeper.

"How long have you been working in the fields?" she asked.

"Five years now."

"You hoped my father's money would get you out of the fields."

"I hoped—eventually—that it might. I wanted to purchase a mechanical reaper. A thresher. Five men can cut two acres in a day. I wanted more."

He didn't think it was possible for her smile to grow any fuller, but it did. She clapped her hands together and spun away from him.

"I can't believe this," she said.

He wasn't quite sure what to make of her reaction. "I realize you must be horrified."

She twirled back around. "Horrified? I'm delighted. I thought you were a lazy no-account waiting for someone to rescue you. Instead you're working hard to better yourself. I respect that."

He narrowed his eyes. "I am titled. That alone should have caused you to have had a measure of respect for me."

Confusion clouded her eyes. "Devon, I honestly don't know what I felt for you. It's not that I didn't respect you. I just didn't feel as though I really knew you. I only knew I wished that I did."

He sighed with resignation. "Well, now you know."

Devon swung the scythe with practiced ease.

He enjoyed the solitude that accompanied him at dawn. The other workers arrived a bit later, so he was alone to work as he saw fit. Usually at a brisker pace than those he hired.

He encouraged them, kept up a steady rhythm as an example, but always tried not to outdo them by much. He didn't want a man to leave his employ because he felt he was being ridiculed or made to look incompetent.

This morning, however, he worked at a slower

pace, his mind constantly drifting to last night.

He hadn't expected his wife to understand. He'd certainly never entertained the notion that she'd curl up in a chair before the hearth and ask him pointed questions about his crops, his yields, and the pattern of his seasons.

What truly amazed him was that she'd not only appeared truly interested in his answers, but she'd apparently comprehended their significance.

A horse's whinny caught his attention. Casting a glance over his shoulder, he saw Gina sitting astride the dark bay mare, holding a wicker basket in her lap.

"What are you doing here?" he asked as he walked toward her.

"I thought it would save you some time if we had a picnic here."

"I'm not certain I've ever heard of a picnic at dawn," he said as he took the basket from her. Although he wished she wasn't here to witness his efforts yet again, he was hungry enough to bring forth his manners. "I rather think it's a splendid idea."

Raising his hands to help her dismount, he noticed they were already grimy and dirty.

"One moment." He wiped them on his trousers, not that it did much good.

"Honest dirt doesn't bother me, Devon," she said quietly.

He looked up at her. "It'll ruin your dress."

"Not this one. It's old enough to go on the rag heap."

Chuckling, he helped her to the ground. Only Georgina Sheridan wouldn't bother to dress in finery for a picnic. She wore no gloves, and the hat perched on her head closely resembled his—a wide-brimmed beastly thing with no adornments whatsoever. He supposed she was more concerned with keeping the slowly rising sun off her face than appearing elegant.

Although he seemed to recall she'd worn a fanciful hat the day before. But then no one was likely to spot her at this time of morning. By the time they'd finished eating and she was headed back to the manor, a few of the villagers would be out and about, but he wasn't overly concerned with them sighting her.

Carrying the basket and a blanket in one hand, with his other hand resting against the small of her back, he guided her to a portion of the field they'd cleared the day before, near evening. He was hard pressed to explain why he was pleased she was here.

She was correct in her assumption—her actions would allow him to lose little precious time. He didn't have to wash up, change clothes, ride back to the manor, eat, ride back to the fields, and change clothes. His clandestine activities were wearisome at times.

He spread the blanket over the ground. Before he could assist her in sitting, she'd made herself comfortable and was scrounging around in the basket. He dropped down beside her.

"Give me your hands," she ordered.

"They're filthy, Gina."

She bestowed upon him a dazzling smile. "I expected that."

She flattened a towel over her lap. Before he could argue further, she took his hand and wiped a damp cloth over his palm, his fingers, and his knuckles. He could well imagine that when she'd begun her journey, the cloth had been hot, because a trace of warmth remained.

Guiltily he gave himself up to her tender ministrations. Margaret had grown to despise his coarse hands. Gina stroked them as though she considered them something of a marvel.

After she'd removed every bit of dirt to her satisfaction, Gina patted his hands dry with the towel she'd placed in her lap.

"Thank you."

"My pleasure," she said, reaching into the basket.

He honestly believed it had been—almost as much as it had been his. He could not fathom the contentment hovering around her, as though she considered eating in a field no different from eating in a park.

"You won't have as much of a selection as you have at home, but I figured what we lacked in choice, we could make up for in abundance," she said.

Home. Strange how he'd never truly thought of Huntingdon as home. His family's ancestral estate. The manor. The albatross around his neck that he dearly loved. But he'd never considered it home.

She set out an assortment of meats and pastries. "No plates. Just pick up what you want and eat it with your fingers."

"How frightfully civilized," he murmured as he reached for a slice of ham.

She brought out a jar wrapped in a towel and promptly poured some into a china cup. With one of her rare gamin smiles, she extended the delicate cup toward him.

The absurdity of sipping his tea as he sat on an old blanket in the middle of a field while the sun was only just clearing the horizon almost made him laugh. All that stopped him was the realization he'd nearly forgotten how.

The last thing she placed before him was *The Times*. Although too many dawn shadows prevented him from seeing the words clearly, he did appreciate her thoughtfulness. He set it aside. For the moment he decided he'd prefer to read her.

Stretching out on his side, he raised himself up on an elbow. He saw little point in pretending to be a gentleman at this precise moment. "What did Mrs. Cooper say when you asked for a picnic basket at this beastly hour?" he asked.

She nibbled on a crumpet. "She did her usual *harrumph*, but when I explained it was to become the new morning ritual she fetched the basket and helped me prepare the food that I wanted to bring."

"You can't bring me breakfast every morning."

"If you don't want to eat breakfast out here, then I'll have it served earlier, before you leave."

"You can't do that."

"Why not?"

"For one thing, you can't change the staff's routine."

"Why?"

"Because it's simply not done."

"Fine. Then I'll cook breakfast for you before you leave the house."

"You can't—"

"But I can. I know how to fix flapjacks, griddle-cakes, sourdough biscuits, gunslinger's scrapple—you name it, I can cook it."

He shook his head in amusement. "Gina, it's not that I think you're incapable of cooking. Rather, you are the lady of the manor and therefore you do not cook."

"It's ridiculous for you to leave the house, work for a couple of hours, and then come back just to salvage your pride. If they're *your* servants, I don't understand why they can't serve your needs when they change."

He supposed she made a compelling argument. "All right. You may instruct Mrs. Cooper to begin serving breakfast two hours earlier."

"Splendid."

He thought he heard a great deal of triumph in her delivery of that one word with a trace of British accent. Perhaps he'd make an Englishwoman of her yet.

He sipped the tea, which was rapidly cooling in the chill of the morning. Sitting up, he hastened to finish the meal, so she could be on her way. No sense in making her suffer any longer than necessary simply because he enjoyed her company.

"What's the wagon for?" she asked. "I didn't notice it yesterday."

"I have a man who tosses in the cut wheat and hauls it to a nearby barn. He was making his first trip when you stopped by."

"I can do that."

He nearly choked on his muffin before forcing out, "Do what?"

"Put the wheat in the wagon and haul it to the barn."

He downed the remainder of his tea in order to unclog his throat. "Don't be absurd." He placed the cup in the basket.

"Then I'll chop the wheat."

He looked over his shoulder at her, not certain if she was infuriatingly frustrating or delightfully charming. "You are my countess. You do not toil in the fields."

"Why not? You're my earl and you do."

"I have explained to you why I must. I take no pride in the fact that I must—"

"You should," she cut in.

"Should what?"

"Take pride in your efforts."

He'd decided. She was infuriatingly frustrating. "My family is made of generations of gentlemen. We do not *have* to labor. They would be horrified to see me do so now."

"I don't think so."

"Because you don't understand Englishmen. Your father wanted better for you. You're not to blame because he didn't search harder for it, but I'll not allow you to sully yourself in the fields."

She placed her hand over his, and everything within him stilled.

"Devon, don't you understand that I admire what you're doing out here? You're trying to save your family's estate with hard work."

"*My* hard work shall suffice. I see no reason for you to labor in the fields."

"But I want to! I've picked cotton from 'can see to can't,' and by God, nothing is harder than that. I've spent too many days to count bent over, plucking bolls with bleeding fingers, while the sun—hotter than blazes—beat down on me. I helped my mother cook meals for a hundred farmhands, scrub heavy iron pots, and haul wagons loaded with cotton to the gin."

"Exactly!" He lunged to his feet and began pacing. In truth he'd had no idea she'd endured all that misery. It sent a cold shiver coursing through him to think about it. Although at one time she'd been no better than he, he refused to allow her to return to those endeavors. "Your father wanted that nonsense to stop. That's the reason he arranged this marriage."

"He arranged this marriage because he knew I wanted children."

His stomach tightened. No wealth, no children. It was the deal he'd cut with the devil—with himself.

She rose and matched him step for step. "He had some notion you know how to treat a wife well, but telling me what you will and will *not* allow borders on slavery. I'm not your possession. I'm your wife."

He came to an abrupt halt and faced her. "Which

means you are entitled to a life of leisure. Why can't you understand that simple concept?"

"Why can't you understand the simple concept that marriage is a partnership? A husband and wife should work together to achieve what they want. They should share dreams and ambitions and goals."

"But none of ours have anything in common."

She folded her arms beneath her breasts. "What is your dream?"

"To restore Huntingdon to its grandeur, to make it worthy of my son to inherit."

She held his gaze. "My dream is for you and the children to be happy. It seems to me if we work together, we can make both dreams happen."

He felt small and spiteful. How could she want his happiness when he was intent on denying her hers?

"Devon, I want to work in the fields."

He waved his hand dismissively. "Fine, then, do whatever you want."

He could at least grant her that small concession.

She smiled in jubilation. "You won't be sorry."

Probably not. But he had very little doubt she would be.

She whistled.

His countess whistled while she raked, bound, and stooked the wheat. Not a soft lullaby but something lively that danced on the breeze and had his men swinging their scythes with a rhythm matching her tune.

And when she needed someone's attention, to his horror she stuck two fingers in her mouth and released a high-pitched shrill that would have pleased an Eastender.

He would have taken her to task for her lack of good breeding and decorum if he hadn't been as entranced by her as his men.

If the gentlemen in London had seen her as she was today, he might have had to fend them off in order to gain her favor.

When she wasn't whistling, she was all smiles and laughter.

He'd thought she'd relaxed somewhat when they'd arrived at the manor, but now she was giddy with delight. Her dark eyes alive with passion, her cheeks ruddy from exertion, her lips inviting a kiss whether she was whistling, smiling, or laughing.

Joyous. She was absolutely joyous, obviously in her element with the arduous, monotonous work. While she had seemed out of place in the ballroom, here she was completely at ease, trudging across the field, going about her work as though she'd been born to it.

He didn't know why that thought took him by surprise. She'd married him to attain the rank of countess, and now she was brushing dirt off her skirt.

He glanced around. His own efforts paled considerably when compared with the results of his workers. Distracted, he was hardly concentrating on what he needed to accomplish.

He grabbed up his scythe and strode toward her.

"Thank you very much. I think you can be on your way now."

She didn't so much as halt. "Don't be ridiculous. It's not even noon yet."

He'd expected her to last an hour, maybe two, not the entire blessed morning.

"You've made a fine showing, but people are beginning to wonder about the lady in the field."

"Let them wonder. It'll make a good legend, don't you think?"

He grabbed her arm to still her movements. "Gina, I didn't mean for you to stay here all day."

She studied him, her nose red from the chill of the morning, her breath forming white wisps that were carried off by the breeze. "I'll leave when you do."

"I shall remain here at least until dark."

"Then so will I."

"We have hours yet to go."

She shrugged, as though his comment was of no consequence. "Time goes faster when I'm busy. I prefer it."

She shook off his hold and returned to raking. For the life of him, he couldn't imagine Margaret out here in a tattered cloak and a floppy hat, with a bead of sweat rolling from her temple down her cheek, a droplet that so closely resembled a tear.

How could she not loathe what his shortcomings forced her to endure?

"I . . ."

She jerked her head around, her brow darkened with a light coating of dirt.

He wanted to apologize, promise her a better life,

thank her for joining him in the fields, but in the end he simply said, "I'll escort you home come evening."

Georgina watched as the laborers wandered off into the dimming light one by one until only she, Devon, and a man named Benjamin remained. If she had been in Texas, she might have thought Devon was trying to impress her with his dedication to his endeavors, but she was in England and knew he'd grown up thinking that working in the fields was beneath him.

She understood now why his shoulders were much broader than his peers' and the reason his clothing had seemed snug. When he'd had it tailored to fit him, he must not have been swinging a scythe with a poetic rhythm. He hadn't been reduced to toiling in the fields.

How could she explain to him that what she'd witnessed today had exalted him in her eyes? Even if she possessed the necessary power of persuasion, he wouldn't want to hear it, wouldn't contemplate believing it.

Class distinctions were innate among his countrymen, passed down through the generations. Devon didn't see his actions as proof of his determination to succeed, to rise above. He saw them as failures.

Her father, however, would have viewed his efforts with the same high regard as she did. He'd mentioned that he'd visited the area. He must have heard about Devon's endeavors. He'd understood that although Devon was willing to marry for money, so was he willing to work for it. The very aspect of Devon's life that he abhorred was exactly the reason her father had deemed him worthy enough for her.

Unfortunately, he'd trusted Devon to care for her to such an extent that he hadn't walked away from the gaming tables as quickly as he should have.

Yet a part of her was grateful that he hadn't. With money at his disposal, Devon never would have revealed this aspect of his life to her. What they had now seemed much more real than what they'd shared in London.

She'd seen Devon in the ballroom, dressed in his finery, on the Thames with his sleeves rolled up. With the exception of their wedding night, when he'd worn nothing at all, he'd never appealed to her more than he did at this moment—with his face streaked with sweat and his muscles straining against the fabric of his shirt as he hoisted the remaining bundles into the wagon while Benjamin guided it along.

She'd offered to drive the wagon so Benjamin could help Devon load it.

"By God, Gina, you've done enough for today," he'd said, not with gratitude but irritation.

She might have taken offense if she hadn't already learned how difficult it was for this proud man to take help of any kind. She hadn't truly understood what it must have cost him to approach her father and offer to marry her in exchange for money. He must have felt as though he was selling himself.

And having bartered himself, he was no better off now than he would have been if he'd never spoken to her father. All he'd gained was a wife who didn't view hard, honest work as a failing.

He strode toward her. "Benjamin has offered to take the wheat to the barn. I'll escort you home."

She fell into step beside him. "If I wasn't here, would you be the one driving the wagon?"

He said nothing as he came to the spot where they'd left their horses to graze all day. He saddled them in silence, her question answered by his refusal to give voice to the truth.

She wanted to punch him for his obstinate behavior.

When he'd finished with her horse, he turned to her. "Yes."

She'd almost forgotten the question. "I didn't think you were going to answer."

"I considered taking that avenue but decided little was to be gained. I'll help you mount."

He bent over, and she slipped her foot into his cupped hands. They seemed much more capable to her now. Was she as guilty as he of judging a person by perceived notions about society? In truth nothing about him had changed, but she found herself looking at him differently now. She was almost ashamed to acknowledge her feelings as she watched him pull himself into his own saddle.

He urged his horse forward, and she did the same. She enjoyed riding beside him. He sat a horse well with an ease that came from knowing he was the master.

"I noticed when I went to the stables this morning that two of the horses were gone," she said.

"I sold them."

"Oh." She turned her attention to the narrow lane. "I keep forgetting how badly you need money."

"I don't much like having debt hanging over my head. With a bit of frugality, we won't go hungry. I appreciate that you are not a spendthrift."

He was becoming little more than a silhouette as the shadows of the night crept in. Still, she gave him a timid smile. "I never could get used to spending money just so it wouldn't burn a hole in my pocket."

"I daresay that would be viewed as a flaw among the ladies in London."

"Never cared much what people thought."

"So I've noticed."

She thought she could see his lips twitching. She'd always enjoyed the last remnants of the day after hours of arduous work in the fields. As much as she'd hated picking cotton, she'd still found satisfaction in it.

"Are you responsible for all the fields?" she asked.

His head turned sharply, and even in the diminishing light she thought he looked as though she'd asked a preposterous question.

"I am, of course, accountable for the two thousand acres that make up Huntingdon."

"I meant are you yourself farming all those acres?"

"Not all. We still have some tenants who work their own acreage. I simply couldn't abide having the land lie fallow when tenants left so I began working it."

"What about Benjamin?"

She could feel his gaze boring into her.

"Are all Americans as curious as you? Or are you the exception?"

"Are all Englishmen as private as you? Or are you the exception?" she asked in as British an accent as she could muster.

He chuckled low. "Although I'm accustomed to dealing with a woman's anger your restrained fury tends to throw me off."

"I'm not furious, Devon. Just frustrated. I'm your wife. I expected to share your life, not be made to feel like a busybody every time I ask a question."

"I expected our lives to run on separate paths."

"I expected them to be joined."

"So I am coming to understand."

She wasn't quite sure if his understanding was for the good or not. "Benjamin?" she prodded. "What's the mystery about him?"

"No mystery. We have an understanding, he and I. He and his family live in a cottage on my land. He oversees the workers when I'm not available."

"And when you are available, you work harder than anyone. Why?"

"Battling my demons, countess. Margaret despised my working in the fields, but I saw no help for it. I doubt I make much of a difference, but it's something, I suppose."

His wife had despised his working in the fields? In addition to his own shame, he'd been forced to endure hers. Was it any wonder that he'd endeavored to ensure she never discovered he spent his days toiling?

The woman had not only been disappointed in their financial status, but she'd not respected his attempt to better it.

"I think you make a great deal of difference," she said.

"Yes, well, we'll see if you harbor the same sentiments when the London Season is upon us and I inform you we cannot afford for you to purchase any new ball gowns."

"My gowns are less than three months old. Why would I need new ones?"

"Women always need new ball gowns."

"I don't."

"No, I suppose you don't," he murmured. "I never know quite what to make of you, countess, but I do thank you for your assistance today."

"I plan to help every day."

"It's not necessary."

"Devon, accept my willingness to help with a bit of grace."

"That's not an easy request for me to honor."

"But I enjoy working."

"Gina—"

"Devon."

"Fine. Do what you will, but at any time you may stop helping and I won't think less of you."

But she'd think less of herself. For the first time since she'd agreed to marry him, she felt equal to the task.

* * *

Devon drew his horse to a halt outside the stables, dismounted, and walked over to his wife. He was surprised the stubborn vixen still sat on her horse.

Wrapping his hands around her waist, he brought her slowly to the ground. As soon as her feet touched the ground, he should have released her. Instead he turned his hands slightly until his thumbs could graze the underside of her breasts.

Night had fallen, but someone had hung lanterns outside the stables, and they cast their glow over Gina. Strands of her hair had worked their way free of her braid. The rich soil was smeared over one cheek. She looked like no lady who belonged in the aristocracy.

Yet she possessed a fierce pride that even now was apparent by the manner in which she held herself. She'd worked in the fields all day. She should have looked withered, not merely weary.

And she certainly shouldn't have appeared enticing or engaging. He wanted to pull her to him, flatten her breasts against his chest, and slash his mouth across hers, tasting her sweetness.

He released her, stepped back, and grabbed her horse's reins. "Head on up to the manor. I'll be there shortly."

"There is no stable boy, is there?" she asked quietly.

He bowed slightly. "You are looking at him, countess. Although Benjamin sends his eldest boy over when I'm not about." He furrowed his brow. "Who saddled your horse this morning?"

"I did."

He swore softly beneath his breath. "Woman, have you no sense?"

She smiled, actually smiled, her teeth showing brightly against the lantern light. "I've been saddling my own horse since I was twelve."

"But as my countess—"

"Devon, stop worrying about appearances. I doubt anyone around here gives a good goddamn."

A good goddamn? Was there such a thing as a bad one?

He was on the verge of asking her when she turned, released a small screech, and stumbled to the ground. He was kneeling beside her in an instant. "What's the matter?"

"My leg is cramping."

"There, you see? I told you." He scooped her up into his arms. "You had no business whatsoever working out in the fields."

She wound one arm around his neck, while with the other hand she attempted to reach her leg.

"Just be still so I can get you to the house," he ordered briskly, alarmed by the situation, wondering if he should send for a physician. He didn't want her suffering.

"What about the horses?"

"I doubt they'll run off. I shall send someone to tend to them."

He took the steps leading into the manor two at a time. As though realizing he would have his way in this matter, she slumped against him, laying her head against his shoulder. He'd forgotten how nice she felt when held completely within his arms. Her simple dress, more suited to working in the fields than attending any social function, had no bustle or bows or anything to prevent him from noticing every swell and dip of her slender body as it pressed against his.

As he turned the knob, he shouldered open the heavy door and caught sight of Winston hurrying into the foyer. "Winston, have someone prepare a bath for Lady Huntingdon. Immediately."

"Yes, milord."

He carried her up the stairs to the bedchamber next to his. Gently he sat her in a chair before the hearth. He slid his hand beneath the hem of her dress and had no trouble finding the knotted muscle in her calf. He swore softly.

She tried to move her leg, but he held it firmly.

"Devon, I can do that."

"As can I," he said sternly, neither in the mood nor possessing the disposition to argue. Not that his tone would have deterred her if she had been of a mind to expostulate.

With a capitulation that he now understood beyond a doubt was totally foreign to her nature, she leaned back in the chair, gripping its arms. How like the blasted woman not to admit she was in a great deal of discomfort.

He kneaded the muscles slowly, gently, until he felt the knot loosening, her leg becoming firm but not hard beneath his fingers. She had such a finely shaped calf. He was tempted to lift her skirt over her knees and press his mouth just below her knee.

What a fool he'd been to speak in anger and disappointment, to deny her his presence in her bed, and in so doing, deny himself the pleasure of her body and the comfort he'd felt from simply holding her on their wedding night.

He lifted his gaze to her face. Her eyes were closed, and her lips were parted the tiniest bit. Her head was tilted at an odd angle, her breathing shallow.

His countess, after her arduous day in the fields, was asleep.

Chapter 19

Barely able to keep her eyes open, Georgina watched the steam swirl around her as the heat from the bathwater eased its way through her tired muscles.

She'd been too distracted by the discomfort to object when Devon had whisked her into this bedchamber. She thought it might have once belonged to the previous lady of the house.

The room was dominated by the bed with its chintz curtains, looped back and held in place by tasseled cords, hanging from square mahogany posts taller than her husband was. Decorative pillows adorned the bed, seemingly in disarray, and yet she felt certain each one had been placed just so.

The massive double wardrobe had a tall mirror in its center. A dressing table draped in muslin and edged with lace sat in a nook before the window. She could see an assortment of bottles resting on top—

probably perfumes. Little silver trinket boxes. Crystal vases, some holding flowers and some not. Dainty chairs and tiny tables that should have given the room a cluttered feel but instead seemed welcoming. And the abundance of framed paintings on the wall made Georgina wonder why they'd bothered with wallpaper.

After the servants had finished scurrying about, bringing up buckets of hot water for the luxuriously long copper tub, Devon had exited through a side door that she was certain led into his bedchamber. This room wasn't masculine enough to be his, but it would have provided him with easy access to his wife.

She didn't want to acknowledge the pang of envy for a dead woman that thought invoked. Nor did she wish to contemplate how desperately she wanted his love.

She wasn't certain when the realization had dawned on her, but she thought she could trace its roots back to London if she thought about it long enough.

She had enjoyed working beside him today. As she'd toiled in the fields during her youth, she'd always dreamed of one day having a man beside her to pick the cotton. Then the war had erupted, taking the dreams with it, far away. No matter how much she reached for them, she couldn't touch them.

Young men and boys had left to fight. Few had returned.

The scarcity of men had made the prospect of

marriage bleak. Then the Yankees had started moving in—damned carpetbaggers. She wouldn't have allowed one of them to court her if he'd been the last man in Texas.

A soft tapping brought her out of her musings and her lethargy. She bade entry, and Martha walked into the room.

"I brought your nightclothes, milady," the housemaid said as she set a bundle on the bed.

Georgina sat up, splashing water over the side of the tub. "Oh, no. I'll need a gown for dinner." She was almost as hungry as she was tired.

"His lordship has said you're to eat in here."

Georgina reached for a towel, and Martha hurried over to help her.

"But I want to eat with the children." Georgina tucked the towel up beneath her arms, wrapped it around her body, and stepped out of the tub.

"The children are coming here to eat. His lordship has instructed us to prepare a picnic on the bed."

Georgina stilled. "He has?"

"He has," a deep voice purred.

With a screech, Georgina spun around, slipped on the wet floor, and landed with a hard thud.

"Damnation!" Devon hissed.

Georgina watched in horror as he strode across the room.

"No!" She held up a hand to stave off his assistance, felt the towel fall, grabbed it, scrambled back, slid, landed on her elbow—

"Stop!" she yelled.

He staggered to a halt, and she realized too late that since he was no longer concentrating on getting to her, he could give his complete attention to looking at her.

Which he seemed to be doing with increasing intensity.

Clutching the towel to her chest left the rest of her embarrassingly exposed. She scooted back and reached for another towel. Her movement must have snapped Martha out of her stunned daze; the maid snatched away her sole protection against his intense glare.

"Oh, milady, this one is all wet. Let me help you—"

"No." Georgina struggled to wrap another towel around her, hanging onto it for dear life. "I'm fine. I can take care of it myself."

"But milady—"

"Martha, fetch the children," Devon said in a voice that sounded as though he was strangling. "I'll see to my wife's needs."

"Yes, milord."

Martha was up on her feet and out of the room before Georgina could draw in another breath.

"You won't see to my needs. You'll turn away," Georgina snapped. The words seemed ridiculous when spoken aloud, especially since he'd seen every inch of her body on their wedding night a lifetime ago, before her father's weaknesses had revealed her husband's uncompromising strength.

Slowly, ever so slowly, he raked his gaze over her with a look she might have mistaken for appreciation if she hadn't known better. Turning away from her, he grabbed the mantel as though he needed something to tether him to the spot.

"I didn't mean to startle you," he said quietly.

"Yes, well . . ." She grabbed another towel, stood and dried herself off. "You did."

He chuckled low. "So I noticed." His laughter faded. "I'd forgotten what remarkably long legs you have."

She stilled. Remarkable? Her legs? Surely he was joking although his voice didn't sound as though he was. It sounded rough and hoarse. If the white of his knuckles was any indication, he was going to leave an indentation of his fingers in the wood. Carefully avoiding the spots of water, she backed to the bed, not trusting him to keep his face averted.

He no longer wore his workman's clothes but was dressed for dinner. The ends of his hair curled, obviously still damp. He'd no doubt been bathing in the next room while she'd been washing up in here. Even with a door separating them, the intimacy of that realization caused her body to flush with heat.

She decided to avoid his comment and change the subject. "It was nice of you to arrange for us to eat here. The children will enjoy an indoor picnic."

She dropped the towel and worked her way into her nightgown. He didn't look as though he'd moved while the material had hidden her face. She drew on her wrapper and knotted the sash.

Sitting on the bed, she wondered if he'd made love to his first wife here—or had he carried her to his bed? She'd never set eyes on his bedchamber, not here or in London.

"I'm decent now," she said, not at all pleased with the breathlessness of her voice.

He faced her, and one corner of his mouth hiked up into a grin. "I thought you appeared decent before."

Unable to think of a witty retort with her skin prickling with the heat of his gaze, she asked, "Was this your wife's room?"

His smile retreated. "You're my wife."

"I meant"—she waved her hand, hating that he had the ability to fluster her—"your first wife. Margaret. Was this her room?"

"Yes."

"Did you and the children have picnics here?"

"We never ate with the children. Ever." He walked to the bed and skimmed his fingers along her wet hair.

She'd completely forgotten about its disarray. She bounced off the bed. "I need to fix my hair."

"Leave it. Martha can see to it when she returns with the children."

She scowled at him. "Don't be silly. I'm perfectly capable of brushing my own hair."

"When will you understand capability has nothing to do with it? You are the lady of the manor—"

"Therefore I should be able to do anything I want, right? And I want to brush my own hair."

She sat in the chair before the dressing table and studied the silver brush, comb, and mirror set out as though never to be used. She glanced over her shoulder. "Was this hers?"

"Yes."

With pantherlike grace, he strolled across the room until he stood behind her.

"Maybe I should pack it away for Millicent." She held his gaze in the mirror. "She might want to use her mother's brush when she gets older."

"She barely remembers her."

"Which will make it all the more special." She stood, turned, and found herself toe to toe with him. "I need to fetch my brush."

"I have one you can use, or we'll send Martha to retrieve yours." He toyed with several strands of her hair. "Have you possession of your mother's brush?"

"Yes, but it's not silver. It's the one we shared when we were poorer than dirt—"

He dropped his hand. "And here you are, poor once again."

"Hardly. I've slept in a shack where you could look through the roof and see the stars. I've been so hungry that my stomach has hit my backbone. I've worn clothes that had enough patches to make them look like a quilt. You continually harp on being poor when you've got two children who make your life richer simply by being. You're just too hard-headed to see that."

He arched a brow. "I do wish you wouldn't sugar-coat the situation."

The twinkle in his eyes made her realize he was teasing. "I need to get my brush."

She started to edge past him, but his hand on her arm stopped her.

"You may use mine." He leaned close enough that

she could smell his sandalwood scent and see the dark rings around the blue of his eyes. "Since you're too hard-headed to follow my conventional wisdom and allow the servant to fetch it."

Gina sat at the head of the bed with her knees spread wide and her feet somehow tucked up beneath her. Indian-style, she'd called it when the children had wanted to emulate her. A most unladylike and undignified pose.

But lounging at the foot of the bed, Devon had never been more entranced.

His children sat on either side of her, regaling her with the events of their day. She hung on every word as though each was spun from gold. She had to be at least as exhausted as he was, if not more, after working in the fields all day, but she gave no hint of it to the children.

She'd brushed her hair to a glorious mahogany sheen that captured the firelight cast by the candle flames. He longed to plow his hands through it, to cup the back of her head and guide her mouth to his—

"Is she, Father?" Millicent asked.

With a mental shake, Devon turned his attention to his daughter. "I'm sorry, Kitten. What did you say?"

"I wanted to know if Gina was going to live in our part of the house now."

Devon's gaze slammed into Gina's. He had brought her here without thinking. She'd scared the devil out of him when she'd collapsed. He'd almost taken her into his room to tend to her but realized at the last moment that the wife's bedchamber was where she belonged.

Where she belonged.

She was his wife, however much he might wish it otherwise.

"I thought we should close off the east wing until we are in a position to have more servants. It will save the staff countless hours of work. If you're agreeable, that is," he said, unwilling to admit the truth: that he simply wanted her closer.

"Say yes, Gina," Noel urged. "Then you wouldn't have so far to run when it rains."

Devon sat up straighter. Why the devil was his wife running when it rained? "I beg your pardon? What are you on about?"

His children's eyes grew as large and as round as saucers, and his wife looked as guilty as sin. He cleared his throat, and both children jumped.

He narrowed his eyes. "All right. What's all this, then? Come on. Speak up. Noel?"

Noel eased off the bed, stood tall, and placed his hands behind his back. "She's afraid of the storms, so she runs here when they come."

He jerked his attention to Gina. "You're afraid of storms?"

"Not her, Father," Noel said impatiently. "Millie."

"Who the deuce is Millie?"

His daughter raised herself up on her knees and planted her hands on her waist. "I am, Father."

"Millie? What's wrong with Millicent?"

"Millicent is a hard name. Who thought it up?"

He glanced at Gina. Her eyes were dancing, and he had a feeling she wore a smile behind the napkin she'd pressed to her mouth.

"I did," he confessed.

"Whatever possessed you, Father?"

This question from Noel, who was looking at him as though he was pondering the merits of having his father placed in a lunatic asylum.

"I was striving to honor the wife of the first earl of Huntingdon. Her name was Millicent."

"Was she pretty?" Millicent asked.

He darted a glance at his wife and grinned. "Her beauty was . . . legendary."

Gina lowered her napkin. Indeed she was smiling, and he felt as though he'd passed some sort of test.

Millicent released a tiny squeal and waddled across the bed on her knees. "Tell us her legend, Father."

She burrowed against his side so his arm came around her of its own accord. She tilted her head back and looked at him beseechingly. "Please?"

"Perhaps later. Tell me why you're afraid of storms," he coaxed.

"Because they're loud and Noel said they took Mummy away."

His gut clenched into a hardened knot. He'd forgotten it had been storming the night Margaret had died. He slid his gaze to Noel. His son looked petrified.

Gina tugged Noel onto the bed and slipped her

arm around him. "Storms frighten me as well, so Noel keeps us company in Millie's bed," she explained.

She was salvaging his son's pride. The boy was apparently as terrified of storms as his sister. What had he told Noel when his mother died? That she was gone?

While Millicent had remained in the nursery, Noel had stood stoically at his side during the funeral. Devon had thought Noel understood about death. Or perhaps he'd simply hoped the child did because he didn't know how to explain it.

"The storm didn't take her, did it, my lord?" Gina prodded softly.

Her question snapped him back to the present. He drew Millicent more snugly against his side. "No, the storm had nothing to do with her passing."

"What's a passing?" Millicent asked.

"It's when a person . . ." *Died* seemed such a harsh word. And then he would have to explain death. His children might come to fear not only storms, but sleep as well. How did one explain?

"Goes to heaven?" Gina offered.

"Yes, quite right." He gazed into his daughter's trusting blue eyes. "It's when a person passes from this world into heaven." He looked at Noel. "The storm didn't take her. She went away because she was very ill."

"And she loved you all very much," Gina added.

Yes, Margaret had loved the children. He'd never doubted that fact. But she'd never crept into their beds when it stormed or insisted they share meals or traipsed about the countryside with them half-naked. Or half-clothed for that matter.

He wished he could stop comparing the two women he'd married. He'd loved Margaret beyond reason.

And yet he was coming to realize he *liked*, enjoyed Gina so much more.

Sitting before the hearth in his room, his legs outstretched, Devon lifted his glass to the painting in a mock salute. Unwilling to part with it, he'd brought it from his London home. "You would have never set foot in a field, much less worked in one. I wonder, my sweet, if we might have been happier if you had not found our financial fall from grace so difficult to accept."

He downed the amber liquid, relishing its scorching path along his throat. The only light in the room came from the candle burning on the mantel. Shadows danced around him.

Theirs had been declared a love match. And he had loved Margaret. Enough so that her weeping had torn at his soul, her tears had flayed his heart.

Until the final year of her life when her disappointments in him became too great, and she wrapped the cloak of a sacrificial martyr around herself so tightly he could not work it loose. Not with promises, teasing, the touch of his lips, or the caress of his hands. She became an iceberg in a frozen sea of disappointments.

He ignored the light tapping on the door that led

into the lady of the manor's room. But he should have known Gina was simply announcing her intent to join him, not requesting permission to enter.

As though she was a willowy wraith, she glided into the room.

"Are you all right?" she asked.

He'd been unusually quiet after discussing Margaret with the children. He'd expected her not to notice but was not surprised that she had.

Lifting the decanter, he poured more amber liquid into his glass. "How long have you been sleeping with my children?"

"While you were in London, it rained here, and I discovered that the storm made them anxious." She perched on the edge of the settee. "Sometimes it's easier to face our demons with someone beside us."

"Is that the voice of experience speaking?"

She bestowed upon him a secretive smile that led him to believe she harbored mysteries of her own. He watched as she studied the portrait above the hearth. He was astounded by the complete appreciation that washed over her features.

"Is that Margaret?" she asked.

"Yes."

"She's beautiful." She pressed her hand against her throat. "No wonder you still love her."

Did he still love her, or did he just love the memory of what they might have shared?

"What illness did she have?" Gina asked, her brow furrowed with concern, as though his first wife still suffered.

"Disillusionment. Disappointment. Marriage to

me was not all she thought it would be." Throwing his head back, he tossed down his drink, then set his glass aside. "I should think you would commiserate with her. After all, sweeting, this marriage cannot be what you thought it would be when you laid out your terms and I so readily agreed to them."

"It's not what you thought it would be either." She eased down to the floor—the floor, for heaven's sake—and wrapped her arms around her drawn-up knees. "I wonder if any relationship ever is."

"You're quite the little philosopher."

She dropped her chin to her knees. "You never spoke to the children about Margaret's death?"

He placed his arm along the back of the settee and shifted uncomfortably. "No. Millicent was only two, Noel five. I suppose I thought they would simply understand. I certainly never meant for them to fear storms. Strange how a child's mind works," he murmured distractedly.

"I think everyone's mind works strangely."

He studied her. Her slippered feet, her long fingers, the collar of her nightgown that rose to her chin, her dark eyes. He loathed comparing her to Margaret, for there was no comparison to be made in either physical beauty or temperament.

Leaning forward, he braced his elbows on his thighs and lifted the thick rope of her braid, which had fallen over her shoulder. He brushed it over his lips, as though the insignificant action could help him make sense of her. Her hair smelled of flowers.

"You wanted a child, so you married me. Yet

when I refuse to seek your bed, you toil in my fields. I don't understand you, Gina."

"As much as I wanted a child, I was more concerned with making my father happy. He thought he'd somehow done me a disservice by dragging me along on all his business ventures. His finding me a husband who knew how to treat a wife well was his attempt to make amends." She lifted her shoulder. "I loved him with all my heart. For so long he was all I had."

"For him you married an irascible earl?"

"I didn't know you were irascible. I only knew you were desperate. I suppose I should be unhappy because my father gambled away his money."

"Quite so."

"Only I'm not unhappy. His love brought me happiness, never his money."

"Are you telling me that you find no joy in the purchase of a new gown?"

"Certainly there is a surge of joy, but it's fleeting."

"Ah, so you need an abundance of money, so you can experience constant surges of joy."

She shook her head. "You're missing my point."

"No, my little philosopher, you're overlooking mine. Money is a means to an end. In my particular circumstances, I carry the burden of ensuring that the estates that the Crown of England bestowed upon my ancestor for his acts of heroism and loyalty are maintained in a manner that represents the grandeur he earned.

"It is not simply a matter of failing Margaret, but of not upholding my share of the coveted heritage."

The light and shadows created a moving tapestry over her features as she seemed to consider his words. He knew now that her weathered face had been earned in fields much like his. It bothered him to find something they shared, especially this.

She was a commoner exalted to the pedestal of nobility by marriage. While he was nobility tumbling toward the common because of poverty.

Reaching out, he stroked his thumb over the crevices that fanned out from the corners of her eyes. Lines he'd thought had been created by laughter. Now he suspected her squinting at the sun had formed them.

"I hear the sun is harsh in Texas."

"Everything is harsh in Texas."

"Then what draws people to it?"

"It's a wonderful place for nurturing dreams."

"Do you not think dreams can be nurtured here?"

"I think dreams exist wherever hope thrives."

He gave his lips a wry twist. "Ah, yes, my little optimistic countess. I suppose today you saw the fields as half harvested whereas all I saw was the work that remained to be done."

"You had to see the beauty of the fields, their abundance, the way the crops rippled in the breeze. Success as far as the eye could see."

He dropped his hand to his side. "I suppose it depends upon where you're standing. If I were a tenant farmer, I could appreciate the success of it. But *I* should not have to look at it so closely or care so damned much that the crops are harvested before the next rain. You weren't raised in my world. You can't fathom my shame."

"No, I can't. I only know I'm glad I hitched my wagon to your star."

Watching as she rose to her feet and strolled from the chamber, he fought the urge to call her back. Hitched her wagon to his star indeed.

His was but a falling star.

Chapter 20

Georgina lay beneath the thick comforters in her bed in the east wing.

After visiting with Devon in his bedchamber, she'd been unable to erase the image of him sitting where he could gaze with ease at the immense portrait of his wife hanging over the hearth. She'd returned to the room that smelled of the woman he loved.

She wanted to be magnanimous, to be joyous of heart, but it hurt to see his love for another, to see it everywhere she turned, to always be reminded that she was here only because of Devon's need for funds.

She'd been unable to convince herself to remain in the bedchamber that served as a shrine for his deceased wife.

So she'd crept through the house as though she had something to hide, her bare feet pattering over the cold marble.

Once inside her room, she'd pulled aside the draperies so the moonlight could spill through the window. Now the fire burned low in the hearth.

She contemplated easing out of bed, dashing over the cold floor, and placing a little more coal in the fire. But losing the warmth of the bed for what she would gain wasn't worth the effort.

She'd never actually answered the children when they asked if she'd sleep in their wing. Tomorrow she would find an excuse to give to them regarding the reason that she wanted to remain here.

She swept the end of her braid across her lips as Devon had done earlier against his.

For a while she'd thought he was going to kiss her.

Heat poured through her with the memory of his gaze touching her face as though it was a caress. She had wanted him to touch her. To tell her that having her with him in the fields that day had lightened his burden.

To the very depths of her being she had loved watching Devon work. There was something incredibly intoxicating about the way a man's muscles bunched and knotted as he swung a scythe.

Her respect for him had grown with each passing hour. She'd come from a society that judged a man by the sweat he worked up. She couldn't understand why Devon placed such a high value on not having to labor.

She much preferred laboring in a field to dancing in a ballroom.

She'd forgotten how much she enjoyed the scent of dirt and freshly cut crops, the feel of the wind riffling her hair and cooling the sweat on her skin.

When her father had returned from the war, he'd had grand plans to improve their lot in life. She and her mother had traveled with him. It was then that she'd begun to feel uprooted. She'd never been comfortable on their travels, had always longed for the comfort of sleeping in the same bed, eating at a familiar table, sitting in a room that carried the scent of those she loved.

But not a room that carried the scent of her husband and the fragrance of the woman *he* loved.

And she had no doubt that Devon still loved the woman. His voice had a deep timbre whenever he spoke of her. It mattered not that Margaret had failed to appreciate his efforts.

He apparently still loved her deeply. Why else would he be staring at her portrait?

He seemed willing to accept that the woman had not lightened his load but had preferred to add to it. Georgina supposed it was because Devon and Margaret were of the same ilk. They understood the subtle nuances of the aristocracy as she never would.

She could not fathom the things they valued. The scales were so unevenly tipped. She and Devon were so different. How could she ever find happiness if she remained here?

She heard the door to her room open. She held her breath as soft footfalls echoed around her.

Peering through her eyelashes, she watched as he hunkered down in front of the hearth, grabbed the poker, and stirred the embers.

He had to have gone to Margaret's bedchamber

first, and after finding it deserted, had come in search of her here. Why had he bothered?

She liked his silhouette, the manner in which the orange glow from the fire outlined a portion but not all of him. He added coal to the fire until the flames danced higher and sent out warmth that crept across the room to create a cozy sense of well-being.

He unfolded his tall, lean body and walked to the bed, stopping just short of her. With her lids lowered, she barely breathed.

"I take it you prefer the distance between us," he said quietly.

He'd been in his room, staring at a portrait of his wife, the true love of his life. How could she compete with that memory?

"I can't sleep in the bed where you made love to your wife."

"I see. That was rather heartless of me to think you would be comfortable there."

"Not heartless. I just prefer it here."

He stood for the longest time, unmoving. And when he finally left, she wished he hadn't.

Chapter 21

Devon did not find looking over his ledgers nearly as gratifying as looking over his wife, where she sat in a chair before the window. Her head was bowed as she read *Jane Eyre*.

She had been reluctant to join him in his domain. He'd convinced her the light was better. Then the dark clouds had moved in, and she stared more at the gloomy day than she did at her book.

He wondered what she was contemplating. He'd gone to the bedchamber adjoining his to simply gaze upon her. This remarkable woman who seemed unable to fully comprehend his world, but whose own world seemed remarkably sane.

He'd listened as she'd explained to the children that the east wing of the house seemed a trifle lonely, and therefore she'd decided to stay in her bedchamber there, but she would always be available to them, especially during storms.

They had readily accepted her explanation.

While he knew the truth. His dear departed wife made his current wife uncomfortable.

"Devon?"

"Yes, countess?"

She ran her finger along the edge of the book. How he wished she was trailing it over his face. He wanted to make love to her with a desperation such as he'd never known.

"You'd mentioned wanting to better the life of the people here, of their children. Do you have a plan?"

"I need to provide opportunities other than working in the fields, because they can better themselves by moving to the cities where industry is thriving." He shook his head. "I'm not in a position to simply give. I've been looking into ways to lure the industries here. Unfortunately, I need a way to help them that will also benefit me."

Her head came up. "That's good business sense."

"Is it indeed?"

She blushed but continued to hold his gaze. "Have you ever considered investing in land in Texas, getting into cattle? You could send the area boys to Texas to work the land and cattle. I know a couple of men who I'm sure would be willing to teach them what they needed to know."

"That Magpie fellow you mentioned."

She smiled winsomely. "Yes, he's one of them."

"I suppose there's some merit to pursuing this avenue. Kit's certainly done well over there by all accounts."

A soft rap on the door caught his attention and he bade entry.

Winston stepped in. "Milord, a missive has arrived for the countess."

Gina popped out of the chair, took the letter, and tore into it as though she was expecting a bauble. Devon watched as her gaze traveled over the words, joy illuminating her features with each passing moment.

She released a small squeal and crushed the letter against her bosom.

Her excitement certainly piqued his curiosity. "What is it?"

She faced him with unadulterated love reflected in her eyes. The beauty of her gaze was mesmerizing. He wanted her desperately now in this room, in every room. Slowly he began to rise.

"Jake is coming!" The only sound in the room was the crackling of paper as her fingers tightened their hold on the letter. "Father must have made travel arrangements for him before he died. Oh, my God, I've missed him so much."

He felt as though he'd taken a blow to his midsection. He gripped the desk. The love she held for this man was incredibly evident. "Who the devil is Jake?"

"My very best friend."

"Jake who?"

"Just Jake."

"One of those fellows with only a solitary name?"

"You could say that." Her smile grew so large that he was surprised her jaws managed to stay hinged. "Lauren's bringing him. I have to tell the children."

She fairly flew out of the room, leaving him to wonder why she looked as though her soul mate had just risen from the dead.

"Father, do you know Jake can do tricks?" Noel asked.

Sitting with his back against a tree, one leg stretched out, the knee of the other raised, Devon studied his wife as she sat among the flowers with his daughter a short distance away. Her smile blossomed over her face as she listened intently to Millicent's ramblings.

Was his daughter carrying on about this Jake fellow as well?

"Indeed. So he's somewhat of a magician, is he?"

"Gina says he's especially talented at making things disappear. She says he'll be arriving any day now."

"I can hardly wait," he responded dryly.

"Neither can we. I'm ever so glad you brought Gina to us. I think she's beautiful. Don't you, Father?"

Beautiful? At first glance, no. Perhaps that was where he'd made his mistake in the beginning. He hadn't taken the time to do more than glance at her.

Her beauty wasn't visible on the surface. It was like an underwater spring, discovered only if someone went searching for it, its warmth and crystalline purity a gift bestowed upon the discoverer.

Devon had not bothered to look beyond what was evident to all.

Like still waters, she ran deep, his wife. She possessed a giving heart that revealed itself with remarkable kindness. She had brought his children back into his life, but more importantly, she'd lured him into theirs.

Bedtime stories and comforting tuckings-in were now a ritual. Dinner conversations were lively, moving beyond recitations of daily achievements to include discussions of artistic works and political events. His son, though only eight, had a grasp of economic conditions that was unnerving.

Noel would not make his father's mistake of waiting to inherit before pursuing his dreams. With the fields yielding a bounty of harvest, it was quite possible that he would not have to inherit his father's debts.

"Yes," Devon said solemnly, "I do think she's beautiful." In ways he was only just beginning to appreciate.

During the week, Gina had continued to work beside him, never once complaining about the early hour or the long day. As she labored, she wore her bedraggled hat and a smile.

Good God, how was it that the woman could constantly smile? Had he ever known anyone who was as filled with joy as she was?

Suddenly Gina jumped up as though she was as young as Millicent. Holding his daughter's hand, laughter dancing on the breeze, she walked toward them.

"Let's fly kites!" she called out.

"I feared she'd never say it was time!" Noel cried

as he hopped up and grabbed one of the kites leaning against the tree.

Gina had insisted they let the picnic fare settle in their stomachs a while before they took to the kites. Devon hadn't thought it would make much difference to their digestion, but he hadn't wished to spoil the festive mood by contradicting his wife.

Although he'd schooled his face not to show it, he was almost as anxious as Noel to set the kites on the breeze. He hadn't toyed with a kite since he was a lad no older than Noel. Bending, he picked up the remaining kites, the larger one painted a bright red, the smaller one a deep blue.

He'd sat in the day nursery last night and observed his wife and children as they'd worked on their creations, using sticks and scraps of newspaper. Lord knew where Gina had found the paint and where she garnered the enthusiasm to give so much to his children every night.

"Mine, Father." Millicent held out her small hands, her eyes glittering like jewels.

"Do you require assistance getting it up?" he asked as he handed her the kite.

She shook her head and ran off.

Gina took the red kite from him. "She will need help," Gina said softly. "The best way is to make it seem as though she's helping you."

"How do you know so much about managing children?"

She gave him her knowing smile. "I used to be a child."

"So was I, but I haven't half your understanding of children."

"I don't think you were a child. I think you were born an adult."

"Touché."

"It's up! Look, Father! Gina! It's up!" Noel shouted.

His kite was dancing on the breeze with its long tail of ribbons fluttering madly.

"Those bows look familiar," he murmured.

"They came from the gowns my father purchased for me. The gowns look halfway decent without them, and I didn't think he'd mind seeing them bring such joy to the children."

"Mine won't go!" Millicent cried as she ran a few steps, stopped, and ran a few more, clutching her kite the whole while.

Devon was on the verge of coming to his daughter's rescue when Noel said, "Here, Millie. Take mine. I'll get yours up for you."

He watched with aching pride as his son handed his kite to Millicent and then took off at a rapid pace, releasing her kite to the wind.

"They're such lovely children, Devon," Gina said quietly.

He cleared his throat of emotion. "Indeed they are."

He turned his attention to her. "Do you require assistance getting your kite up?"

"Are you kiddin'? We fly kites back home."

She left him then, heading away from him toward the openness of the field as though she was one of the children.

Crossing his arms across his chest, he leaned against the tree and watched as she loped across the field, laughing as she went, lifting her arm, releasing the kite, allowing the wind to snag it and carry it toward the clouds.

Georgina loved the unmistakable instant when the wind accepted a kite into its keeping and sent it soaring. Slowing to a walk, she turned back and watched the kite dip and twist. It was such a simple thing, standing here, holding the string, while the kite moved very little after it reached its height, but she loved it all the same.

She lowered her gaze from the sky to the land, to Devon, standing beneath the boughs alone. She'd been so entranced helping the children make the kites, showing them by example as she worked on hers, that she hadn't considered he was being left out. He hadn't offered to make his own but had simply observed them through the evening.

She'd been surprised he'd stayed with them the entire time. They'd made such a mess in the day nursery with their paste and newspaper and the old paint she'd located in a shed.

She'd planned this picnic to include all the family, had been thrilled when Devon had agreed to accompany them. But although he was here, she didn't feel as though he felt he truly belonged. Just as she did not feel that she belonged in the bedchamber next to his.

Waving her hand, she called out to him, "Come here!"

She saw his hesitation before he shoved himself

away from the tree and strode toward her. Long strides, even and confident. For all the worries he carried on his shoulders, he seemed more at ease here in the country, more real, than he had in London, where he was constantly under the scrutiny of his peers.

As he neared, she extended the ball of twine toward him. "Did you want to fly it?"

He studied her as though he hadn't quite grasped her meaning, and then some emotion—gladness, she thought—quickly flickered across his face.

"What say we do it together?" he suggested.

"All right."

He walked behind her and put his arms around her, closing his hands snugly over hers. She wished neither of them had been wearing gloves—or shoes, for that matter. He pressed his chest to her back, and she could feel the buttons on his vest and the watch chain that dangled outside the pocket.

Even for an event as relaxed as a picnic, he dressed in his finery. Yet she was beginning to see through the elegant façade to the man beneath it. She was much more comfortable with this man who worked in the fields than she'd ever been with the gentleman in London. Yet they were one and the same.

"Do you know what I'd like to do?" she asked.

Devon could think of any number of answers as he stood with her in his arms. She fitted perfectly. He'd only have to lower his head a bit, and he'd have access to the enticing spot behind her ear, a place he knew from experience was incredibly sensitive.

Her fragrance teased his nostrils, and he remembered how the scent had grown stronger when heated with passion.

He'd been a damnable fool to exile himself from her bed, and to announce his intent had been even more ill considered.

She jiggled her hands. "I want to let the kite fly higher."

Ah, he'd forgotten she'd asked him a question, hadn't realized he was grasping her hands so tightly that she was unable to release more of the twine. He loosened his hold. "My apologies. I didn't realize I was holding it quite so securely."

She glanced over her shoulder, her smile bright enough to put the sun to shame. "I don't blame you. I'm always afraid I'll lose it. What do you think would happen if we let go?"

"I should think it would crash to the ground."

She twisted her head so she was again looking at the kite, the vast expanse of sky.

"I think it would fly forever."

Devon was vaguely aware of the scratching of his quill pen over parchment as he made notations in his ledger, notations that were blotted out here and there as he continually lost his train of thought and stared ahead as though he was a man with no goals in life. He'd stare until the ink dripped from his pen onto his paper, creating a mess that it would shame him to ever show anyone.

But there was no hope for it. He could not keep his mind on his task.

They'd returned from their picnic late in the afternoon. The children had gone to their nursery, his wife to her sitting room. And he'd come here searching for answers that had no questions.

Leaning back in his chair, he brushed his fingers over the quill again and again. It looked rather mutilated after being used as part of his daughter's Indian headdress. He should replace it, but he liked the memory it invoked.

The memory of his daughter—and the memory of his current wife.

At twenty-six, she'd sworn she'd never kiss anyone but him. He had no doubt on their wedding night that she'd been a virgin.

So if this Jake fellow meant so blasted much to her, why hadn't he kissed her—or more to the point, married her?

Was it because—as she'd hinted about his kind—he'd returned from the war defeated? Did he now, for some unknown reason, feel victorious? Had he come to claim what should have been his all along?

The thoughts tormented him as they swirled around him, boxing him in, blocking off the light until only darkness surrounded him. And with darkness came despair.

A discreet knock on his door intruded on his steep decline into melancholy. The door opened, and Winston stepped into the room.

"Have you a moment, milord?"

Setting the pen to paper, Devon tried to make it appear as though he was occupied with important matters and not lost in unsettling thoughts. "Yes, of course."

Winston's visage was more grim than usual as he came to stand at attention before the desk.

"Milord." He cleared his throat.

"Milord, as you instructed, I was on the brink of preparing a bedchamber for our guest in anticipation of his arrival. I thought it prudent to ask Lady Huntingdon which chamber she thought the guest might prefer. She informed me, however, there was no need to prepare one for Mr. Jake. She expected he would sleep with her."

Devon heard a resounding snap and realized he'd broken the pen in two. "Surely you misunderstood."

"Yes, milord, I thought so as well, but when I questioned her on the matter, she insisted that he was accustomed to sleeping in her bed."

Devon's heart was thundering against his chest, while his voice was trapped behind the hardened knot in his throat.

"Milord, I am well aware Americans are ill-mannered heathens with few morals, so I fear I am not fully understanding the situation. I thought perhaps you might clarify it for me."

"Certainly." He stood with such force that the chair screeched across the floor. "Mr. Jake will stay in the bedchamber located at the farthest corner of the west wing." Where he'd have no trouble keeping a watchful eye on the chap.

"Very good, milord." Winston bowed slightly before turning to make his exit.

"Winston?"

The butler stopped and faced him. "Yes, milord?"

Devon knew Winston would never repeat any of

this conversation. A good butler was a discreet butler. "I appreciate you informing me of this situation. Your action in no way reflects disloyalty to Lady Huntingdon."

"Thank you, milord. I sometimes find it difficult to communicate with Americans, and I'm quite certain I am to blame for any misunderstanding that has occurred."

"I'll explain to Lady Huntingdon that we have plenty of bedchambers and no need exists for any doubling up."

"Very good, milord."

Ah, yes, indeed, he planned to explain a good many things to Lady Huntingdon.

"This Jake fellow . . ."

Startled by the unexpected voice, Georgina jerked her attention from the story in which she'd been lost and looked toward the doorway of her sitting room. Devon lounged against the frame. Yet even in his carefree pose, he did not give off the aura of one relaxed.

Quite the opposite in fact. The harsh lines in his face, the intensity of his gaze led her to believe he was a man on the verge of snapping in two.

"What about him?"

He shoved himself away from the doorjamb and took a step toward the fainting couch, where she lay with pillows at her back providing comfort as she read.

"He will *not* be joining you in your bed."

"Of course he will. He's used to sleeping with me."

He narrowed his eyes into dark and dangerous slits. "You were untouched when we wed, I'd swear it, and you claimed to have never been kissed. So how is it that this Jake fellow sleeps in your bed but leaves your innocence intact?"

Merciful heavens! He completely misunderstood her relationship with Jake, and yet she could not prevent herself from taking advantage and teasing him a bit. She slowly, carefully set the book aside.

"I assume it's because he prefers bitches."

He looked as though she'd just doused him with a bucket of cold water. "Pardon?"

She fought back the urge to laugh at his bewildered expression and simply shrugged. "He's attracted to bitches."

Something close to sympathy filled his eyes as he stated firmly. "But you love him."

"Yes."

He knelt on the floor beside her and cupped her cheek with tenderness. "How could he prefer a termagant to you?"

Her chest tightened with the gentleness in his voice, as though he sought to comfort her for a rejection he thought she'd experienced. She'd wanted to have a little fun with him, and instead she was coming dangerously close to making a fool of him. She shook her head. "Devon—"

"He's here! He's here!" Noel's voice echoed down the hallway.

Devon was unprepared for the jealousy that slammed into him as Gina hopped out of the chair, gladness reflected in her face.

Noel burst into the room with Millicent in his wake.

"I spied Lord Ravenleigh's coach from my window!" he yelled before darting back out, Millicent quickly following.

Gina turned to him. "Devon, about Jake—"

"You'd best go greet him."

"Yes, I need to make sure the children don't startle him with their eagerness into attacking."

Before he could question her about what the deuce she was on about, she'd hurried out of the room. As lord of the manor, he knew his duty was to follow and welcome the fellow. And if the fellow thought he was going to have the liberty of placing a hand on his children, he was going to learn right quickly that he did not—with the assistance of Devon's knuckles, if necessary.

Once outside, he made his way to the bottom of the steps, a short distance away from Gina. She'd joined the children, who were waiting impatiently, hopping from foot to foot, in the drive.

He did not wish to interfere with their excitement. Still, it troubled him somewhat to witness it.

The coach rolled to a stop. He could see Lauren through the window. The footman hurried forward and opened the door.

A blur of black leaped from the carriage with a resounding bark. Gina fell to her knees, and this mass of ungainly legs and frantically waving tail proceeded to lick her face while she ran her hands over its ugly head.

He looked back toward the carriage. Lauren had alighted. The footman had closed the door. So where the deuce was this Jake fellow?

"Oh, Jake!" Millicent cried as she giggled.

Devon snapped his gaze to his daughter, who was petting the beast.

"Isn't Jake splendid, Father?" Noel asked, his face beaming with delight.

With dawning realization, Devon stared at the creature in their midst. No wonder he preferred bitches. He was a damned dog!

He couldn't prevent the laughter that erupted without warning from deep within, from someplace where he'd been hoarding joy. It burst through to claim its freedom with such force that he had to sit on the steps, his sides aching, as he laughed with an abandon he'd never before experienced.

Gina twisted around, her eyes wide. His children stared at him open-mouthed.

"Bitches indeed," he said, gasping for breath.

Still on her knees, she worked her way to him. "I didn't mean to deceive you. When I realized what you thought—"

"You little witch, you taunted me."

Smiling, she nodded. "It was too good a prank to resist."

"You beguile me, Gina, by God, but you do."

* * *

"You beguile Huntingdon," Lauren said.

Sitting on a bench, watching the children toss sticks for Jake to retrieve—one of his tricks—Georgina furrowed her brow. "He was only caught up in the moment. He believed—and I didn't confess otherwise—that Jake was a man who slept with me."

He'd laughed, actually laughed when he'd learned that Jake was a dog and not a man. She hadn't meant for the little deception to take place, but no harm had come of it.

And she'd heard his laughter. Had he laughed like that with his first wife? Had she been able to bring such joy to his days?

"I wouldn't be surprised if he's fallen in love with you."

She shook her head. "He's never declared his affections." But then she'd told him not to, had never considered the possibility he could love her.

"Well, I need to be off," Lauren said as she rose.

Gina followed suit. "You could stay the night. We have lots of room here."

"No, I want to return to Ravenleigh. It always takes me a while to settle in once we return from London. We returned later than usual this year because Mother was hoping I would settle on someone."

Gina wound her arm around Lauren's as they strolled toward the waiting carriage. "Is there someone who's taken your fancy?"

"No one I can't live without."

"It might be better to look for someone you can live with."

"When we left Texas, when I left Tom, I thought I would die. It hurt so badly. I realize ours was a youthful love. I seriously doubt it would have stood the test of time. But I wouldn't mind feeling the same sort of excitement that came over me every time I laid eyes on him. I was always simply so glad to *see* him. I just don't feel as though I could settle for less."

And yet Devon had. Once he'd known a great love. With Georgina he'd forfeited love in exchange for wealth. Now he had neither.

And the realization hit her that she had settled as well.

Devon had loved a woman whom Georgina was convinced did not deserve him. As far as she was concerned, Margaret had been spoiled. When Devon had needed her the most, she'd turned away from him. And yet he continued to worship her. Her portrait hung in his bedroom where he could look at it each night before he went to sleep.

Georgina had tried to make their marriage into a partnership. Yet it remained about as cold as any business arrangement.

She couldn't deny that she enjoyed being with Devon. She treasured the smallest of shared moments. But it suddenly dawned on her that she was settling for crumbs while Margaret had benefited from the sumptuous feast of his love.

Devon was right. Perhaps it hadn't been wise to take a taste of dessert first. In London, he'd given her a glimpse of what their life together might have been. He'd been warm, caring, and considerate.

She'd altered her expectations because of her father's failings. How unfair to her and unfair to Devon.

In the past few weeks, she'd come to realize that she had a great deal to offer a husband: her unwavering support, her constant belief in him, and her undying love.

Because God help her she did love him.

And perhaps that was the reason that his not loving her had begun to hurt so much.

Strange how once she'd been willing to accept him without his love. But having witnessed all he'd given to another, she could no longer ask her own heart to do without. She deserved the kind of love that Devon and Margaret had shared, the kind of love that Lauren was willing to wait for.

Leaving the children would be almost unbearable, but surely they would recover quickly, especially after Devon found someone else to love. Children were resilient. Noel and Millicent deserved to grow up in a house filled with warmth. She wanted them to experience what she and Devon could not give them.

She would soon be twenty-seven, and she'd never put her own needs, desires, and wants ahead of anyone else's.

It was long past time that she did.

She would remain with Devon until she'd given him what her father had promised—a financial leg up.

Then she would set them both free.

Chapter 22

The bonfires burned into the night, illuminating the harvested fields and the many people who had worked to ensure the yield was good.

With Gina's hand on his arm, Devon strolled among the throng of merrymakers. Millicent clung to Gina's other hand while Noel walked beside Devon. His son continually reached out to pat Jake as he lumbered along. Gina had assured Devon that the dog would enjoy the outing. Jake seemed as eager to please as his mistress was.

Gina wore the enticing blue dress she'd worn the day he took her boating on the Thames. This evening she appeared more lovely than she had then.

More lovely.

In London he'd never expected that he would associate that particular sentiment with his wife. But she was lovely, lovely beyond measure, her face alight with joy as the men of the village and those of the fields stopped to doff their hats whenever they passed.

She knew them all by name and asked after their health, their happiness, and their families. Her absolute joy was mesmerizing. He could have watched her all night and not grown tired of seeing the emotions passing over her features.

She was without a doubt at home here. No seeking out fronds behind which to hide. She identified with these people, because she'd come from the land. She respected them more than she did those of the aristocracy.

And in so doing, she respected him.

So he found it easier to respect himself. Perhaps his own labors in the fields were not something of which he should feel ashamed. Perhaps the calluses on his hands were not signs of defeat as much as they were badges of victory.

He caught sight of Benjamin, his wife, and his five sons standing at a nearby table, gathering up food. Devon guided his own family toward them.

"M'lord," Benjamin said with a toothy grin as they approached. "Good of you to bring your family."

Gina squeezed Devon's arm before giving all her attention to Benjamin. "I'd like to meet your family."

Benjamin's eyes widened before he caught himself. "Certainly, m'lady. Certainly."

Devon listened as introductions were made. Tonight class distinctions were blurred, lost in the shadows. He should have been appalled.

Instead he was grateful Gina had insisted they bring the children. It was good for them to be aware that all the benefits they might enjoy in the future had its roots in these people.

Once introductions were finished, Devon gave his attention to the man who had worked almost as diligently as he had. "I'd like your eldest, Timothy, to begin working in my stables on a permanent basis."

Benjamin's chest puffed out, the lad's face brightened immeasurably, and Benjamin's wife looked as though she was close to weeping. To Devon, it was a small gesture. To them, he knew that they felt their son was moving up in the world—from the fields to the lord's stables.

"Very good, m'lord. He'll be there bright and early in the morning."

"Come with him, Benjamin, and we'll work out arrangements for his future."

"Aye, m'lord." Reaching out, he ruffled his son's dark hair.

Devon heard the lilt of flutes and fiddles traveling on the gentle wind.

As Benjamin and his family wandered away, Devon steered his family with a purpose. His family. He'd never felt such completeness. Not with Margaret.

She would have been appalled at the thought of coming here tonight. As for the children, she never would have allowed their presence. She understood her place in society.

Gina defied convention, charming him in the process. She put on no airs. How was he to have ever known he'd find that attribute so enchanting?

"Why was he frightfully glad about working in the stables, Father?" Noel asked.

Ah, trust his son not to overlook anything. He was a sharp lad, and Devon felt his own chest expanding.

"He's moving up in the world. He'll live on the premises, learn. Perhaps in time, we'll take him into the house and allow him to serve as your valet."

"Noel is perfectly capable of dressing himself," Gina said.

"That's not the point, countess. As much as you despise our hierarchy, I must admit to there being a method to our madness. We provide positions that allow people to better their lot in life. You will find a hierarchy even among servants. They do not see their assistance in our lives as belittlement but rather as evidence of their worth. I hope that in time, as we place ourselves back on an even keel, I shall be able to do even more for those here."

She looked at him as though only just seeing him for the first time. "I hadn't considered all that."

They neared the circle of bonfires. At its center, people danced with seemingly little rhyme or reason. The dances of country folk did not resemble the stateliness of the waltz or the complexities of the quadrille, where even there one's place in society was reflected.

The fires shot sparks into the air. Millicent squealed with delight. Devon lifted her for a better viewing, and she wound her arms around his neck, her eyes glowing with joy, her smile revealing her latest missing tooth.

"Can Millie and I dance, Father?" Noel asked.

She quickly twisted, placed her palms on either side of his face, and said, "Yes, please, Father?"

He cast a sly glance Gina's way. She bobbed her head. He wasn't quite as sure of the appropriateness of the request.

As though sensing his hesitation, she asked, "What can it possibly hurt?"

What indeed? He almost mentioned that it simply wasn't done—but then neither was a nobleman working in the fields as though he were a commoner. He could not help but feel that the world he knew was on the cusp of change. How long before marrying heiresses would give way to other means of restoring wealth?

"Do you think you can determine the proper steps?" he asked of Noel.

"Yes, sir."

"Very well, then." He lowered Millicent to the ground. "Have at it."

Joining hands, with the dog in tow, they raced to the edge of the dancing couples and began to do little more than skip around. Devon had a strong urge to pull his wife into his arms and hold her as he'd held her when they'd flown the kite. But that action, that thought, was entirely inappropriate. He was after all still the lord of the manor.

He could see the toe of her shoe peering out beneath the hem of her skirt, tapping the ground in lively rhythm to the music.

"I'm so glad we came," Gina murmured.

"I wasn't certain how it would go over with you

and the children. I've always come alone before."

She snapped her head around, locking her gaze with his. "I wouldn't have thought you'd come."

"It's the celebration of harvest. It's important to these people, and therefore my presence is expected."

She narrowed her eyes. "You're not here because you want to be? You're here because of your society's rules?"

"Quite right." Although to himself he readily admitted that he enjoyed the celebration, would have attended even if it wasn't expected.

She shook her head and looked away as though disappointed in his answer.

"My wife and children are here, however, because I enjoy their company."

She returned her attention to him and gave him a wispy smile. "I'm glad."

"As am I. You see at long last I have a partner with whom to dance." He held out his hand in invitation. "Shall we?"

Her eyes widened along with her smile. "Do you know the steps?"

"I rather think we can manage, you and I. We've done quite well so far."

He wasn't certain if it was a trick of the bonfires or the night, but it looked as though tears welled in her eyes just before she placed her hand in his and averted her gaze. What a sensitive woman she was, his wife.

He escorted her toward the madness, surprised to discover how much he was anticipating joining in.

"Father, do you need me to teach you the steps?" Noel cried out as they walked past.

He winked at his son. "I think I've got it."

Then he took his wife into the center of the throng, and they danced with wild abandon, not with the stiffness of the balls in London.

Her laughter wove through the music, her smile grew larger, and her eyes sparkled with merriment.

And she was his. Before he realized what he was about, he'd offered up a silent thank-you to Nathaniel Pierce.

Pride could be a man's strength or his weakness. Its perception depended on one's perspective or where a man stood in relation to his place in the world. Pride could keep a man from giving up when surrender was an easier course. Or it could cause him to shore up his defenses and act without consideration for the consequences. Pride was an asset that sometimes turned on a man and became a liability, as it had with Devon.

In his thirty-four years of life, he'd discovered he had a great well of pride, which defined who he was, who he perceived himself to be.

At times it dictated his actions more than his conscience or his reasoning did.

It was more powerful than lust, desire, or love.

It spoke in moments of anger and trapped him by words that would have been better left unsaid. Because of its brashness, in order to now claim what he wanted, he had to devise an explanation that would allow him to obtain what he so dearly wanted—without causing his pride to suffer. He wanted from Gina what she gave to the children: her unbridled love. And in order to attain it, he would willingly grant her wish.

Standing before the window in his library, he heard the door click open.

"Winston said you wished to see me," Gina said.

He wished to do a great deal more than that. Slowly he turned from the gray clouds hovering on the horizon and smiled warmly. "Indeed I do, countess. Please join me."

Bowing slightly, he made a gesture toward the padded leather chair that rested before his desk.

The light blue gown she wore today was a plain affair, lacking bows or frills. Still, it suited her perfectly. He had discovered of late that it was her very plainness that appealed to him. Her simple manners were open and honest, her smiles genuine, her laughter riveting.

How was it that upon first meeting her he'd failed to notice the tranquil beauty that enveloped her?

She sat and primly folded her hands in her lap, giving him her undivided attention, as was her way. While others hurried through life with a passing comment or a brusque nod in acknowledgment, she managed to make a person feel as though no one else existed on the earth, as though at that precise moment, held in her uncompromising gaze, nothing and no one were more important.

Little wonder the children and servants adored

her and that he found himself doing what neither of them had ever expected he would do.

He was falling in love with her.

He darted a quick glance at the ledgers strewn over his desk, wondering briefly how to explain himself without butchering his pride. He gave his throat a sound clearing so he wouldn't squeak like an overanxious schoolboy. He met his wife's gaze.

"I have been studying the ledgers, projecting the future. Your assistance in the fields has made a notable contribution. I foresee our profits at this point in time as being rather small, but I do see them growing—to the point that I will consider us financially solvent in a short while."

She scooted to the edge of the chair, her smile blossoming. "That's wonderful, Devon."

"Indeed. Your father told me that with you by my side I would know unlimited wealth. It appears he spoke truly."

She shook her head. "You managed it all on your own."

He held up his hand, noted the trembling, and closed his fingers into a fist. "I believe that we managed it together. As a result, it seems only fair that I honor the bargain I made with your father. I anticipate slowly acquiring wealth. Therefore, Gina, I shall ensure that you acquire a child."

He had expected delirious joy on her part, not the withering away of her smile, the deep furrowing of her brow, or her retreating against the back of the chair.

"I'm not sure I understand exactly what you're saying."

"That I shall begin visiting your bed with the express purpose of getting you with child." To his own ears the words seemed cold.

To her they must have resembled a block of ice, because she could not have looked more stunned if he'd tossed her into a river in the middle of winter.

Slowly she rose, her hands clasped tightly enough that the white of her knuckles showed. "I suppose I should have told you sooner that I've decided to return to Texas."

His heart stuttered. "Pardon?"

A sad smile flitted across her face. "You made a pact with my father. He failed to live up to his end of the bargain. I wanted to make restitution. But you didn't need me, Devon. You didn't need him. You've had the power all along to make Huntingdon something grand, an estate worthy of your heir. I can't compete with the memories of Margaret. She was beautiful beyond description. You know what it is to marry for love. How you could possibly have settled for less this go round is beyond me.

"I had an emptiness in my heart that I assumed having a child of my own would fill. It was my greatest desire. But the emptiness no longer exists. Although I'm not their true mother, I love your children as though I were. And loving them as I do, the greatest gift that I can give them is to set their father free, so he can once again find a woman to love.

"Therefore I thank you for the generous offer, my

lord, but I assure you in time we'd both resent my accepting it."

In stunned silence he watched his wife stroll from the room as though he'd merely invited her to join him on a picnic.

She was leaving him?

For all her talk of hitching her wagon to his star, she didn't want him. In many ways, his current wife's betrayal was much worse than his first wife's had been.

He'd thought that through Gina's eyes, he stood tall because of who he was and his accomplishments. Not because of what he was. Not because of his title. Not because of an accident of birth. But because of his unwillingness to accept that what his father had left was all he would ever have.

With her at his side he'd felt wealthy, even though he possessed less than he had when he married her.

Dear God, he'd even begun to fancy himself in love with her.

Spinning around, he glared out the window. The dark clouds were rolling in. The storm would be here by nightfall, but it paled when compared to the tempest twisting inside him.

For all he'd worked so damned hard to acquire, he'd never in his life felt so incredibly destitute.

Gina galloped over the rolling hills as though the hounds of hell were baying at her heels, threatening to bite her horse's flanks.

She could hardly fathom his dispassionate offer.

His uncompromising glare and harsh words that

awful day in London when he'd announced he'd no longer be visiting her bed had cut her to the bone. Today he'd offered to give her what she'd thought she most wanted: a child.

Although his children had filled the aching void in her heart, she still desperately desired her own child. She wanted to place her hand on her stomach and know life blossomed within her. She wanted to feel the subtle movements. She wouldn't even mind the pain that accompanied childbirth, because she was certain it would fade to nothing in her memory the instant she held her child in her arms.

But as much as she wanted a child, she'd come to realize in the passing months she wanted Devon's love more.

She brought her horse to a halt and looked out over the fields where she'd lived some of the happiest moments of her life. Tears washed down her cheeks. She was tormented by the knowledge that he would never love her as she did him. The memory of his deceased wife would always stand between them.

But to leave him would break her heart.

Yet how could she not leave when she knew that staying would shatter it as well.

When he'd made love to her before, she'd not fathomed the true extent of his love for his first wife. Now that she'd lived in the woman's shadow for months, she knew she could never again lie beneath the woman's husband—and pretend that it was her that he cared for.

* * *

"Milord, the stable boy informs me Midsummer Moon has returned."

Sitting at his desk, rubbing his brow, Devon thought it was an odd statement for Winston to make, but he was so absorbed by Gina's revelation that she planned to return to Texas that he didn't give any thought to the reason he considered it odd.

He understood his wife so little. She dusted when he wasn't looking—he knew she did, because he'd caught her at it, unknown to her—she scrubbed, she'd planted a nice-sized vegetable garden. She'd worked in his fields, threshed his wheat . . .

"Milord?"

He lifted his head and glared at his butler. "I'm striving to concentrate here, Winston."

"Yes, milord, I can see that you are. It's just that . . . Well, milord, Lady Huntingdon has not returned."

Everything within Devon stilled. "What do you mean she hasn't returned?"

A crack of thunder echoed, causing the panes of glass to rattle. Winston cast a furtive look at the window. "She took the horse out for a ride, milord, but only the horse has returned to the stables."

"You think she was unseated?"

"I don't know what to think, milord."

"Bloody damned hell." Devon shoved himself to his feet with such ferocity he sent the chair crashing to the floor. He strode across the library. "Fetch my coat."

"I have it here, milord."

He reached back and grabbed the coat, not waiting for Winston to assist him but simply thrusting his arms into it as he quickened his pace. He was halfway across the foyer before the tiny voice stopped him.

"Father, there's a storm," Millicent said.

He spun around. Both children stood at the bottom of the stairs, Jake sitting between them, his tongue hanging out.

"We want Gina, Father," she added.

"I know you do, Kitten," he said, crossing back to them and kneeling before them. "I'm off to look for her now."

"Where is she?" Millicent asked.

"I don't know. Did she happen to mention where she planned to go riding?"

"No, Father, but she should have come back before the rain started," Noel said.

"Yes, I'm sure she meant to." He didn't want to upset them by mentioning the horse had but she hadn't. "That's the reason I'm going to look for her."

"Jake could help you, Father," Noel said with utmost seriousness. "He finds us when we play hide and seek."

"Indeed." He glanced at the dog. He thought it highly unlikely that he could sniff out anything in the rain.

"You just have to give him something of hers to smell so he knows who you want him to search for," Noel explained.

"Undoubtedly unnecessary at this point." He placed his hand on each child's head, communicating assurance, wishing to lessen their fears, a touch that would not have occurred to him before Gina had arrived to so absolutely unsettle his life.

The woman who had no place for rules in her life.

Thunder echoed around them. He turned to Winston with more confidence than he felt. "Have a bath prepared for the countess. She'll no doubt look like a drowned cat and be quite cold once she returns."

The dog released a little whine. Such a large creature to emit such a helpless sound. He stopped himself short of patting the beast's head and murmuring words of comfort to it. It was an animal—but he knew that reasoning wouldn't have stopped Gina.

She gave love to everyone and everything. Had he ever known anyone who possessed an unlimited capacity to love?

He stood and strode through the foyer to the front door.

"Find her, Father," Millicent called after him in a voice reflecting her age and her fears.

"I shall, Kitten," he called.

"Promise?"

"Promise."

A promise that was proving difficult to keep under the circumstances. No one knew where she might have ridden. No one noticed from which direction the horse had returned.

Devon searched the gardens, the area around the stables, the land on either side of the path that led to the main road. The rain continued to fall, lightning periodically lit the black sky, thunder shook the air, and his trepidation increased.

Rivulets of water created shallow pools around

him. If she'd landed face down, if she'd lost consciousness, if the water rose around her, would she drown? He'd heard of drunken men drowning in inches of water.

Where the deuce was she?

She might not care what he thought, but she wouldn't stay away on purpose. She wouldn't want to worry the children. The children, of course. She wouldn't want to worry them.

And yet she was contemplating leaving them. Leaving him he could well understand, but to leave the children? He couldn't fathom why she would even consider it.

Margaret wouldn't. . . . Margaret. By God, how often did he think of her? How often did he speak of her to his current wife? What sort of fool was he?

And yet none of the thoughts, none of the spoken words reflected happiness. They all revolved around Margaret's disappointments, his failing to make her happy.

With his constant references to Margaret he'd managed to make Gina miserable.

Gina, who possessed a far greater capacity to love than any woman he'd ever known.

Gina, who did not look to others for her happiness but created it herself.

Gina who would never leave his children unless she'd truly convinced herself it was in their best interest—unless he'd allowed her to believe they would all be happier without her.

Her father had spoken of wealth beyond imagining. Devon realized now that he possessed a deplorable lack of imagination, because where Gina was concerned, the wealth *was* immeasurable.

Out here, searching frantically, he wouldn't know if she'd returned to the house, which she'd no doubt already done. He'd been looking for an hour, scouring the nooks and crannies.

She was such a skilled rider. He could not fathom that she'd be unseated. He tried to convince himself that another logical explanation existed. She'd no doubt dismounted so she could inspect a plant that took her fancy, as she was wont to do. Perhaps a clap of thunder had startled the horse and caused it to bolt. She'd no doubt trudged home while he had been searching.

But somberness greeted him when he walked into the manor. He couldn't explain it, but he felt it long before he saw anyone, before anyone knew he'd returned.

The manor had never felt so empty or forlorn. The grief upon Margaret's death had not hovered this thickly, this ominously.

Margaret again. He needed to exorcise her memory. She was his past. Gina, he desperately hoped, would be his future. If he could only convince her to stay.

Thunder resounded, and a shudder rippled through him.

He caught sight of Winston striding toward him. "Has she returned?"

But the answer was clearly written on Winston's face.

"No, milord."

"All right, then. Gather up some lanterns. It's black as Hades out there."

"Yes, milord."

He rushed up the sweeping staircase. He had to appear unworried, had to keep his escalating fears under control. It would not do for the Earl of Huntingdon to show panic.

Gina would no doubt chastise him once he found her. He could hear her now, ordering him, "Show it, if that's what you feel."

Strange how her voice was ensconced in his mind. He could carry on a conversation with her without her being present. How long would that ability continue if she left him? If she did indeed return to Texas?

She was no doubt bluffing.

He entered her room. The open trunk sat near the foot of the bed. Far from empty. How could he not remember that his wife did not bluff?

Where was she?

He strode to the bed and snatched up her nightgown. Soft against his fingers, as comforting as she was. He didn't have to press it against his nose to smell her scent wafting around him.

She was everywhere in this room. Her subtle fragrance somehow managing to fan out over everything.

How like Gina, with her quiet ways and her penchant for creeping behind fronds. How like her in the final tally to exhibit such a presence that he could see her, smell her, hear her as though she stood before him now.

He marched from her bedchamber along the hallway, down the stairs, across the foyer, up the stairs, and into the day nursery. It was long past time for the children to be abed, but here they were sitting before the hearth, Mrs. Tavers closing the book in her lap.

Gina had even managed to win the old bat over. Before her influence, the governess would have ordered the children to bed regardless of circumstances. Now bed did not happen until their stepmother tucked them in.

Devon held his son's earnest gaze. "Do you truly think Jake could find her?"

Terror was evident in his son's eyes before he straightened and took on the mantle of the heir apparent, displaying a confidence Devon thought he probably didn't feel.

"Oh, yes, Father, I'm sure of it."

Devon thrust the soft flannel toward him. "Her nightgown."

Noel took it, knelt before the dog, and pressed it against its muzzle. The dog's tail began thumping the floor with a force that might have been dangerous if anyone happened to get in the way.

"Find her, Jake," Noel ordered. "Find her."

The dog took off at an ungainly lope. Noel extended the gown toward Devon. "Take it with you, Father, so you can remind him of her scent from time to time."

Devon shoved it inside his coat. Her scent wafted up and around him, comforting him.

He would find her, by God, he would.

* * *

He found the dog at the door in the foyer, throwing his gangly body against it as though he intended to break it down. Devon attached a leash that he'd located, left over from the days when he had hounds, and they were off, the dog straining against the restraint.

But on this moonless night he couldn't risk losing the dog as well.

A short while later he sat astride the gelding, cantering over the fields, carrying a lantern that Winston had brought him. When he'd left the estate, he'd seen a half-dozen lights floating in the darkness as his servants searched for their mistress.

His first stop had been Benjamin's cottage. Devon had tried to explain the situation coolly, but fear had continually crept into his voice. Fear, dread, loneliness. He'd never in his entire life felt so alone.

He thought he'd been alone when Margaret had turned from him. Only now did he realize that with her, he'd always been alone.

Ah, he'd loved her. Her gentle beauty, her genteel nature. He knew he'd loved her. But she'd never challenged him, frustrated him, worked beside him, given to him far more than he'd ever given to her.

Theirs was a polite marriage, a proper relationship. So utterly boring he wondered now how it was that he'd never noticed before.

Sparks, fire, ice, chills. Laughter, smiles, yelling. His marriage to Gina followed no rules. He never knew what to expect. He only knew he found it exciting.

Once Benjamin understood that Devon was looking for Gina, he'd sent his nine-year-old son to the homes of the other laborers, alerting them to the need to gather and search for Lady Huntingdon.

Devon had watched the young boy run off into the rain, no umbrella, no jacket, no shoes upon his feet, taking off with nothing more than a quick bob of his head and a "Yes, sir."

Ah, yes, these people who were good enough to work his fields . . . He suddenly realized that they were the very best friends he had. As the search continued and expanded, he could only see the increasing number of lanterns, not those who held them.

Devon did not delude himself into thinking they'd come quickly in order to ease his burden. They were here, just as he was, desperate to find the woman who had become an indelible part of their lives, a woman with whom they'd talked, laughed, and worked.

A woman who cared nothing for rank or privilege but simply cared.

Devon drew his horse to a halt and dismounted. With muddy, wet paws, Jake leaped on him, barking feverishly.

Devon pulled the now soaked gown from inside his jacket. He'd allowed the dog to sniff it a dozen times now. He doubted it had any scent left except for the fragrance of rain, but he could hope, with everything in him, he could hope.

"Find her, Jake," he ordered with urgency, as though the dog understood not only the words but the importance. "Find her."

Jake took off, a sharp tug on the leash nearly

pulling Devon's arm from its socket. He left his horse where it stood. So many people were in on the search he had little doubt someone would be by shortly to tend to the gelding.

The dog stopped, bayed at the darkness, and took off again. Devon held the lantern high, but the light didn't fan out a great distance. He could barely see the dog's wagging tail.

But he heard a change in Jake's bark. A subtle difference that made him question his sanity, as though he actually thought the animal was communicating with him.

Then he spotted it. The light from the lantern caught something pale, something not shadows. Something that didn't disappear when the lantern's glow fell across it.

Gina.

As though sensing all was not well with his mistress, Jake lay beside her, his head across her ankles, his bark giving way to a pitiful whine.

"Benjamin!" Devon yelled just before he dropped to his knees and held the lantern over her. Her eyes were closed, her face incredibly pale. He touched her cheek. Cold. So very cold. She lay at such an odd, twisted angle. He wanted to straighten her, but he was afraid, so frightened of doing more harm than good.

"You found her, m'lord," Benjamin said as he knelt on the other side of Gina.

"Look at her, Benjamin. She's all broken. My dear wife is all broken."

He heard his father's resounding voice echoing in

his mind, "Chin up!" Only he didn't want to keep his chin up. He wanted to weep, pull her close, hold her tightly, and beg her to be all right.

"I'll fetch a wagon, m'lord."

Devon nodded, unable to think clearly. "And fetch a physician. I'm afraid to move her without his consent. I don't want to cause more harm."

"Aye, m'lord, I'll send someone."

"And pad it—the wagon. Mattresses, blankets—get blankets out here." He set the lantern aside and tore off his coat, gently spreading it over her inert body. Hoping some of the warmth it held from his body would seep into her.

"Here, m'lord, use this as well."

He glanced up to see that Benjamin was offering his coat as well. Worn and patched. Strange how in a moment of crisis the lowliest piece of clothing served as well as the most finely made garment.

Devon placed it gingerly over his wife as Benjamin headed off at a run.

Word spread that he'd found her. One by one the men he'd worked beside in the fields came over and handed him their coats before leaving him alone with his wife.

Eventually she lay beneath a mountain of rags, and Devon had never in his life been so grateful for so little.

Once the physician had arrived in the field and examined Gina in the pale light of a dozen lanterns, he'd deemed her unbroken—at least her body. He wasn't aware of her spirit, of the manner in which

Devon had unwittingly battered and bruised it with his constant references to Margaret.

For all his education and learning, the doctor didn't seem to know that a person could look whole on the outside and be nothing but shards of broken dreams on the inside.

Devon knew. God, how he knew. He wasn't certain if he'd ever been whole on the inside. He'd just always given such a good imitation.

With the utmost care and tenderness, he'd placed Gina on a mattress in the wagon. Dampness surrounded them as he'd lain beside her, wrapping himself around her, trying to buffer her from the lumbering swaying of the wagon as it rolled over the fields. Occasionally the wheels sank into the freshly turned earth until the farmers shoved the wagon on its way, each one saying, as if on cue, "She'll be all right, m'lord. Not to worry."

But he was worried. Standing at the foot of his bed, gripping the bedpost with icy fingers, his clothes drenched, he watched as the doctor examined his dear Gina more closely. He'd noticed a bruise forming on her side along her ribs before the servant slipped a fresh nightgown onto her.

The doctor had proclaimed nothing broken there. Now he was gingerly running his fingers along her scalp, over her face, beneath her chin. Lifting her eyelids, he squinted his eyes as he stared into hers.

"She's got a rather nasty knot on the back of her head," he murmured. "But her eyes react to light. That's good."

Devon swallowed hard. "But she hasn't stirred since I found her. Why doesn't she wake up?"

The physician straightened, scratched his head, and heaved a melancholy sigh. "I fear all we can do at this point is stand vigil." He glanced at Devon. "You should get yourself into some dry clothes before you catch your death."

How could he explain that without her life mattered not? As much as he'd grieved over Margaret's passing, not once through her illness or after her death had he felt that he could not go on.

"What am I to do for her?" he asked.

"Keep her warm, keep things quiet. Send for me should you notice any change."

"How long before she'll wake up?"

"That, my lord, I can't say. A few hours, a few days. I shouldn't think it would be long."

"And if it is?"

"Let's walk across that bridge when we get to it, shall we, my lord?"

It was long past midnight by the time the physician took his leave.

As he'd known—he wouldn't have known before Gina had come into his life, but he knew now—the children were still wide-eyed and awake, lying in their beds, afraid to sleep because the storm continued. He gave them the important task of sitting with Gina while he changed out of his damp clothes.

With Gina in his bed, he'd taken his clothes into his former wife's bedchamber. He wanted Gina in his own bed, not closeted away at the farthest reaches of the house, not in the bedchamber that had once belonged to Margaret.

His body was numb from the cold, his spirit numb from worry. She would not have ridden carelessly. Something must have startled the horse, and perhaps Gina had been too distracted to notice until it was too late.

Quite right. He could well envision that scenario.

Once he was properly dressed, he stood in the doorway that separated his room from Margaret's. A stupid tradition that dictated a man and wife should have their own chambers, their separate beds. When a man dared to enter, he was letting it be known in no uncertain terms that he intended to bed his wife.

Where was the spontaneity of it? The wooing, the uncertainty, the moment when all became clear because two bodies shuddered with need?

And what of the nights when a man was weary beyond belief and simply wanted to fold himself around the woman he loved.

He did love Gina, more than life itself. But would she believe him when she seemed to have so little faith in her own worth?

How did a man show a woman that he loved her, heart, body, and soul? Oh, he well knew the art of courtship. He knew the right things to say, the right manners to project. He was possessed of courtly grace.

He could write the book on how to give the appearance of love.

But what did he know about actually showing it?

He heard the whispers of his children as they sat

on the bed, one on each side of Gina. One touching her face, while the other held her hand. Noel speaking and then Millicent.

Precious children. Healing. His greatest assets. His most magnificent joy.

He would sell himself, settle for unhappiness, accept shame, he would humble himself before his peers if need be. For them he would sacrifice anything.

Just as he would for the woman who now lay between them.

The knowledge hit him in the center of his chest, caused an ache in his heart, a chasm in his soul. He wasn't certain when he'd fallen madly in love with her.

She would fault him for not knowing the exact moment, but the feeling was such a part of him he knew it had taken root *long* before it had fully blossomed and he'd become aware of it.

Did she love him? At all?

Did a woman work in the fields and thresh grain without complaint for a man she didn't love? Margaret had claimed to love him, but she'd withdrawn from him, had never considered working beside him, lessening his burden.

Gina lessened his burden simply by standing beside him. She needn't have worked in the fields. But she had. Because her nature was to give—everything within her.

She gave to him, the children, the servants, Huntingdon. She asked nothing in return, expected nothing. "She can't hear you," he said quietly.

The children snapped their heads around.

"But what if she can, Father?" Millicent asked.

"Her last memory is falling from her horse. It might give her nightmares," Noel explained. "We wanted to give her something better to dream about."

He cocked his head to the side. "Come, you two need to go to bed now."

As if on cue, thunder rattled the panes.

"You can sleep together in the bed in the next room," he offered.

They scrambled to the floor, approaching him warily. He didn't think they were frightened of him but afraid of losing the woman whose unconventional manners were such a delight.

Millicent stumbled to a stop, her eyes growing wide as she stared at the large painting above his hearth.

"Is that our mother?" she whispered.

"No, silly goose," Noel said before Devon could respond. "Our mother is lying on the bed in here."

Angling his chin in challenge, Noel met his father's gaze and held it. "Isn't that right, Father?"

By God, Devon had never known such pride. His son was going to make an exceptional earl. He would know society's rules but not be master to them. "You're quite correct, son."

"Does that mean we can call her Mother when she wakes up?" Millicent asked.

Not if but when. When she woke up.

It seemed both children were holding their breath. He had a feeling they weren't asking his permission but simply informing him of what they intended to do—in a most diplomatic way.

"I think that's a splendid idea. Now, into bed with you."

He followed them into the next room, tucked the blankets in close to them, and lowered the flame in the lamp until the shadows danced around them. Straightening, he studied the cherubs in the bed. The children had never been in his room. His youngest didn't know what her mother looked like.

Ah, yes, she did, he corrected himself. She knew her mother had mahogany hair and rich, dark brown eyes.

"I love you," he said quietly.

"And Mother, too?" Millicent asked.

He nodded once. "And Mother, too."

Now if only she would awaken and he could convince her to stay.

Devon pulled a chair close to the bed. He considered lying on it, drawing Gina into his embrace, but he'd messed up royally. He'd been afraid of showing her what he felt.

And here he was, greedy for her love. Wanting it so desperately, he'd do anything to have it. Anything. Anything except make her unhappy.

How was it that a person could want something so badly he'd be willing to give it up? It made no sense, but then so little did when it came to Gina.

So he sat in the chair, facing her. He took her callused hand in his. They were such a pair. Not at all as the aristocracy should be. But he realized with sudden clarity that they were exactly as they should be.

He pressed his mouth to her fingers, long, slender, graceful, but strong. Capable of soothing his frustrations, gentling his children, working his land, arousing his passion.

"The children seem to think you can hear us." He was surprised by his voice. It sounded like a plow grinding its way against rock embedded in the soil. Rough and grating. Rasping.

He molded his lips around her knuckles, just shy of where the ring he'd given her rested. The garnet seemed to wink in the lamplight. Truth and constancy.

How was he to have known the truth revealed his love to be constant?

"I would rather live as a pauper and have your love than live as a king and know your disdain. Your father told me you would make me a wealthy man. I thought he spoke in terms of material things"—he shook his head—"but he spoke in terms of love.

"Wake up, Gina, wake up and tell me what you require for happiness, and I will give it you. Anything that you wish, all that you wish.

"Do you truly want to return to Texas? I shall let you go without ever revealing the cost. And if you choose to stay, I shall forever be grateful. I love you as I've never loved anyone. Your strength, your courage, your determination, your wisdom.

"Don't die, sweeting. You turned my world upside down and taught me that love has no boundaries. Don't die."

Chapter 23

Don't die.

The litany swirled like a gray fog into the black void where she'd sought refuge from the throbbing pain in her head.

At first it had come to her in the voice of a child, sweet, innocent, beseeching. Then it had drifted away. And when it had returned, it arrived with a deeper timbre, anguished.

Don't die.

As though she had a choice. As though the decision was hers to make.

She became aware of the firm grip on her hand, the damp and warm breath wafting over her fingers, the soft mouth pressed against her skin.

Slowly she opened her eyes to the dimly lit room. A bedchamber. But not hers. One she'd visited only once. *His.*

Even the low light caused her head to ache. She

didn't dare move her head for fear of increasing the pain.

She slid her eyes slightly to the side, and there he was, sitting beside her, holding her hand. The bearded stubble of his face shadowy and thick. His hair stood out at odd angles as though it had been wet and left to dry on its own with no one bothering to take a brush or comb to it. He'd never looked so unkempt.

His eyes were red and swollen . . . and . . . what was that?

Gingerly, she reached out and touched his eyelashes. "You overlooked a tear."

He bestowed upon her the sweetest smile she'd ever seen.

"You're awake," he rasped, his voice thick with an emotion she didn't dare try to name. He pressed his mouth to the back of her hand. "Thank God, you're awake."

"What . . . happened?"

"You took a spill. Three days ago. Wait here."

As though she had a choice. She watched him stride across the room. She'd never seen clothes so wrinkled. Were the servants not doing their job?

He opened the door and said in a hushed voice, "Winston, her ladyship has awoken. Fetch the physician."

He closed the door quietly, returned to the chair, reached for her hand, and then as though thinking better of it, gripped the chair. "Are you thirsty?"

She nodded, regretting the movement as soon as she'd completed it. He poured water into a glass.

Gingerly he lifted her head and carried the glass to her lips. She sipped slowly. Nothing had ever felt so welcome as the cool water slid past her parched throat.

"Not too much, now," he chided gently before easing her back down to the pillow.

He set the glass aside and then looked at her as though he had a thousand things he wanted to say but couldn't think of a single comment at the moment.

"In your room I saw your trunk. You were packing to leave?"

Everything came rushing back then. Her trunk. The whole of her life packed inside. Disappointment. Needing to leave. Wanting to stay. How could she leave the children? What would they think?

She'd always thought better on horseback, so she'd gone for a ride to argue with herself. To leave—to stay. To welcome him into her bed, knowing he loved another.

She shook her head slightly. "I decided I couldn't leave the children."

He looked wounded somehow, disappointed.

"Did you want me to leave?" she asked.

"No," he answered hastily.

"I mean not unless you want to," he amended. "I'd rather you didn't, but I understand if you feel you must. I've hurt you with my careless disregard for your feelings." He plowed his hands through his hair. "You needn't make any decisions at this precise moment. We can work out the specifics once you've recovered."

She rubbed the spot on her finger his tear had dampened and wondered why he had wept.

"Jake rescued you!" Noel said, his face beaming, as though he'd somehow been responsible for Jake's feat.

"Did he?" Georgina asked, feeling well rested after three days.

"With a little help from Father," Millicent rushed to assure her.

She shifted her gaze from the children sitting beside her on the bed to the man standing solemnly at its foot. This evening he was once again the lord of the manor. Shaved. Every hair combed into place. His clothes pressed.

"Jake's a hero!" Millicent said.

"We made him a medal," Noel told her as he held up a silver disk with a ribbon threaded through a hole someone had punched in it. "Father allowed us to use the lid to a trinket box."

The lid looked to be real silver. "How generous of him," she said.

"It's time for you children to be off to bed. Say good night."

Millicent leaned toward her and pressed a kiss to her cheek. "I'm ever so glad you're all right, Mother."

Gina's heart constricted and tears welled in her eyes.

"Father said we could call you Mother," Noel explained. "If you'd rather we didn't, we won't."

She slipped her arms around both children, holding them close. "No, no. I'm so glad you want to. I love you so much."

"As we love you," Noel said.

"Father loves you, too," Millicent said.

She jerked her gaze to Devon. His cheeks were burning-red.

"That's enough, now. Your mother needs to rest," Devon said sternly from his position of guardian.

"But you said—" Millicent.

"I know what I said. Off with you now."

The children scrambled off the bed and scurried out of the room. Devon remained at his post, hands behind his back, reminding her of their days in London when he'd been so formal with her that she'd thought she might shriek.

"You gave them permission to call me Mother?" she asked.

"I thought it high time. You are more of a mother to them than Margaret ever was."

She glanced toward the hearth. She'd noticed the bare spot on the wall shortly after she'd awakened.

"Where's the portrait of Margaret?" she asked.

"I had it placed in another room. I don't want the children to feel as though I have no regard for her, but I determined that her portrait no longer belonged in here."

"I see."

"Do you? When I offered to give you a child and you preferred not, I was quite stunned and chose to believe that you rebuffed me because you loathed the thought of intimacy with someone who worked in the fields.

"I failed to take into account your generous heart, your affectionate nature, the manner in which you give so much of yourself and ask for nothing in return. For all that you seemed to accept that I worked in the fields, for all the respect you claimed to have for me, I had none for myself."

"I more than respect you, Devon. I've fallen in love with you. I thought I could accept that Margaret would always be the love of your life—"

He moved quickly to the head of bed, sat on the edge, and placed his thumb over her lips, silencing her. "She *was* the love of my life . . . until you."

Her heart tightened. "You promised never to lie to me."

"Then hear the truth, Gina. I did love Margaret. She and I were well suited, cut of the same cloth, so to speak. But our happiness was fleeting. She came to despise me and all I stood for.

"She found my touch abhorrent. She made me feel less of a man. I came to dread our moments together, because I always saw disappointment in her eyes.

"Her beauty went no farther than the surface."

Gina closed her eyes as he leaned closer and placed a kiss at her temple.

"Do you remember the condition upon which you agreed to marry me?" he asked.

Opening her eyes, she held his gaze. "No lies."

"Exactly." He bestowed upon her a warm, sensual

smile as he framed her face between his work-roughened hands. "So, my dear countess, heed my words. You instructed me to never tell you that you were beautiful when you were not. I swear to you I have never known a woman who possessed more beauty than you."

Tears stung the back of her eyes. "Devon—"

"I am not yet finished. You commanded me never to tell you that I love you when I cannot. That condition is also voided because I do love you, Gina, more than I thought possible to love anyone. You quite simply . . . take my breath.

"Let me make love to you," he rasped. "Allow me the privilege of showing you how truly beautiful you are."

She shook her head. "Not in this bed."

"This is my bed, Gina," he said quietly before he touched his lips to hers. "I swear to you no other woman has ever been in it."

He settled his mouth persistently against hers, his tongue waltzing with hers. He didn't carry the scent of the fields with him this evening but she inhaled his raw masculine scent, such a part of him that the most expensive of colognes could only add to its allure but not hide it.

She scraped her fingernails along his nape, up into his scalp, his curling hair clinging to her fingers as he pressed her more deeply against the bed. She was vaguely aware of him loosening the buttons on her nightgown as he increased the urgency of his kiss, deepening it. He slid his hand inside her gown until he could close his hand around her breast.

A throaty rumble escaped him as he tore his mouth from hers, lowered his head, and latched his lips around her nipple, his tongue circling even as he suckled. Whimpering, she arched her back to give him easier access.

"You are so enticingly sweet," he murmured.

And so incredibly hot. She was burning with the passions he elicited with his touch. As though he was equally ablaze, he shot up and made quick work of removing his clothes while she, trapped beneath the blankets, wiggled as she tugged her gown off her shoulders, past her hips, over her feet.

"I would have gladly done that for you," he said as he threw back the covers, exposing her nakedness to his appreciative gaze. "But I see there are advantages to its already being done."

He stretched out beside her, the length of his body pressing against her, his smile warmer than she'd ever seen it, incredible to behold. "I take this image into my sleep every night."

"You do?" she asked breathlessly.

"Ah, yes, countess. Our night in London haunts me. I was a fool, punishing us both for what could not be changed. This evening I intend for us both to receive our just rewards."

He blanketed her mouth with his as he rolled over her, wedging himself between her thighs. Although he supported himself on his elbows, taking care not to crush her, she loved the weight of his body over hers, adored the feel of her legs wrapped around him.

He trailed his lips along her throat, his tongue

swirling over her flesh, sending delicious sensations rippling through her.

She admired to a much greater degree the firmness of his muscles as she skimmed her fingers over his arms, his shoulders, his back. Now she understood how he'd gained those muscles. She knew how they looked as he swung a scythe and tossed sheaves onto a wagon. She knew the difference between flesh wet with sweat and that damp with desire.

He took his mouth on a journey around one of her breasts and then the other. Slowly, enticingly, with no hurry attached to it. Only a sense of appreciation.

She felt the desire building between her thighs. She lifted her hips, pressing against his stomach, seeking some sort of surcease and finding none. "Devon?"

"Easy, countess, all in good time. A harvest does not come to pass a day after planting."

"It might if you were the sun," she reflected breathlessly.

He chuckled low. "You think?"

He eased lower and she twisted against him. "Devon—"

"You're not yet ripe enough, sweeting."

She was on the verge of declaring she was nearly bursting when he kissed the inside of her thigh, his breath hot against her sensitive skin, stealing her voice, her breath, her thoughts.

And then he placed a kiss at the heart of her womanhood, and she felt as though molten fire was sluicing through her. His velvety tongue swirled with abandon that turned to purpose. Her shoulders curled off the bed as the pleasure increased.

She tightened her fingers around strands of his hair, needing something to keep her anchored as she burst into full bloom, her body shuddering almost violently and yet with such incredible rippling sensations she could only think of her reaction as joyous.

He stilled at the same moment she did, turned his head to the side, and pressed his cheek against her curls. Her harsh, erratic breathing grew shallow as a contented smile spread over her face.

Through lowered lashes, she watched her beloved lift his head, grin at her with pure male satisfaction, and ease himself up and over her.

She flattened her palm against his slick chest, effectively stopping him. "Turn about is fair play."

"Gina—"

"I really want to, Devon," she whispered as she rose up and gently pushed him off her.

He landed on his back and threaded his fingers through her hair, bringing her mouth to his. He tasted of her, had sipped of her nectar, and now she wished to do the same for him.

She began her journey slowly, hesitantly, but willingly. She loved this proud man who fought to remain equal to his peers, never realizing that he stood far above them. This father who adored his children. This husband who had sought to spare her shame and in the end had allowed her to work beside him, had made her a partner in the marriage, not simply an observer.

She wrapped her hand over him and lowered her

mouth. With the first contact he twitched, his breathing labored, his fingers tightening their hold on her hair.

"Gina . . . ah . . . sweeting . . ."

He sounded as though he was strangling, and for reasons she couldn't explain, her own pleasure increased. She slid her mouth over him.

"Come here, vixen," he rasped. "Now."

With a triumphant smile she allowed him to guide her hips as she mounted him. The feel of his fullness never failed to amaze her. The rightness of two bodies joined as one. The joy of moving in tandem.

She lowered her mouth to his, their tongues darting and thrusting in rhythm with their hips, the tempo increasing, the pleasure mounting . . .

Until they cried out in unison, their bodies jerking forcefully before quivering. Satiated, she relaxed completely and sprawled over him.

He lifted himself up slightly, grabbed a sheet, and spread it over them before kissing the top of her head. He folded his arms over her as though he intended to hold her for the remainder of the night, the remainder of his life.

"I want you in my bed," he murmured.

"I am in your bed," she reminded him.

He slid his finger beneath her chin and angled her face until their eyes locked. "This business of your bedchamber, my bedchamber is ludicrous. I want you in my bed every night. Even if you've no desire to make love. I want your scent wafting around me. I want to be able to curl around your warm body any time I wish."

"Every night?"

"Every night."

A smile blossomed over her face. "I think I can accommodate that request."

Epilogue

Seven years later

"Once upon a time, in a land across the vast ocean, an Indian maiden—"

"Not that story, Father," young James Nathaniel Sheridan interrupted, his blue eyes bright. "Tell us the story about the lady of the fields."

"Yes, please, Father," Edwina Devona Sheridan pleaded. "It's my most favorite of all the legends."

"I seem to recall telling you the story last night," Devon reminded the two children nestled against his sides as he lay on the bed, pillows at his back. They'd been born on the same night six years earlier. Trust his wife to begin with efficiency and make up for lost time in gaining the children she'd always desired.

"But I never tire of hearing it," Edwina said.

"Do tell it to us, Father. It's the reason I enjoy coming home," Noel chimed in. Home from school for the holiday, he was lounging on the floor, his fingers buried in Jake's thick fur.

He was a good-sized lad, having often worked beside Devon in the fields. More alarming, however, was his recent announcement that he wished to study veterinary medicine. Devon had a feeling that the days of the idle aristocracy were rapidly vanishing.

Yet he could not help but feel a burst of pride that at fifteen his eldest son had the confidence to seek his own path in life. He would, of course, inherit the title one day, but he had no plans to sit around waiting for it to be handed to him.

Millicent looked up from her latest fashion magazine. "There's no hope for it, Father. You might as well get on with it. You know they won't settle in to sleep until you do."

"Very well." Clearing his throat, he drew James and Edwina closer. He so enjoyed this nightly family ritual.

"Once upon a time, in the land of England, there was an impoverished nobleman who woke up each morning, looked out over the land, and saw only what it would not yield. He worked the fields each day but resented each swing of the scythe.

"And then one day to his utter amazement a lady appeared in the fields. When she looked out over the grain, she saw the dreams that could be harvested with hard work. So each day she stooked the wheat that he'd cut. And as she did, she whistled. In time, others came to the fields simply to listen to her tune of merriment.

"But they soon discovered that if they helped with the harvesting, the lady's tunes became merrier and the harvesting went more quickly and the lord became more wealthy.

"And as he became more wealthy, so did they.

"During the harvest feast, the lord approached the lady of the fields and asked her why she'd worked day after day in his fields.

"'Why, my lord, because I love you,' she answered, as though he was a silly twit for being too dense to figure it out himself."

Edwina and James giggled while Noel and Millicent grinned. Devon gazed at his smiling wife as she rocked two-year-old Gregory. The lad had already drifted off to sleep. He supposed he would have to repeat the story tomorrow night.

"Finish the story, Father," Edwina prodded. "This is my most favorite part."

"Ah, yes, the ending to our tale," he murmured, looking deeply into Gina's eyes. "Following her declaration, in the middle of the fields where the seeds of their love had been planted and taken root, he lowered his mouth to hers and she stole not only his breath but his heart."

"And they lived happily ever after!" the children cried in unison.

Devon smiled warmly with satisfaction. "Indeed they did."